SKULL VALLEY

SKULL VALLEY

David Martin Lins

SKULL VALLEY

First Edition
Copyright © 2021 David Martin Lins

eBook ISBN 978-1-7365970-0-2
Paperback ISBN 978-1-7365970-1-9
Hardcover ISBN 978-1-7365970-2-6

Cover design/Lorin Petrazilka
Line Editor/Lee Clarity Consulting
Developmental Editor/Stephen Prat
Formatting/DTPerfect

DavidMartinLins.com

For Dad.

DAY ONE

"WHAT WAS COVETED IN THE PAST,
WILL BE COVETED AGAIN."

—

MARK TAYLOR

1.

IF I'D KNOWN WHAT WOULD HAPPEN over the next several days, I'd have filled my gas tank, trusted my dad, and stocked up on Peanut M&M's. Instead, I was telling ghost stories around a campfire.

"Whenever a farmer turns the land, there is still a good chance they'll find human bones."

The two remaining middle school kids just stared at me as the fire flickered in their horrified eyes. Finally, the girl smiled. "You're makin' that up."

"About a hundred-fifty years ago," I whispered, "two tribes battled over the land."

Addison and Jessie—the other two counselors—extended me some rope, but seemed concerned with how far I'd take it.

"Why would anyone fight over some random spot in the middle of nowhere?" the boy asked.

"Dude!" The girl punched him in the side of his ribs. "It's his hometown!"

"Because it's the only place stuff will grow in this part of Arizona. So when a drought hit, the dirt was like gold."

"They killed each other?" the girl asked. "Seems kinda harsh. I mean, they coulda just shared."

"Did people make sure everyone had enough toilet paper when that virus hit a few years ago? No. They didn't. People don't always work together when all hell breaks loose."

"Lukas." The other junior counselor, Addison, admonished me with nothing more than my name.

"Point is," I went on, "Skull Valley's got a bloody history."

"Point is," Addison jumped in again, looking just as good in camo pants and a hoodie as she did in that blue prom dress last year, "Skull Valley is a beautiful little community hidden in the Sierra Prietas."

"I like your description more than his," proclaimed the seventh-grader who'd adopted Addison as her big sister for the week. "Where is it?"

"About twenty miles west of here."

"Did you say Skull Valley is beautiful?" I sneered. "Maybe if you like places where you have to drive thirty minutes to get a candy bar, your phone doesn't get a signal half the time, and your power goes out with every strong breeze."

4

"You're exaggerating. And I like it," Addison tried to agree to disagree.

"That's because you've only lived there for two years now. After I graduate, I'm gone."

Even in the campfire glow, Addison's growing exasperation was obvious.

"Where'd you live before that?" her self-appointed sibling asked.

"Newport Coast." She saw the blank faces. "It's a neighborhood just north of Crystal Cove State Park in California."

"Wait." The boy perked up. "Is Newport Coast near Newport Beach?"

"Yeah," Addison flashed her natural smile. "It's actually part of it. The southern end."

"My grandparents take me there every summer. You must be *crazy* rich."

Her face flushed in the firelight.

"I wouldn't say we're rich."

"Rich people never think they're rich," the kid said, throwing a pinecone into the fire.

"I'm from Taos, New Mexico," chimed in Jessie, the senior counselor present at the fire, trying to move the conversation along with random facts. "It has a really cool art scene. That's why we moved there."

The logs kept burning under the clear night sky at BWC, on the north edge of Prescott.

"I don't understand why we can't have our cell phones." The boy broke the silence.

"Because a cell phone would distract you from the natural beauty that surrounds us," responded Jessie.

"Whatever."

"No. She's right." Addison jumped in. "People dream about living where I used to live. But I always looked forward to summer camp near Big Bear."

"But *why?*" asked the girl.

"Because the beach is always crowded. But when I was in the mountains, there were moments when I couldn't hear anything but the wind." She smiled broadly at the memory. "Or see anything but the stars."

"Sounds boring," the boy groaned.

"You might think so, Bobby." Addison knew his name. "But I always found it peaceful. Still do. And that's why I'm a junior counselor."

"Cool!" exclaimed lil' sis, who nodded before turning to me. "What about you?"

"Me? I needed to make some cash this summer."

My answer didn't seem to get me points with Addison, who flared her eyes at me as if to say, "Can't you *try* to be nice?"

"At least he's being honest," Bobby—*or was it Robby?*—shrugged.

"You think I wasn't?" Addison said with another flash of her smile. "Alright, just listen for a minute."

She waited as we went silent.

"Okay. What did you hear?"

"The fire crackling!" exclaimed her little friend.

"The wind in the trees," Jessie jumped in, lending support to Addison's effort.

"A car driving by." Bobby-Robby was determined to be a little snot.

"True," Addison acknowledged, "but it was only one and it was in the distance. I guess what I'm saying is, sometimes, it's good to unplug from all the noise so you can hear yourself think."

Jessie took the sales pitch and ran with it. "And, my young friends, trees produce oxygen. We breathe in oxygen." She paused to take a dramatic inhale. "Simple math. Since there are more trees than people in this forest, the air is rich and healthy here."

"But that doesn't mean it has WiFi."

The little jerk wouldn't quit and I was done.

"Why are you here if you're so miserable? Huh? Is it because your parents needed five days of peace and the only way they could get some was to send you off to a camp?"

The boy's freckled face tremored an instant before he stood and stomped toward his cabin.

"Bobby," Jessie called after him.

"Jeez, Lukas! Do you have to be so mean?" Addison was angry and darted off in pursuit.

"Can't tell me I was the only one thinking it." I had tried to defend her and it backfired.

Jessie moved to sit next to me. "Hi there, Mr. Sensitivity," she whispered. "Nice to meet you. I should fill you in. That kid? His parents are in jail and his grandparents are raising him."

2.

JESSIE TOLD ME I NEEDED TO speak to the kid and try to make it right before he told his grandparents and the camp had to deal with the aftermath, so I immediately reconfirmed his name was indeed "Bobby." I mean—I owed the little punk that much.

I walked into the mess hall. Ponderosa Pine cafeteria set up for about two hundred that had seen better days. A few members of the kitchen staff were still cleaning up after the final dinner of the week and in the far corner, Bobby had been sitting at a table and looking out a black window. Ben was Jessie's corresponding senior counselor and was sitting next to the boy, silent. I slowly zig-zagged between the tables and wished Jessie had realized I was the least qualified person for this task. Ben noticed me first and shook his head, apparently briefed on what I had said.

"Could I have a minute with him?"

Bobby looked from the window. "Oh great. You." He wiped his nose with his sleeve and looked back toward the darkness.

Ben stood up and moved to within inches, "Try not to make it worse."

"Thanks. I think Jessie is still at the fire if you hurry."

I sat next to Bobby as Ben walked away grumbling.

"What do *you* want?" Bobby didn't look away from the window as he said it.

"Jessie told me about your parents."

"Seriously?" His voice cracked. "Great. Now everyone in the camp thinks my parents are felons."

Because they are. "No, man. Only a few staff members know." And after a beat, "I obviously didn't know."

We sat there without a word for a while.

His eyes moved to the space halfway between the window and eye contact. "You don't have to sit with me. I'm fine."

"I'm not leaving before I apologize."

"Said I'm fine."

"Maybe, but I'm still sorry for what I said."

"Okay." Still staring out the window.

"Listen. I know it's gotta be hard."

He finally looked back at me. "How would you know?"

This time, I was the one who turned and looked out

the window for a second. "Addison was right. This is a good place to hear yourself think, especially in hard times."

"She likes you, ya know," looking out the window again.

"I don't know what the hell you're talking about."

"Addison. She *likes* you. And I don't think you're supposed to swear in front of campers."

"She's just nice to everybody. Even jerks like me."

"You *are* a jerk." But the kid smiled.

Every light in the mess hall shut off at the same time. Every industrial appliance hum from the kitchen went silent. The windows that had been so dark were suddenly the only source of dim light. Once again, clear skies and moonlight were a blessing when an outage hit the mountains.

"What's going on?" Bobby asked, the pitch of his voice higher than normal.

"Power went out. Nothing to worry about. It happens up here sometimes. Usually during a rainstorm, but not always. We've got generators for the big buildings and flashlights so we can find our way to the cabins. Most of the campers are in the cabins already."

"Ironically, it's almost lights out anyway," Ben said as he approached in the dark. He was slapping an old flashlight into his palm. It finally flickered on.

"Plenty of moonlight to get to the cabins anyway," I answered. "Power will be back up before morning."

"The bus will still be here in the morning, right?" Bobby asked, his voice still betraying him.

"Nothing to worry about there, buddy. You'll be home by lunch tomorrow." Ben slapped him on the back. "Now, let's get you to your cabin." The three of us began to cautiously make our way back between the tables, following the weak beam of Ben's light.

A voice from behind the kitchen doors could be heard asking why the generator hadn't kicked in. Then, someone else said something about their cell phone.

"Guess it knocked out the cell towers," Ben guessed. "Must be a big one."

"This place keeps getting better and better," Bobby muttered in response.

All the power.

The generator.

Cell phones.

We exited into the cool night, headed for Bobby's cabin, and were about halfway down the short path when labored footfalls rapidly approached from our left. Ben's eyes went wide as his flashlight's weak beam failed to show the source of the noise.

"Ben! Is that you?" a voice approached from the shadows.

"Jessie?"

She ran up close enough to be identified in the light.

"Dang, girl!" Ben smiled. "You almost scared the kid half to death."

"I wasn't the one who was scared." Bobby looked up at Ben.

Jessie, breathless, was still focused on Ben. "Need a favor."

"Anything." *Way too eager. Would've maybe had a chance if he learned a bit of subtlety.*

"Justin asked me to go pick up some ice from town to keep the food cold until he can get the main generator up and running, but I think my battery's dead. Can I take your truck?"

"Uh. Sure." He dug around in his pocket and produced the keys. "Want me to drive you?"

"No. Once you get—"

"Does that happen often?" I interrupted.

"What?" Jessie asked.

"Do you have car trouble often?"

"It's only two years old. Graduation present." She glanced at Bobby, then back at me. "Did you take care of the situation?"

It took a second to remember what she was even talking about. "Uh. Yeah. Can I go with you?"

"No freaking way, kid." Ben laughed, still holding his keys.

"I understand why Ben is needed here, but that's gonna be a lot of ice and you could use a hand," I reasoned.

"Are you even eighteen?" Jessie asked.

"Yup," I lied. "Two months ago."

"Fine. Let's go. We've got to hurry."

"No, no, no," Ben objected.

13

"I won't take advantage of him." Jessie winked before swiping the keys.

As we made our way to the staff parking area, I was pretty sure Ben had nothing to worry about. This probably wouldn't be a long trip.

The automatic locks on Ben's four-year-old Dodge Ram wouldn't work, so Jessie pulled the manual key out of the key fob, unlocked it the old fashioned way, and reached across to let me in. She pushed the engine start/stop button. Nothing happened.

"Seriously?" Jessie groaned. "What's going on?!"

I jumped out of Ben's truck and ran to my own.

I pulled out the keys for my 1979 baby blue Toyota Hilux and got behind the wheel. She started right up. I shut it off quickly.

That's when I knew. The power wouldn't be coming back on. The bus wouldn't be coming. The world just changed.

3.

JESSIE POUNDED AGAINST THE WINDOW INCHES from my ear. I opened the door and pushed out.

She stumbled backward. "What are you doing?"

"Where's Justin?"

"What's going on?"

"No time. Where is he?"

"He was out back behind the kitchen, trying to get the generator going."

I bolted off back toward the mess hall, the moonlight filtering through the pine.

"Justin!" I hollered out as I approached. "Justin!"

"Who's that?" asked the man with the shaved head who was in charge for the week.

I jogged into view. "We've got a situation—"

"Ah, Lukas. I know buddy. Working on it. I need you to get back to your cabin." He turned back to the generator.

"Sir? The power won't be coming back on for quite a while."

He looked back. "Buddy—"

"Listen! I think we're dealing with an—"

"Only an outage. Nothing more. Get back to your cabin. That's where you're needed."

"Ration food from the fridges first."

"Lukas. Stop."

"Then go through the freezers. Lastly, the dry goods. Protect the hand pump. It's going to become very valuable. Figure out who—"

"Enough! What the hell is wrong with you?"

Several of the counselors and junior counselors had made their way toward the mess hall, and Addison was among them. I looked around in disbelief. "Fine. Good luck."

I walked up to Addison and laid it out. "I've got to pick up a few things from town. I'll have to move fast before things get crazy—"

"What're you talking about?"

"Hey! Kid!" Justin yelled. "Do I need to fire you? Stop trying to cause a panic."

I ignored him, staying focused on Addison. "I don't know what caused it, but I think we are dealing with the after-effects of a high-altitude electromagnetic pulse. If it's something else, it won't be good either."

"Your dad." she said it as if it explained away my ravings.

The other counselors began whispering as I continued, "If we don't get back to Skull Valley in the next few hours, it might become infinitely more difficult very soon. Come with me."

She looked taken aback. "You heard Justin. It's just an outage."

"Addison? We don't have time. You can come with me now or I'll be done in Prescott within thirty minutes and passing the camp heading home. I'll look for you. If you get out to the main road and flag me down, I'll pick you up. If I don't see you, I'll keep driving." I turned and started toward the parking area as quickly as the moonlight would allow.

"What about all the campers?!" Addison called out.

Justin thinks he can handle it. Let him.

4.

PULLED OUT OF THE DIRT LOT while a few other counselors were scrambling into their cars and trucks, presumably to see if they would start, and to determine if I might've actually been right.

I arrived at the main road and cautiously turned south toward town. No cars in sight. Must've been less traffic, thanks to the big event taking place at the high school football field. It was a hometown special for a local kid all grown up and turned celebrity survivalist. My parents had known him and I didn't have the impression they thought much of him. Nevertheless, a good portion of the town had probably been there when everything went dark. Truth be told, I'd probably have gone if I wasn't on the job. People change, right? And the guy was the real deal from the Youtube clips I watched when my parents weren't around. Now? Hopefully, he'd be of some help.

As my eyes continued adjusting to the moonlight, I saw a few people walking on the opposite side of the road. Four silhouettes I couldn't make out, yelled to get my attention. I looked away and didn't slow down. This wasn't a time to help everyone. A person needed to save themselves and their loved ones. Lucky I only had one or two.

I had to swerve to the left as I rounded a bend in order to avoid a dead sedan in the shadowy darkness. And the road became more congested every few blocks, every stationary car already abandoned. I saw a few people walking and another on a bicycle. In the three miles I drove, there were only four other moving vehicles.

Don's Supplies came up on the left. An aged, free-standing building with fencing that extended to abandoned buildings on each side. There were more silhouettes standing at the front door. They all spun to watch the sight and sound of my little pickup. I didn't slow, but turned onto the next left and took the alley leading back behind Don's before pulling up next to an ancient Jeep Cherokee. I shut off my truck, quietly made my way to the back door, and knocked hard. The noise was a risk, but I needed Don to hear me.

"Come through that door and I'll shoot you!" The unmistakable sound of a pump action. "Don't want to hurt anyone, so don't make me!"

"Don! Don't shoot! It's Lukas!" I moved five feet to the left of the door.

There was a thoughtful pause.

"Where is your dad?" the old voice interrogated.

"My guess is he's with my uncle!"

The door's bolt lock disengaged and pulled inward to reveal an elderly man with thick-rimmed glasses and white wisps of what used to be a brown widow's peak. The room was lit by a single candle. "Get in."

Don Wilson had one rule in his store—no cursing. Maybe that's why he got along with my dad so well. That, and the fact that my dad kept a running account at his store since running accounts at stores were a thing.

"Why are you out and about?" he asked as he bolted the door behind me. "I would think you'd know better."

"I was working at BWC. Came straight here to see if Dad still had any money in the account." I looked around the musty old store that was full of hunting and camping gear, but survived on ammo and secondhand guns of every variety.

"Not as much as you'll need." He seemed to chew on something before continuing. Someone kept slamming on the front door every few minutes. "Tell you what, I'll make you an offer."

"Name it."

"You help me get as much in my Cherokee as we can cram in. Then, you can take whatever you can fit."

"Deal." We both understood there'd be limited time before the general public realized what was happening and a small mob descended on the place. The ones out front would only be the beginning.

We crept back out to the alley and opened the back of the Cherokee and got to work. Before long, we discovered the fastest method was for Don to remain in the store and point out what I should take next. Within minutes, his truck was becoming loaded down with a variety of guns, enough ammo to last well beyond his expiration date, a tent, a sleeping bag, water purification tablets, gasoline canisters, some MREs, ropes, matches, and more.

Within minutes, I walked back in and he asked, "Truck just about full?"

"Yeah, but we can probably fit a few more things." I was eager to keep going.

"Your turn, son. Grab anything you want. I'll help you carry it out."

"Mr. Wilson, you should go."

"Stop arguing with me." He smiled. "I've got most of the guns."

"Okay. I'll grab what I think my family needs. You grab what you *know* we'll need."

He responded by going straight to the firearms section.

I cleared the remaining MREs, water purification tablets, and gas canisters. I swiped a small mountain of water-proof matches before grabbing other random supplies. The bed of my tiny truck was filling quickly. Too quickly. I determined I had room for a few more weapons and tools. Don had already carried out the remaining handguns, rifles, and shotguns. As he came back inside for more, I picked out two saws, a hatchet, and a large axe.

I kicked open the door and took a single step before something slammed into my gut. I doubled over, dropping the tools. It was dumb luck they didn't land on either of my feet. Still bent at the waist, my eyes cleared and realized two large boots were standing a few inches away. As I slowly straightened, another fist slammed into my cheek, sending me to the ground. How I avoided a broken jaw—or a concussion—I'll never know.

I looked up from the ground. The man had a square jaw and a body chiseled from flint. Behind him was a much thinner man, who had set a pistol on the tailgate and seemed to be frantically searching for corresponding ammunition.

Don's voice, from inside the store, "Lukas? You need anything else?"

The big guy stepped toward me and raised a single finger to his lips. He didn't take his eyes off me as he lowered and picked up the hatchet and addressed his associate in a low, powerful voice. "Loaded yet?"

"Sorry. Had to find the right ammo," the higher, raspy voice replied.

"Christ, Stevie. Took ya long enough."

The door swung inward and a shotgun pumped within

a single second. Mr. Wilson emerged and swung the shotgun toward the larger man. I was still curled up on the ground, between the two. "Hey! Superman! Toss the hatchet to the side and back away from the boy!"

He tossed it but didn't take a step. The other guy shook while trying to load his gun.

"And you over there! Set it down or your bodyguard here gets it."

Stevie started to lower it when the big guy spoke up. "You won't shoot us, Grandpa."

"Just because I don't *want* to, don't mean I won't. Your little friend needs to set the gun down. Now!" The handgun was set back down on the tailgate.

"Calm down." The big man had his hands raised. "There is plenty to go around here."

"Forgive my suspicion of your motives since you punched my young friend before taking his hatchet. Lukas? Roll away from him before you get up."

I did as I was told, grabbing the hatchet from the dirt.

"And you," he turned to the man at the back of my truck, "get over here with your buddy."

The man began to nod before snatching up the pistol and diving behind the far side of my truck.

The big man took a single step forward before Don swung the shotgun back in his direction. "On your knees! Fast!" The man could tell Don meant it and complied.

I leapt to the near side of my truck, got on all fours and

looked under the truck. I made out the shape of the gun-man's feet facing the back of the truck and didn't waste the opportunity. I took the hatchet and whipped it underneath the belly of the truck with as much force as I could summon. I hoped the blade would land, but the handle skimmed the man's heel and skittered into the dirt. Didn't matter. It distracted him for an instant.

"What the—"

I barrelled around the back of the pickup and propelled myself into his back like a missile. He landed full force on the gun. It didn't go off. Don came around the front of the truck and aimed the shotgun. I rolled off the man quickly.

Don hesitated.

"Shoot him!" I yelled.

"Lukas. Step away." Then, he addressed the man, "Friend? If you even flinch without permission, it'll be the last thing you do." I could hear the big man running away on the other side of the truck. Don didn't care. This man was the bigger threat now, thanks to the loaded pistol.

"Lift yourself up with one hand," Don instructed precisely, "While you slide that gun to the side slowly and carefully with the other."

This time, the man did as he was told.

"You should shoot him," I urged.

"Never kill a man unless you have to, son. Now get the gun. Then, get some rope."

We hogtied the man right there in the dirt.

"Don, I'd ask where you are headed, but… " I motioned to the man in the dirt who looked dumb enough to follow us once free.

"Oh," Don grinned. "I doubt you'll ever see me again."

"Untie me! I won't do nuthin'!" The guy pleaded.

I ignored him. "Well, good luck. Wherever you're going."

"You too."

"I swear!" Stevie wouldn't give up. "It was Kyle's idea!"

"And thank you for all of this." I gestured toward the loaded Hilux.

"Son, if you hadn't been here to help me, I would've been loading up when this thug and his big brother showed up. And I might not be breathing right now. So thank *you*." He paused a brief moment. "Anyhow. We need to get out of here."

"I never hurt nobody! I only wanted a few things. I was gonna pay you!"

Don finally looked at him. "Good news. You manage to untie yourself and everything is free." The old man looked back to me and gave me another warm, grandfatherly smile.

"Bye, Mr. Wilson."

"Lookin' like your dad was right all along."

I just gave a curt nod before getting in my truck and revving it to life. He waited for me to pull out first.

I turned out of the alley and onto the side street when I spotted Kyle staring at me from the shadows of a small dirt lot. I kept my foot on the gas. The guy was just waiting until Don and I had left to see if his accomplice was still alive and gather up whatever we'd left behind.

I turned again onto the dark main street that would lead back past the camp and immediately noticed an increase in foot traffic. People had begun congregating outside of their homes in small groups of concerned discussion and gossip. Power outages were one thing, but when cell phones go on the fritz and cars simultaneously stall out, it grabs the imagination of the entire community. Time was running out.

5.

APPROACHING THE CAMP ENTRANCE, I SLOWED a bit and scanned both sides of the road. Didn't really care whether or not she was there, but I made a promise.

Fine. I might've cared a little.

Didn't see her—or anybody—so I began to accelerate again. A half mile past the entrance, a shadow was walking the same direction on the opposite side of the road. I squinted for detail. Camo pants and a hoodie pulled up over the head, but I couldn't see her face.

I drove twenty yards beyond the figure and skidded to a stop. I grabbed the gun and jumped out of the car. I yelled back, "Who are you?!" The figure froze. I raised the gun. "Who *are* you?!"

"Lukas! Put it down! You're freaking me out!"

I dropped the gun to my side. "Are you crazy? Do you have any idea how dangerous this is?"

She was jogging up. "You didn't show. I had no other choice."

"So, you were gonna walk?"

"Well, yeah." She slowed to a walk, opened the passenger door, and slid in.

I stood there a brief second on the roadside in exasperation before getting into the driver side. I set the pistol between us. Looking out the windshield, "I had the safety on."

"Good thing it was me then."

"I had time." I shifted into drive again and we drove a good six blocks, before I parroted her words, "What about all the campers?"

She took a deep breath. "I know. I'm not sure we're doing the right thing here."

"Hey." I glanced over. "Don't."

"What?"

"You can't go with me, and then feel guilty about your decision."

"I can make whatever decision I want. I can feel however I want."

She was right, but I couldn't afford the stench of guilt or second thoughts clouding my mind. I drove in silence a full awkward minute before, "Why did you leave the camp?"

There was another full minute of silence before the quiet response: "I need to make sure my parents are alright."

We were about three miles down the road when we passed a young family of four walking in the opposite direction.

"Shouldn't we help them?"

"No."

"But they had two little kids."

"We're headed the other way and I'm not using a drop of gas more than I have to."

"Lukas." There was a pleading in her voice that made me want to stop. And I would've loved to play the hero for Addison. Any high school boy would. But tonight, we didn't have time.

"Addison," I didn't dare take my eyes off the road on the open road, "I'm getting you to your parents and getting home. That's the deal."

"Okay." With a single word, she sounded broken. And I hated it.

A mile further, we passed an abandoned minivan. Neither of us mentioned it. What made it worse? I knew there was no way we'd make it another eight miles without running into somebody else.

6.

THE TWO-LANE ROAD WOUND THROUGH the sloping hills where only a scattering of trees and cactus grew above three feet. I needed to conserve as much fuel as possible, so we topped out at around thirty miles per hour in the darkness. More importantly, I didn't want any supplies flying out of the back of the truck and I needed time to react if a car was stalled out somewhere ahead. The last concern was almost a guarantee. The road wasn't highly traveled at this late hour, but there were bound to be a few vehicles. The next car was in our lane and had been heading in the same direction. As I swerved to its left, a near miss, Addison squeaked.

"Did you see anybody?" she asked.

"Nope. Might be up ahead." I lied as I slowed to twenty. "They were going in this direction."

"If they are going in our direction and they don't look like trouble, will you pick them up?"

"I'll think about it." With my adrenaline still pumping, I tried to sound calm and in control by saying, 'Your safety is my priority, Addison.' Instead, I *actually* said, "You are my safety, Addison."

She looked at me.

Such an idiot.

"Your safety," I formed the rest of the sentence carefully, "that is my priority."

"Oh."

I knew I'd let the last few years turn me into a bit of a jerk, but I never fully appreciated what a moron I was until that moment. The same moment, two motorcycles came into view, laying on their sides, straddling two thirds of the road directly ahead.

I slammed on the brakes to keep from running them over and potentially disabling my truck. We wobbled left and skidded to a stop in the dirt slightly off the left edge of the road. A cloud of dust filled the windshield. A flash of something moved through it. I reached for the pistol. It wasn't there.

Addison saw what I was doing. "By my feet!" She started for it when there was a knock on her window. Addison screamed.

"We need your help!" A young woman with a pixie cut yelled through the window. "Please help my boyfriend!"

I unbuckled and lurched for the gun, removing the safety as I sat up. "Back away from the window!" I yelled.

Addison straightened to make sure she was out of the line of fire.

The woman wouldn't stop. "My boyfriend needs your help!" She looked frantic.

"Back! Away!"

"Please don't leave us here." Her voice lowered, but could still be heard through the window. "He's really messed up."

"Where is he?!"

Her face suddenly went from panicked to stone. "Pointing a gun at the back of your head."

I didn't have time to react before a metallic clink tapped the window inches behind my head. A deep growl barked, "Are you gonna help us or are you two going to spend the rest of the night on the side of the road while my girlfriend and I drive off in your Tonka truck?"

The woman took a step toward the back of the truck, putting Addison between herself and my aim.

"How can we help?" Addison said breathlessly from the passenger seat.

"Roll down your window!" the deep voice thundered from somewhere behind me.

I did as I was told.

"Put the safety on and throw the gun and your keys out the window." The voice had lowered.

I let out a slow exhale. With a slow shake of the head, I

removed the keys from the ignition and tossed the keys and the gun.

A giant of a man with a woodsman beard stepped up to my door and placed his hands on the window frame. He was country strong and his tank top revealed massive arms brandishing an impressive collection of ink. Between his meaty right thumb and index finger was a small rock.

His wife scrambled around the back of the truck and picked up the gun, flipping off the safety. "Got it!"

"You were *bluffing*?" I looked over at the man as he tossed the rock into the yellowing grass behind him.

The man backed from the door as his wife stepped beside him. She didn't raise the gun.

The man looked at me. "Will you help us now?"

"How can we help?" Addison repeated.

"Need a ride to Prescott," the man rumbled.

"And I get to keep the gun," the woman added.

"Babe," he looked to her.

"It might come in handy."

"No," I said, barely above a whisper.

"Excuse me?" The big guy almost looked humored.

"Lukas?" Addison, concerned.

I turned to her, "When I drove into town to get the supplies, I was attacked. It'll be worse now."

"What're we talking about?" The woman cocked her head.

"Do you have any idea what's going on?" I hadn't even considered they might not.

"All we know is that both our bikes shut off at the same time," said the big man. "That doesn't happen. I thought maybe someone messed with 'em when we caught a late dinner back in Yarnell."

"But then..." The woman trailed off with a look to her boyfriend.

"Neither of our phones worked."

"And we aren't talking about coverage." She shook her head. "They were dead."

"So, when we finally heard a car coming toward us from the south, we tried to flag it down."

"It was some kind of classic car—"

"Late sixties Camaro. Cherry," he said with a wistful smile.

"Trey." His girlfriend tried to get him to focus.

Trey's smile vanished. "Punk didn't even slow down."

"Then a big truck drove by."

"A 1960-something International Scout," Trey remembered proudly.

"Who cares, Trey!"

"Details are important, Pumpkin."

She turned to look at him. "Well? You gonna tell 'em why you call me that, too?"

He shrugged his mountainous shoulders. "When I met her, she wasn't blonde. Her hair was dyed red."

"Rhetorical, Trey!"

"Was it dark?" I asked.

"Yeah. It was only minutes ago," she answered.

"No. The truck."

"I think so. I don't know the precise color, though."

"Which way was it headed?"

"Same direction as you."

"Had to be…" Addison looked at me.

"Probably rounded up his kids and started forming a trailer park militia by now."

"Hey!" It was Pumpkin. "You gonna tell us what's goin' on?"

"Power's out." I thought simple would be best.

"But that doesn't explain—"

"This is something different," I went on. "Bigger. And it isn't coming back on for a while."

"Here's the problem, buddy," Trey spoke up. "You say you won't drive us the rest of the way to Prescott because it isn't safe. But, I say my girlfriend and I aren't spending the night out here. And my girlfriend happens to be holding the deciding vote in her right hand. How do you suggest we settle this?"

"We give you a ride to Skull Valley," Addison chimed in. "It's where we're headed."

"Ain't nothin there. Rode through it on the way," Trey responded.

"It's where we live," Addison told them. "And you can stay with my family until this gets fixed. I've got a house with plenty of room."

I shot Addison a look. She had a great heart, but her offer was dangerous.

"What? You got a better idea?"

I leaned toward her to whisper.

"Hey!" Trey boomed. "You got something to say, say it!"

"Fine." I turned back to Addison. "Two crazy motorcyclists ambushed us and stole our gun."

"Desperate for help." Trey interjected. "Not crazy."

"Now, they are threatening us."

"Leveraging the gun to get somewhere safe for the night," he corrected.

"You invited them to an infinite sleepover."

"As soon as we are able to get back home, we'll be on our way."

"And by the way, every mouth to feed will make survival of the community that much more difficult, and by the looks of him, Trey is the equivalent of three."

"Now you're just being hurtful." He took a step toward my open window.

"I'm sorry, but it's all true. And how do you think her parents will react? 'Hey, Mom! Hey, Dad! I brought home a few members of a Hell's Angels gang!'"

"They have clubs, jackweed." Trey clenched his jaw. "Not gangs. And we aren't members of a club."

"They could've killed us," Addison pleaded. "They aren't bad guys."

"There isn't room. We need everything in the bed of the

truck. Especially if we are taking on two more people."

"Only until whatever this is gets resolved," Trey interjected.

I shook my head, staring out the windshield. "You have no idea."

"Do you drive stick?" the woman addressed Addison.

She hesitated. Looked at me. Then looked back at the woman. "I do."

"Okay. Here's what we're gonna do. Romeo! Get out of the truck."

"Hell no."

She raised the gun. "Get out of the truck. And Juliet? You slide over behind the wheel. I'll take the passenger seat and keep the gun on you so Romeo doesn't get any ideas. Boys? You ride on the tailgate. We'll cruise nice and slow to Juliet's house."

"My name is Addison."

"Mine is Emily." She smiled sarcastically. "Now that we're Facebook official, can we get moving?"

I thought about sitting on the open tailgate, but once the little truck lurched forward, an avalanche of supplies would've pushed us right off our seats. We opted to perch ourselves atop the closed gate, hoping Addison could maintain calm acceleration despite having a gun pointed at her.

Once the ladies were in the cab, I climbed up first. When Trey hopped on, the truck, which was already riding exceptionally low, sank even lower on his side. He banged his hand against its side. And the truck eased into a roll.

As it gradually picked up speed, Trey looked over at me. "Hey, dude. I'm sorry for all this. Allison is right, we aren't the bad guys."

I didn't return the look. Instead, I stared out into the moonlit landscape. "Addison."

"Huh?"

"Her name is Addison."

"Addison." He locked in her name while looking at the road rolling inches beneath our dangling feet. "What I haven't decided yet, is if *you* are one of the good guys." He looked back over at me.

"Everybody's the hero in their own mind," I said, more to myself than Trey.

"Sure, bud, but some of us aren't delusional."

I let the miles pass in silence. I was fairly certain our new reality was about to reveal quite a bit about all of us.

7.

A S WE CLIMBED A RIDGE ABOUT a mile outside of town, I had a
thought.

"Hey. We need to stop for a sec."

"And why would we need to do that?" Trey inquired.

"I'd rather not get Addison shot."

"Pumpkin ain't gonna shoot her." He nudged his head
toward me. "You might be a different story."

"Not by her. By the guy you saw drive by in the truck.
Or one of his kids."

"Explain. Now."

"Stop the truck. Have your wife point the gun between
my eyes while I explain. I don't care. Stop the truck before
we get too close."

He leaned and squinted at me, trying to read my face. Then, he slammed on the side of the truck.

"What?" Emily yelled from the passenger seat.

"Tell Addison to stop a second!"

"Why? You okay?"

"Yeah! Just do it!"

Emily said something unintelligible in the cab and the truck slowed to a stop next to Skull Valley's cemetery. A fenced-off patch of land that looked down at the distant town from the near edge of the ridge.

Trey hopped off the tailgate and the little truck's shocks jumped back up into place with a groan. He turned. "Well? Spill it."

As I got down, Addison slid out from the driver's seat. Emily reached over and pulled the keys from the ignition, before getting out of the passenger side.

"Listen. Skull Valley isn't your average place," I began. "You went out of your way to ride through it because it's scenic, but you could've gone straight from Yarnell to Prescott and skipped it altogether. If people live there, it's because they don't trust most people, they enjoy solitude, or they are hiding from something."

"What's your point?" Emily snapped.

"When something like this goes down, take any lack of trust and multiply it. There are some families there who've been preparing for something like this for a very long time. No one will be passing through on their way somewhere else." Something occurred to me. "That guy. The one who drove right past you. How fast was he going?"

"Pretty fast," she conceded.

"His name is William. He didn't stop because he doesn't know you and he doesn't trust you. And he was rushing to get back to his home."

"To check on his family."

"Yes. That. And then to defend his town."

"No one loves Skull Valley more than William," Addison confirmed.

"And we are the first to arrive behind him," I added.

"But he knows you two. What's the problem?" Trey asked.

"First problem: We have to make sure whoever is watching the road recognizes us before they shoot. Second problem: once they can see us, we have to convince them that we aren't your hostages."

Emily thought for a second. "Uh huh. I get it." She smiled. "I'm not giving up the gun."

"You're going to have to."

"Emily." It was Addison, voice as calm and confident as it had been at the campfire. "You can trust me. We won't leave you behind."

"Girlfriend? You seem nice enough. But I don't know you and the only person I trust is standing right over there." She glanced at Trey.

"I trust her, Pumpkin."

41

"With our lives, Trey?" She gave him the side eye.

"I don't trust this guy. But if you are asking if I trust her? Well, I do." He shrugged his shoulders. "I think we should trust her. It's the safest way to do this."

Emily looked at him for a few more moments before rolling her eyes in resignation.

"God help me. But don't give it to your boyfriend." She took a few steps and handed the gun to Addison, who handled it like it was made of something toxic.

"I'm not her boyfriend." I said it quickly so I wouldn't have to hear her say it.

Addison rolled her eyes.

There was a sound in the darkness. I couldn't tell how close it was. Never could at night. We all looked in its direction until Trey spoke the words for all of us with, "Let's get moving."

I took the wheel, Addison had the gun in the passenger seat, and the young bikers rode on the tailgate as we rolled toward town. The purr of the engine and the wheels pressing over pavement were the only sounds.

We were approaching the unofficial northern border of the community. What appeared to be a small levee in the moonlight, was actually a raised railroad track that intersected the road on a bridge barely wide enough for the two lanes. It formed an ideal point of defense. People with weapons could lay atop the tracks and see anything on the road all the way back up to the cemetery. And the only way a vehicle could enter from this direction would be under the tracks. Anyone in a vehicle would be blind to what awaited them on either side of the road the moment they crossed under.

I hoped William was still busy fortifying his little home and giving instructions to his family, but I feared we had taken too long and Skull Valley was no longer a town you could freely pass through.

I slowed to a near-crawl as we came within the last twenty yards. To our right there was a sign: "Skull Valley." A smaller sign had been attached to its bottom: "Home of Travis Beck." The pride of our town for everyone but my parents.

My eyes wandered back from the sign to the road and saw it—William's flat steel trailer straddled the lanes inches from the far side of the underpass. I eased to a stop.

A voice, deep, but young, called from above, "Lukas! That you?"

I leaned out my open window and into the dim moonlight. "Yeah! That Conor?"

"Yeah. Who's with you?"

"Are you the only one? Where is the rest of your family?"

"Dad is talking with the few others who weren't in Prescott. Liam has the south end of town, Sophie has the old road." He paused. "Lukas! Who is with you?!"

"Addison is next to me—"

"Addison?" Conor's voice went the slightest bit higher.

"And two people who needed help are riding in the back."

"Strangers?"

Addison stuck her head out the passenger window. "Hey, Conor!"

"Hi, Addison!" I could hear his smile.

"I've known Trey and Emily for some time!" Addison lied with a lack of specificity. And I'm sure it pained her. "They ride through town a couple times a year!"

"But they aren't from here…" Conor considered.

"Conor!" Addison's voice got louder. "We're coming in! It's no less my home than yours!"

"Addison." There was more resignation than protest in his voice.

She hopped out of the truck and motioned back to Trey for help. Together, they walked under the tracks and Trey pulled the trailer out of our lane before whispering something to Addison. She punched him in the shoulder. He chuckled.

I rolled through and stopped again. Addison hopped back into the passenger seat before Trey moved the trailer back into place and took his spot next to Emily.

"Thanks, Conor!" Addison yelled out her window.

8.

WE ROLLED FURTHER INTO TOWN. Metal guardrails rose to border the road on each side as it curved left in the darkness. The rail on the left gave way to a defunct single-pump gas station. We turned right onto a smaller road. On the right, we passed one of the smallest elementary schools in the state. Light was flickering from behind two of the windows.

I didn't stop to investigate. Probably an impromptu community leader meeting already in progress. My priority was dropping off Addison and her two best friends before getting my truckload home.

I glanced over at Addison. "What did Trey say back there?"

"Huh?"

"You punched him in the shoulder back there. Why?"

"It was nothing."

"Well. He said something."

She shook her head and looked skyward. "He said it looks like Lukas has some competition."

I wasn't sure what to say.

"Never mind. Told you it was nothing." A tone that said the topic was no longer open for conversation.

As we ventured further down the dead-end road, a stone arch gate came into view on the right. It was almost opulent in its juxtaposition to the barbed wire fence running up to it on both sides.

Addison got out and swung the gate wide. Once she crawled back in, I continued up the private dirt drive to her expansive home at the edge of the foothills.

In the shadowy night, the home looked like something Frank Lloyd Wright might've designed. Angles. Concrete. Glass.

The front door swung open and a powerful beam of light struck me flush in the eyes.

"Who the hell is on my property?!"

"Dad!" Addison yipped. "Relax, would ya?"

"Addie?" The beam swung to the passenger seat. "We weren't expecting you until tomorrow."

We both got out of the truck.

"Dad? Do you know what's going on?"

He pattered down the steps, adjusting his designer glasses as he descended. "Well, let's see. My little girl, who should be at BWC tonight, is arriving home before dawn with a local boy."

"Hey, Mr. Forrester." I said it more to remind him I could hear him than as a greeting.

"Hello, local boy."

"Dad! You'll thank this local boy once you realize what he did!"

"I can't imagine—hey! Who the hell are you?!"

I turned to see Trey standing behind us. He waved. "Hi, Pops."

"Sebastian?" Addison's mom emerged from the door holding a flashlight of her own. "What are you doing out—"

Addison gave a little wave in the darkness. "Hey, Mom."

"Addie?" For a second time in less than a minute Addison was blinded.

"Hey, Mom." Trey's burly voice through a smile.

"Ahhh!" She jumped and clutched her chest.

"Not helping." Addison said over her shoulder, before turning back to her parents. "Mom? Dad? Lukas saved me tonight and these two need our help."

Sebastian waved his hand dismissively. "A, I don't know what that means—*he saved you.* B, Hell, no."

"Dad. Mom. I'm going to ask you again. Do you even know what's going on?"

"Yes." Addison's mom pursed her lips and shook her head. "I was in the middle of a *Housewives* marathon when the power went out. And remember the backup generator your dad promised us would work? Yeah," she shook her head violently, "nothing."

"I'll call them in the morning, Corrine."

"Sure. If the phones suddenly start working again."

"I told you. We need to get a good night's rest. Power will be restored by morning."

"They have no idea." Emily walked up to Trey's side and put her arm up on his shoulder.

"Pardon me, Walmart?" Addison's mom asked with condescension.

Trey bristled. "What did you say to my pumpkin?"

"Trey." Emily said it like a warning. "You don't have to defend me against the likes of her."

"Trey! Emily!" Addison commanded their attention before lowering her voice and extending her hand, palm to the ground. "Please wait here a few minutes."

"We had a deal," Emily reminded her.

"I know." Addison turned to her parents. "Mom? Dad? Let's go inside. There are some things you need to know." She looked to me. "Lukas, thank you." A hint of a smile before turning and walking past her parents and into the house.

Addison's mom looked at her father, who shrugged. They followed their daughter through the door.

"Charming family," Trey deadpanned.

"How the hell did those two raise that girl?" Emily wondered aloud.

"I've wondered that for two years," I answered, still staring at the door. I looked over at the couple and thought for a minute. Then, I walked to the back of the truck, grabbed a compact pistol, found the right ammo, and quickly loaded it to capacity. I walked over to Trey and extended the gun.

He threw his hands up and took a step backward. "Whoa, whoa."

"I need you to use it if…" I stopped myself.

"What?" Emily cocked her head.

"Forget it."

"No." She waited. "Tell us."

"If you're going to be staying here, I want Addison to be safe."

"Ahh," Trey said with a knowing smile.

"Never mind." I turned to put it back in the truck.

Emily reached out and grabbed my shoulder. I turned as she said, "We can do that for you." She reached out her hand and I gave her the gun.

As I walked back to the driver's side of the truck, Trey whispered to Emily, "Told you so, Pumpkin."

The Toyota revved to life and I drove it back to the gate, but instead of turning left back toward the center of town, I turned right. Further down the one-way road as the night crept closer to dawn. To where it ended. To my home.

9.

THE LITTLE TOYOTA JOSTLED OFF THE last of the pavement and onto the dirt that signaled a change in ownership from the county to my family. Up ahead, the farmhouse was dark, but that didn't mean Mom was asleep. Every second of battery life, every centimeter of candle wax, and every unlit match was to be conserved. In her eyes, the bullets in the gun I'd just given away would be a much bigger sin than the gun itself. Every bullet is a one-shot deal. That's why I had no intention of telling her about my recent donation.

I eased in next to the house, between Mom's old Bronco and Dad's classic Jeep and shut off the truck. I had barely opened the little truck's door before my mother had wrapped her arms around me in a tight embrace.

"You alright?" She whispered in my ear, not easing the embrace. She was almost fifty, but her strength hadn't waned in the slightest. She was lean, but country strong.

"Yeah, Mom. I'm fine."

She backed off enough to allow me to exit the truck and grabbed me by the shoulders. "I love you and I'm relieved you're alright." She smiled for a brief moment in the darkness. Then, it was gone. "Let's get moving. Not much darkness left. Inner keep."

Without argument, I said the words. "Inner keep."

Our family had planned for as long as I could remember, in case of any scenario that required hunkering down, we would share supplies with the community and do our best to help hold the town. The outer keep. But if Skull Valley fell—from within or without—the family would retreat to our home against the local mountains. We would defend it with our lives, and with the supplies we held back from the wider community. When I was little, I thought it was cool to imagine our rickety old farmhouse as a castle. Now I just thought it childish. And selfish.

Dad didn't know what would happen, but he had always been convinced *something* would. The possibilities were endless. San Andreas finally giving way and destroying the majority of California. The overdue La Palma fault giving way and causing the Canary Island tsunami to devastate the eastern seaboard. The Juan de Fuca fault decimating the Pacific Northwest coastline. The Yellowstone supervolcano blackening the skies. The exponential increase of extreme weather caused by climate change. The loss of individual rights as our country slid further toward an all-powerful and centralized government. A resulting second civil war. Solar flares that had the power to take down our power for over a year. And electromagnetic pulses caused by atmospheric detonations from anyone able to get their hands on the right weapon. The list went on and on.

But now that something catastrophic *had* happened? Well, refusing to help strangers was one thing, but we'd need this small town to be as strong as possible to survive for any extended period of time. And, yeah, I guess there were people beyond my family that I cared about.

"Lukas?" Mom's voice called me back to reality, even if it felt anything but. She was frozen at the back of the truck, looking at my haul. "Exactly where did you get all this?"

"As soon as I knew what was going on, I headed to Don's."

"Lukas!" she yelled with an admonishing tone.

"I didn't steal it. He let me in and we cut a deal. I helped him load up. In return, I could take from whatever was leftover."

"I'm just upset you headed back into town." She considered something. "Crap."

"What?"

She didn't respond.

"Mom. What?

"If he took all he could and left you the rest, he's thinking the same thing I am."

"This won't go away anytime soon."

"I mean, I knew it. But hearing Don knows it too just makes it more…" She hesitated. "Real." She swallowed before nodding, somehow steeling herself. "Where did he go?"

"Didn't say. There were two bad actors on the scene by that point."

"What?!"

"We handled it. Tied one up and the other ran away. It was best to keep our destinations to ourselves."

"Honestly, son." She shook her head.

"I'm fine. I helped Don, and look how much more we have now."

"Listen. I don't care about extra supplies. If something had happened to you…what would I even be defending?"

I hated her words. Like I was still five. After all, I'd moved quickly. I had gotten the supplies. I saved an old man's life. I'd gotten Addison home. And I was here now, to defend my mom. Not the other way around. For the first time in my freaking life, I'd pretty much been heroic. With the exception of all the people I'd refused to help.

Without waiting for my assistance, she began unloading the back of the Toyota through the side door to the house and spreading it across the living room floor.

"Mom." She stopped to look at me. "We don't have to unpack it. We could just bug out."

"I'm not leaving your father," she declared before going back to her mission. The message was clear. She would entertain no further discussion.

It wasn't long before every minute brought a fraction of additional light to the impending dawn and I was beginning to feel hazy from pulling an all-nighter. Back at Don's, I had moved so quickly, he eventually just got out of my way. Here, I struggled to keep up with Mom's pace. I was certain she hadn't slept either, but there wasn't any visible evidence.

Finally, everything was in the house. The Toyota was empty and the keys were in my pocket.

Mom surveyed the haul now covering the floor for a moment, taking stock. "Did anyone other than Don and the two thugs see all this?"

"Addison Forrester. I gave her a ride back from camp. And two other folks who I brought back to town, Emily and Trey."

"Who?"

"Two motorcyclists we met on the way here—"

"Okay. Six people."

"Conor saw it, too."

"William's boy?"

"Yeah. William already had him posted at the railroad overpass."

"Then William will know soon. Which means the town will know soon. Damn it."

"There was nothing I could do."

"Other than cover it with a tarp."

"Don took all of them." I said defensively. I decided mentioning the fact that Addison's parents might've gotten a glimpse was a bad idea.

"It's fine. We can skim whatever we can get away with and the rest will fortify the outer keep."

She seemed completely disappointed.

So much for being the hero.

"Lukas? You did well." She must've seen something on my face.

"Should we sort through it and move whatever we can get away with downstairs?"

She took the hint and moved on. "Once that's done, we need to steal a few hours of sleep. I imagine a knock on the door will wake us up."

DAY TWO

"WHEN THINGS FALL APART AND OTHERS FIGHT FOR CONTROL, BECOME THE GRAY MAN."

—

MARK TAYLOR

10.

MOM WAS RIGHT.

I woke up from my too-short siesta to the sound of someone pounding on the door. I rolled off the couch I'd passed out on and scrambled for a gun, but I was too slow. Mom was already opening the front door.

"Good morning, Conor. What's the news?"

"Hi, Mrs. Taylor." He was wearing a baseball cap backward atop his athletic build. The perfect jock. He looked to me with a nod. "Hey, Lukas. Uh. There is going to be a meeting in an hour at the school. We are asking everyone to be there. I volunteered to let everyone know on your road."

Of course he did. It included Addison's house.

"Thanks for letting us know." Mom went to shut the door.

"You'll be there, right?" He quickly asked, poking his head toward the space between the door and the frame.

"Thank you, Conor." She shut it on him.

I moved to the window and looked out in time to see him get on his mountain bike and head back toward town.

"They'll want everyone there, Mom."

She turned to look at me. "You're going. Remember, we just entered a new world and the pecking order is about to be established. I want to know what everyone says. Observe as much as you can. When the meeting is over, be the first one out of there. I'll be finishing up preparations."

"If you don't go, it'll draw attention."

"If I go, it'll draw more. They'll ask what I think." She smiled a bittersweet smile. "And I'd rather not tell them what I'm thinking."

"Which is?"

"I'd love it if everyone lives through this, but when it comes to my family's survival, it comes first; anyone else is a secondary concern."

11.

APPROACHING THE ELEMENTARY SCHOOL FELT LIKE an alternate universe. People of all ages walking on foot from every direction. A few on bikes. One kid on a skateboard. No one with a working car was wasting precious gasoline to travel less than a mile or two.

I pulled the bill of my baseball cap a bit lower as I neared the front entrance. I didn't want to be noticed. I wanted to watch the show. My parents always taught me that pressure brings out the worst in most people. Skull Valley was now facing pressure like it had never known before. No air conditioning. Limited clean water sources. Gasoline joining the endangered list. Refrigeration was a memory. Everyone, a potential thief. Worst of all? Complete information isolation from the outside world.

Without knowing how long it would last, we were the newborn nation of Skull Valley. And we were about to draft our constitution.

"Lukas?"

I spun around to see Addison. She was walking toward me with her parents close behind. I imagined her mother's disdain at the prospect of mingling with the common folk. Her father was dressed neatly. Too neatly for the potential apocalypse.

"Hey, Addison." I usually could put together a decent sentence or two, but in Addison's presence, I turned into a blabbering caveman.

"Get any sleep?" she asked as her parents continued into the school.

"Maybe two hours. Then Conor tried to beat my door down."

"Ha." She smiled. "Mine, too."

"I bet."

Her cheeks seemed to flush, and for once, I didn't like it.

"My two favorite townspeople!" Trey exclaimed as he walked up with Emily. They were getting looks from every person heading in. Mostly, it was Trey's menacing frame that was drawing the attention.

"Morning." I didn't mind Addison's company one bit, but I didn't need last night's band to get back together. It wasn't helping my plan to be incognito.

"Where were you?" Addison asked her new lodgers.

"We… uh…" Trey stammered.

"Your mother asked us to hang back a few minutes." Emily cut to the chase.

Addison's eyes went wide with obvious outrage. "What did she say? Exactly?"

"I tuned out after ten seconds to be honest with you," Trey grinned.

"Don't worry about it," Emily shook her head. "We were comfy in the garage. We can deal with her attitude."

"You shouldn't have to. I'm so sorry."

"I think they're about to start the meeting," I cut in. Addison's parents being pretentious idiots wasn't exactly earth-shattering news. At least not to me.

"Let's get in there, then," Trey motioned to the door.

The cafeteria was the biggest room in the building and only fit two-thirds of those in attendance. The rest of us were relegated to the hallway. With no door leading into the cafeteria, hearing wouldn't be an issue, but I wanted to see the action. I wanted to read the faces.

There was a series of three loud bangs and Trey jumped. I noticed Emily rubbing his massive back.

"I want to thank all of you for coming this morning!" *Predictable.* I could picture William Sinnot's red face behind his small glasses. "We have a few things on the agenda this morning!" He seemed to pause for dramatic effect. "We will share what we know. Next, we will share our suggested plan. Then, we will open it up for questions and concerns. Finally, we'll hold our first election."

A quiet murmur spread throughout as people wondered why they were allowing William to take charge already. To his credit, he seemed to anticipate the feeling.

Three more loud raps on a table.

"Listen. I don't want any of you to think for a second that I'm somehow assuming control. Fact is, someone had to organize this gathering right away. We will vote on leadership going forward at the end."

"Is that really necessary?" someone asked. "How do we know power won't come back on within days or even hours?"

"We'll get to that," William said. "But we are sitting on a rare patch of fertile land. Most of us have septic systems. Many of us have hand pump wells on our properties. There are several streams that run through the area. Even if this isn't a long-term emergency, there are enough preppers and panic-driven individuals in populated areas who will be heading our way. And if it lasts as long as some of us suspect it might, they'll just keep coming."

"Not really calming us down, William!" another member of the sparse community shouted.

I nudged my way ahead a few feet until I had a view of the proceedings.

"Okay, then. Let's get to it," William pulled out some

notecards. "I want to thank my kids who spread the word about this community meeting. They were exhausted from keeping watch through the dark hours of the morning and are now home sleeping. I also want to thank those who are watching to the north, the south, and the old road as we meet.

"There will be a sign-up sheet available at the end of this meeting. Please only sign up if you have firearms experience and you are willing to defend our community with the skills that come with that experience. Now. We don't know what is going on or why the power is out—"

"It's more than power!" someone shouted.

"The North Koreans did it!" someone else shouted.

"Terrorism, probably," another said.

William rapped on the table again. I was pretty sure he had purchased a gavel decades ago in anticipation of an excuse to use it.

"The point is—the point is, we don't know what is happening and we don't know with certainty how long it may last."

"With respect," Addison's dad said with authority. It was his normal voice, but with added volume, enunciation, and even a touch of bass. "With respect. It is almost certainly an electromagnetic pulse caused by an atmospheric blast set off with the express purpose of shutting down our power grid and communications."

"Told you it was that Kim Jung guy!" the citizen said, taking credit.

There was a disruption in the crowd behind me before Trey leaned over my shoulder and asked, "He get all that from his little girl?"

"Yeah," I whispered. "But I doubt she knew he'd do this."

"Now," William tried to regain his authority. "The whole town knows I've been preparing for a day like today for quite a while. Along with Lukas and his mom." It was the first time he had acknowledged me since my father's funeral. "So, not trying to toot my own horn, but I know quite a bit. And yes, it looks like what you are describing, but we can't be certain."

"I mean no offense, and I am certainly not presuming expertise in all things related to our current situation, but you cannot deny, given what stopped working, like newer vehicles and more complicated electronics, and what still works, like non-LED flashlights and the like, that it points overwhelmingly to precisely what I have claimed." Addison's father held his ground.

"Well." William paused. "It does, but like I said, we can't be sure."

"Similar to how a medical professional might diagnose an underlying disease by looking only at the collected symptoms. We have enough symptoms to move ahead with a proper course of action." William opened his mouth to say something, but the authoritative voice of Sebastian Forrester continued. "William? We owe you a debt of gratitude for protecting our town thus far. We owe you a debt of gratitude for gathering everyone this morning. Now, we must move forward with the knowledge that the power and communications we have lost will not be restored any time soon."

The room murmured its assent.

Perspiration became visible on William's forehead. "Okay. Alright. I appreciate your input. May I share my immediate suggestions?"

"William. Of course." Sebastian made a broad gesture to the assembled. The townsfolk William had lived next to for fifteen years, suddenly belonged to a man who never mingled with them a day prior.

William addressed them. "I believe we must maintain a perimeter. I believe we must determine how our resources are to be shared. I believe we must establish who is allowed in. These are the priorities."

"Agreed," Sebastian interjected. "We need to determine how to best keep everyone within the perimeter safe. We must determine what force we feel is sufficient to guarantee that safety. We must take stock of our collective resources. We are blessed. We have your family, William, and another..." He scanned the room, before finding me toward the back. He added what almost looked like a genuine smile, "Lukas! There you are!" He turned again to his new constituents. "Lukas and his family have also prepared well for emergencies such as this. Two families who have done so much. Truly a blessing."

Dad warned that our efforts would make us a target, but judging by the look on William's face, he didn't foresee how quickly others would put claims on his well-known preparations.

Sebastian went on. "And let's face it, our divided government is not going to have an adequate response for this. And even if it did, a small community this remote wouldn't be anywhere near the top of the priorities. So I'm certain you were going to suggest some sort of vote to determine temporary leadership. Please." Again, he bowed ever so slightly and took a step back.

William blinked at him for a moment before finding a hint of composure. "Actually, yes." He pushed up his glasses. "Well. Yeah. I mentioned that earlier." He paused. "We need to take a vote for who will be the person ultimately responsible to make the quick decisions, because make no mistake, there will be decisions that need to be made before a consensus can be reached."

"But it can't—under any circumstance—turn into a dictatorship." Sebastian interrupted.

"Of course not!" William exclaimed, completely on the defensive.

"The individual should always be subject to an immediate vote of no confidence if necessary."

"Well." William struggled to think quickly. "There would be logistics to think through on how that could be done, but yes. Accountability would be important."

"Paramount." Sebastian finished.

I looked over and saw Addison. She wasn't looking to the spectacular dismantling of one Mr. William Sinnot at the hands of her father. Instead, she was looking at her feet. Flushed.

"Okay. We agree on that point," William fumbled for footing. "And we all agree that we don't have a lot of time. We've got a lot to get done before another night without power. We should vote. And I'd like to humbly suggest myself." There was no audible support. Silence. "I've already moved to secure the perimeter. I've already called this meeting. As has been mentioned, I have prepared as well as anyone for this scenario."

"Who is gonna run against you?" someone questioned.

"I say the other guy should be an option," someone else suggested.

"I'm sorry, me?" Sebastian, quick to pounce.

"Why not?"

"Oh. That wasn't my intent. I fully recognize William here has been part of the community much longer than myself."

"Yeah? And that tree out the window has been here longer than him, but that don't mean I'm voting for it to take charge!" someone remarked to several laughs.

William looked wounded.

"Okay. Fine." Sebastian raised his open hands. "But only because you need someone to run against William to make it official. But because this is still the United States of America, I suggest only citizens of Skull Valley who are of legal voting age should participate."

"Fair enough," William assented sheepishly.

In the interest of time, it was decided those eligible should crowd into a classroom and a show of hands would determine the winner.

As the adult citizenry herded into the class and the door shut behind them, the foursome from the night before found one another. Emily looked at Addison and said, "Looks like I'm going to have to be nicer to you."

Addison, with arms now folded, "Why's that?"

"Because you are about to be the daughter of the President of Skull Valley."

Without a word, Addison looked back at the floor.

Trey leaned close to me and whispered, "And it sounds like you might need to scamper home and hide a few things."

"Not worried about it." Mom was working on it as we spoke.

After a few minutes, the door swung open and the herd made their way back out. As the chattering people slowly filed into their previous posts, William joined the crowd. Sebastian stood before them. Addison turned and darted out of the room. I wanted to go after her and make sure she was alright, but I needed to stay. I needed to know what Mom and I would be facing from within.

"Everybody! Everybody!" He reached for William's gavel, and in the most painful moment for William yet, he asked, "May I?"

William nodded.

Three sharp raps and the crowd quieted again.

"Everyone, I am humbled. This was not what I was expecting, but I'll honor your wishes. Since time is of the essence... William? If you would be willing, I would like you to be my head of security."

"Well..." William was still reeling.

"Folks? Is anyone more qualified than this man? We need you, William."

William Sinnot looked around the room for a brief moment. He weighed the disappointment of the public rejection he'd endured with his desire to be needed. "Yeah. I can do that."

"I know you can." Sebastian rolled on. "Lukas!"

Hearing him call me out almost made me jump.

"I'd like to ask you to be my youth representative. I'll need you to help me determine how to best use the youth of our community. While this is still the United States and voting wasn't your right, these are extreme circumstances and I'll need to know what the young among us can contribute."

I shook my head. "With all due respect. I'm not exactly the homecoming king around here. I'm probably the least qualified teen in town."

"Nonsense. Addison has told me great things about you.

And there is the issue of your family's knowledge. I'll need to pick your brain regularly, for the good of the town."

"I really don't…"

"Son!" Sebastian raised his voice slightly. "If we are going to get through this, none of us can be afraid to step up when called upon. Even if we didn't ask for it. Follow my example here."

I had to hold back a dry, sarcastic laugh.

"Son." His voice lowered again. "This isn't a request. You can do this. I'll be calling on you." He finished it with that smile again.

Trey whispered from behind my shoulder, "Keep your enemies close."

I tipped my head to look back. "I'm not his enemy."

"Is the feeling mutual?"

"Remember to sign up and help protect Skull Valley." Sebastian looked to William. "How did you say it? People willing to defend our community with the skills that come with firearms experience?" He looked back to his people. "William can't keep us safe without your help. I know none of us want to think about it, but things might get dangerous around here."

12.

I LEFT TREY AND EMILY BEHIND and headed straight for William. He was standing near the sign-up sheet for perimeter security, shell-shocked.

"Mr. Sinnot."

He looked at me and his eyes took more than a moment to focus. "Ah. Lukas. The sheet is on the table right there."

"No. I mean, yeah. I'll be signing up. But I wanted to say I'm sorry. I would've voted for you."

"Ehh." He waved me off. "It's for the best. This way I can focus on what's most important."

I nodded, allowing him to save face. "Maybe you're right." I wanted to tell him to head home and hide what he wanted to keep for his family, but I couldn't be sure where his alliances landed. I stepped over to the sheet, grabbed the pen and signed my name.

A giant hand gripped onto my shoulder. It was Trey.

"Hey. We're heading back down the road."

Emily took the pen from me and signed her own name.

"You don't need to do that," I whispered. "You're sleeping in a garage."

"The seats in the Land Rover are plenty comfortable," Trey confided. "Don't tell 'em."

"They're gonna know with you drooling on the headrest like that," Emily laughed.

"Check on Addison, would you?" I asked. "She didn't seem too happy about something."

"I saw her scoot out of here," Emily noted.

"Don't worry. We'll check on her," Trey added, before putting his arm around Emily and joining the departing crowd.

Most of the assembled had made their way out the front double doors of the school when Conor walked in, stood a few steps inside the doorway, and peered in all directions.

"She ain't here, brother," I called to him.

"Hey, Lukas. What'ya talkin about?" He approached through the stragglers.

"Addison left as soon as her dad was elected new king of the castle."

Conor cocked his head and furrowed his brow. "Explain."

"Sebastian Forrester. Addison's father. The town elected him—"

"But my dad…"

"He ran against Mr. Forrester. But your dad was asked to continue to be in charge of perimeter security."

"Addison's pop? That doesn't even make sense." His prematurely deep voice cracked. "He hasn't said more than ten words to this town since he built that ugly fortress."

"Conor!" He turned to see his dad approaching. "What are you doin' up? You should be sleeping another three hours."

"Couldn't, Dad. Woke up and couldn't fall back asleep. Wanted to come down here and…"

William inhaled deeply through his nose and put his hand on his son's shoulder.

It was only when they stood side-by side, that you could see the slightest resemblance. I imagined Conor and his sister took after their mom. The youngest was a little mini me. Poor kid.

"What happened, Dad?" Conor searched his father's face.

"It's better this way." He leaned in to whisper, but I could still hear him. "While Richie Rich over there has to deal with gas rations, curfews, and bureaucratic nonsense, we'll be doing what really matters—keeping the town safe." His eyes moved to me. "Lukas. I need you to relieve the old road in three hours. Identify whether or not any approaching individuals are townspeople or not. Townspeople welcome. No one else." He leaned close. "No one. If they don't stop and you have time, yell for backup. If you don't, stop them. The shift will be six hours. Bring your own food and water."

"Sir?" I tried to hide how I felt about the order. "Stop them?"

"No one who didn't live here before… gets to live here now."

"I get the bridge again, right?" Conor asked a bit too eagerly for my liking.

"Of course." William slapped his oldest son on the back. "Prescott is the nearest population center and the northern entry point will almost certainly be the first to see significant action. But I've got an idea to make it a bit more secure. Let's go."

I stood there for a moment, wishing I could convince Mom to help me pack as much as possible and get out of here while we still could. At this point, I figured Addison might even want to join us. Not likely, but a guy could dream.

"Lukas!" It was the new king. "Thank you for agreeing to help me." He walked up and put his arm around my shoulder. The physical assumption felt rooted in power. And I didn't like it.

"Yeah." I decided to take some power back. "Did you see your daughter leave? She looked upset."

"She'll be alright. Her mother is looking for her." He smiled smoothly. "Hormonal teenager."

"If you say so. She looked *really* upset."

His face hinted at the slightest worry.

Punch landed.

"Hey listen," he continued. "We need to talk about what your family has that will be of help to the community."

"Can't right now. Your head of security asked me to prepare for my first shift on the wall."

"Maybe I'll go talk to your mom then."

I smiled, "Good luck with that."

Sebastian Forrester had seen the truckload the night before. But he had no clue about our food stores. He didn't know my dad maintained two thousand rounds for a Beretta, a Winchester shotgun, a Winchester rifle and a heavily modified AR. And he definitely didn't know about the shelter.

13.

I DROPPED ONTO THE RICKETY COUCH in my living room, unsure if I was more exhausted from a lack of sleep or the soap opera my little town had already become.

Mom made her way up from the basement.

"Lukas! That better be you!"

"Put down your gun and make me some lunch!" I yelled with a smile.

"That can't be my son because he'd know better than to say something like that!"

She walked around the corner and placed her Beretta on the coffee table.

"Mom. I got you plenty of new toys from Don. You should keep any gun no one has seen hidden for now."

She bent down in front of me and took my chin in her

hand. "Listen, son. You don't need to give me advice. And never refer to these as toys." Then, she smiled as she looked back at the Beretta. "And this is my favorite." She let go and straightened, "So. Tell me what happened."

"There were a few twists."

"Go on."

I let myself fall sideways on the couch, my head heavy on the armrest. "Let's see. If there is a knock on the door, it will probably be the new guy in charge of Skull Valley."

She looked down at me. "Why'd William be paying us a visit?"

"Not William. Like I said, 'twist.'"

"Okay." She processed a quick moment. "Not William. Then who?"

"Mr. Forrester."

"Forrester?! What in God's name?"

"The international man of mystery himself."

"He seems to openly disdain having to live here. The only member of their family worth two cents is Addie."

"Mom. He must've either been a politician or a lawyer, because he came prepared to win the crowd."

"How?"

I sat back up and looked at her. "William wanted control, of course, but Forrester actually used everything I had told Addison. He pretended like he knew everything about EMPs. He owned the room and totally threw William off his game."

"Okay. Well. If he's parroting you, at least he's responding appropriately."

"That's the thing—he's only using it to seize power. He has no idea what he's doing. He basically forced William to be his head of border security and I'm his youth advisor."

"And what is that?"

"I have no clue. Neither does he."

"So, why is he—"

There was a knock on the door.

Mom reached to the back of her waist and handed me a CZ handgun. "Take it. Let him see it." She grabbed the Beretta. "On the other hand, it might be someone selling girl scout cookies."

14.

"WHO'S THERE?" MOM ASKED LOUDLY.

"Ms. Taylor? It's Sebastian Forrester. I'd like to talk if you've got a few minutes."

She opened the door. "Mrs."

"Pardon?" He wiped a bit of sweat from his forehead.

"*Mrs.* Taylor." She held up her hand proudly bearing her wedding ring. "I am busy, as we all should be. What do you need?"

"May I come in?"

"You've got five minutes." She stepped to the side.

He stepped through the threshold and looked around. "So, this is the homestead?"

"Was a lot bigger before Mom sold half of it to you," I said, without meeting his eyes.

"Hi, Lukas. Thank you for agreeing to be of help earlier." His eyes dismissed me and moved to Mom. "Your son has agreed to advise me. But William tells me he also agreed to watch the perimeter." He looked back over to me. "Make sure you leave enough time to take care of your mother, here."

She coughed and shook her head. "What brings you to the end of the road, Sebastian?"

"Two things. Mind if I sit?"

"Yes. As I said, we're quite busy."

Even I was surprised by Mom's aggressive tone. But I was enjoying every second of it.

"Fine. First. Lukas, I don't need a youth advocate or whatever the hell I called it. I need an advisor, but I didn't want to offend all the adults in the room. Face it. You know more about what we are about to face than anyone in that room save William. And he already has a job."

"Mom knows more than I do."

"She wasn't there and you don't have to be a genius to figure out that meant she wouldn't want the job."

"Neither do I."

"Young man. You're no idiot. You know full well how I knew half of what I said at that meeting. I need you."

"Then why'd you run against William?"

"Hey," his voice softened. "He is a good man, but he's no leader. And this community is going to need one to get through the next days, weeks, or even months. People will need to be persuaded to pitch in and to be team players. And that brings me to the other reason I'm here." He turned back to Mom. "The town needs to know we can count on your family to contribute more than your knowledge. We know you have a supply of firearms, ammunition, and various supplies."

"We have prepared, but not nearly as well as the rumors suggest. Truth is, we don't have much. Look around. There's a reason the—what did you call it—homestead... is half the size it used to be."

Sebastian tilted his head. "Come on, Jennifer. I saw the truckload last night."

"I didn't say we didn't have anything. I didn't say we wouldn't contribute what we can. I'm just afraid we aren't quite as prepared as Cheyenne Mountain, or even William's family, for that matter."

"That's not good news." He seemed to be probing Mom's face for any tells.

She gave him nothing until breaking the silence, "But I've got an initial package I quickly cobbled together." She walked into Dad's old reading room and came out with a huge canvas duffle bag. The heft of it was obvious as her sinewy arms strained to set it down. "You'll find it contains two first aid books, several car repair books, a Bible, a few gardening books, several flashlights, batteries, and five long range walkie talkies."

"They still work?"

"They were in a Faraday cage."

"A what?"

"Nevermind."

"Well that's great, but some firepower might be more helpful."

"I noticed you aren't packing," Mom said, giving him a quick look-over. "Any reason for that?"

"We are planning on setting up an armory. I'll get something from it."

"Ahh." She nodded slightly. "But you are vulnerable now. You don't own any guns? You live in the sticks now, friend."

He let out a heavy exhale. "We have several. My wife demanded we get a safe that operates on fingerprint recognition. Now the safe, with all its contents, is a glorified paperweight."

"Oops." Mom smiled before looking serious again. "Well. We can't have our fearless leader walking around without protection. She walked past him and reached above the door to remove a M1911 pistol off a nail. A few days ago, that nail had held a cross.

She held out the classic pistol. Sebastian hesitated. "Is it loaded?"

"Wouldn't be much good to you if it wasn't, but the safety's on."

He took it, inspected it, and thanked Mom, before stuffing it in his waistband.

Mom just gave away our worst handgun.

"Thank you, Jennifer."

"No problem." She nodded, hands on her hips.

"Regarding our armory—"

"Say no more, Sebastian. That is my next project. The three of us have guns that have been cleaned properly. I gave you my husband's. Take good care of it." She took a moment and looked like she was composing herself, probably trying to repress a laugh. "I'm going through the ones Lukas brought home last night. Once I can guarantee their safety, they'll be donated to the cause along with the proper ammunition."

"Excellent to hear." He paused and looked at the duffle on the floor.

"Valuable stuff right there," she said confidently. "As of last night, books are the new Google. As I see it, first aid, car repair, and gardening are going to be pretty important. But not as important as God's word."

"Of course."

"And I figure the flashlights are good for anyone and the walkie talkies will be crucial for each of the perimeter posts."

"And will we need some of those Faraday cages?"

He had no clue whatsoever.

"In simple terms," Mom explained, "it's a sealed metal container with insulation that protects electronics from what happened last night."

"Ahh." He thought a moment. "Is that why older vehicles are still working? Whereas newer vehicles don't use metal exteriors, the older models' metal frames protected all the internal mechanisms?"

"No. They aren't sealed in metal. When it comes to vehicles, it's more about the electronics. The more complicated it is, the more likely it won't work."

"So, can you make me a list of what should still work?"

"Nope."

"Why not?" he shot back.

"Two reasons. One? It's all theoretical, so it has been educated guesswork up until this moment. Two? As I told you, I'm busy. So…"

"Alright. I need to get this stuff back to the school." He moved toward the duffle.

"Is that where you will operate from?" asked Mom.

"Yes. The principal's office will become my office."

Mom shot me a glance.

He went to pick up the duffle and grunted as he lifted it. I couldn't be sure, but I suspect Mom had packed her thickest books to humble William Sinnot when she thought he was going to be the one visiting. And he wouldn't have asked for guns, because that would mean he'd have to give up his own.

"Hey." I jumped up. "I'll leave one of the walkies in the bag and distribute the others. One for each post and one for William."

"That sounds good, but should we conserve the batteries?"

"I think William would agree," I suggested, "we'll need them over the next few days more than ever. That's when we're most likely to have visitors."

Sebastian nodded in agreement. "We've already had a few citizens make their way back from Prescott right after the vote."

Mom's eyes widened with interest. "What did they say about Prescott?"

"Not much has happened yet. Most people were either at home or at the event for the hometown hero." Mom snorted at that. Sebastian noticed. "What? Did you know him?"

"Yeah. Anyway, Prescott?"

"Some looting. If there's been any serious crime, the lack of communications will probably keep it from being discovered for a bit." While he spoke, I unzipped the duffel, removed four of the walkies, and zipped it back up. He went on, "A big meeting at the football field was called by the county sheriff for late this afternoon."

"Alright. Well, thanks for stopping by." She opened the front door and waited expectantly.

"Okay." He hoisted the duffle, attempting to mask the effort. "Let me know when those guns are ready." He headed out the door.

Mom closed it quickly and looked at me. "Load one bag. Food, walkies, and hidden treasure. Visit Dad before you go."

15.

THE SIMPLE HEADSTONE WAS ABOUT SIXTY FEET from the back of the house.

I sat in the yellowing grass. "Hey, Pop." Didn't know why I always talked to him. He wasn't here. But I went on, "Looks like you should've gone all in on the pulse. Yosemite and San Andreas let you down." I tried to think of something else to say. "Mom is making you proud though…"

I sat there in silence a few minutes more before getting up, grabbing the pack, and heading down the road toward Addison's.

I arrived at her stone gate, looked in all directions, and satisfied I wasn't being watched, moved to its left base. Sitting with my back against the stone, I pulled a spade out of my pack and proceeded to dig a small hole in the dirt. Then,

I set down the spade and pulled a gallon Ziploc freezer bag containing a loaded Glock out of the pack. Rechecking to make sure the safety was engaged, I set the insurance policy in the hole, before replacing the turf and patting it down. Having resumed my journey toward the center of town, I was startled by a panicked voice off toward the railroad tracks to the right.

I moved quietly toward the origin.

Then, a second, deeper voice spoke.

I slowed as I crept up behind some scrub brush and silently set my bag down. My hand on the CZ, ready to pull it.

"Give me your name again!" The higher voice shook. I recognized it as Liam, Conor's eighth grade little brother. I raised up enough to see him aiming a gun at Trey.

"Dude. I really need you to stop pointing that thing at me." His shaking paws were raised to each side.

I needed to somehow let Liam know Trey wasn't a threat without startling him. The kid might've been fine on the range, but he had no business walking around with a loaded gun in the real world.

"Get on your knees!" the boy's voice went higher.

"Liam, it's Lukas Taylor," I said it quickly, but calmly.

"Lukas? Lukas? I need your help." His voice was frantic.

"Hey." Trey looked like he was breaking up, his face a ghastly pale. "Please make him stop pointing—"

"Shut up and get on your knees!" Liam shrieked.

"Liam? I know this guy." I extended my hand, palm down, calming. I hadn't pulled my CZ. The situation didn't need more escalation. "His name is Trey. He has been staying at the Forresters' with his girlfriend."

"He doesn't look like your friend." The nerves shaking his voice.

"Dude," Trey panted. "Please."

"Liam?" He wouldn't look away from Trey as I spoke to him. I realized I only had one option. I pulled out the CZ and aimed it square at Liam's lower half. Safety on—not that he'd be able to tell. "If you don't lower your gun—right now—I'm going to have to shoot you through the leg, but I've never used this gun before and I could be as much as six inches off in any direction," he looked over at me, eyes wide, "and that would truly be a shame."

His gun lowered.

"Safety on Liam!" I ordered.

He complied.

Trey dropped to the ground. Sitting, but somehow still needing to hold himself up with a hand to keep from slumping over.

Liam looked back at him.

I covered the distance in a flash, clasping my hands over Liam's, ensuring the gun didn't rise toward Trey again.

"Give me the gun, Liam."

"Why?!"

"Give. Me. The gun." I conjured the authority a seventeen-year-old often holds over a thirteen-year-old.

He released his grip and I yanked it out of his hand.

"Liam. I appreciate you were looking out for the community, but you almost shot my friend." I went about removing every last bullet from his weapon.

"I'm sorry! I didn't know who he was and…and…look at him!"

I did. Trey didn't look the slightest bit scary at the moment. Instead, he looked half-dead.

"Here's your gun. Go find your dad and tell him what almost happened. Tell him we need some identification code or something everyone in the community knows."

"What good does this do without bullets?" Liam asked, looking at his gun.

"You saw what the threat of it can do. Besides. Once I'm convinced you won't accidentally shoot your sister in the dark, you'll get your bullets back."

"Whatever!" He turned and stomped off.

I looked down at Trey. He'd begun to recover, still looking down the tracks. I sat next to him and looked in the same direction.

"You alright, big man?"

"Yeah. Just don't like guns, dude."

"Could tell. Noticed your girl doesn't have the same issue."

"Yeah, well," he picked up a little rock and tossed it down the tracks. "Different person, different story."

"What are you doing out here alone, anyway?"

"We're sleeping in a garage. We don't have a change of clothes. We feel horrible about what we did to you and Addison last night." He glanced over to me, before continuing. "I know everyone is going through a lot, but Pumpkin is my girl, ya know? So, I told her I needed some air. I walked down the drive to pick some flowers I spotted near the tracks on our way back from the school earlier. I know it's stupid, but she loves flowers."

I stood up. "You better get back to that then. See you around." I decided to take the tracks the rest of the way.

"Hey, bro!" His husky voice called out to me. "Thanks."

"Only wanted his bullets," I said without turning around.

"Sure, dude."

16.

BOUT HALFWAY DOWN THE TRACKS toward town, a bush rustled about fifteen feet ahead to the right of the tracks. I stopped silent. My right hand found its way back to the CZ's grip for the second time in a matter of minutes. Then, another rustle and something like a zip.

Sophie Sinnot's auburn hair popped up looking in the other direction. She was William's middle child and only two years younger than me. She turned. "Oh, for God's sake. Can't a girl get some privacy anywhere in this town?" She was tucking in her shirt.

"Were you—"

"Peeing? Yeah, I was."

"But I thought you had a septic system."

She looked in all directions. "Do you see my house?"

She waited a brief second. "Neither do I. And I had to go. You gonna write me a ticket for public indecency?"

"Listen. I don't care where you pee, okay?"

"Good. I'm hoping it's still a free country." She cleared her throat. "Dad said you are covering the old road soon."

"Yeah. Next shift."

"He gave Conor the north end of the highway again and I've got it to the south." She shook her head with disgust. "Like anyone will be coming from that direction."

"Listen, Sophie, I know it's pretty far away, but the Phoenix metro area is only a ninety minute drive and quite a few cars are still working."

"I know, but even if Wickenburg hasn't organized yet, all the people looking for breathing room and fresh water would have to get through Yarnell. And my guess is, Yarnell is totally concerned with the southern edge, the same way we are concerned with our northern border. We've become allies of convenience without much between us. And Yarnell won't be easy to overrun from the south since they sit at the top edge of one hell of a climb."

God, she was good. Yarnell sat at the end of a steep thirteen-hundred-foot climb. They would expect almost all danger to come from that direction because people wouldn't be traveling toward dense population centers at a time like this. Over ninety percent of people getting all the way to Skull Valley would be using the highway or possibly the old road. Over the coming week, at least.

"So here is my issue," Sophie went on, "if you want to keep me in the kitchen wearing an apron and baking muffins for the boys, say so. But don't patronize me by sending me to watch the south."

"I guess the advantage is that you'll be closer to home and your toilet."

"Good, because that's so crucial to my feminine sensitivities, you a-hole."

"Oh." I reached in my pack and pulled out a walkie. "This is for the southern post. In case you need back up. Or to keep you updated on the north and the old road."

"Oh good. I can hear what I'm missing." She snatched it from me.

"Turn it on when you get there, okay? It's a simple single channel."

"Fine. Maybe I'll pretend to flirt with you. Keep myself entertained by making Conor angry."

"Please don't. I don't think your brother is my biggest fan as it is."

"You're his only competition, ya know."

"For what?"

"Never mind. And I'll pretend to flirt with you if I want." She looked up at me. "Be careful, okay?" She slapped my shoulder before turning and walking off.

"Did you use hand sanitizer after—"

"Nope!" she said without turning around.

17.

WHEN I ARRIVED AT THE NORTHERN POST, William was barking directions at Conor, Liam, and several other volunteers. The single trailer barrier had been replaced with something far more complex. Now people wishing to enter the community could freely drive under the railroad bridge but would emerge on the other side, penned in by two trucks on each shoulder, end to end. At the end of each of the second trucks were two more trucks crisscrossing the road, side by side, facing opposite directions.

Conor spotted me and made his way over, guzzling a canned coffee drink. "Pretty intense, huh?"

"Looks like something out of *Mad Max*." I glanced at his drink.

"It has milk in it. Working my way through anything

with dairy first." He lowered his voice. "Besides, I'm operating on a lack of sleep and the kick won't hurt."

"Hey, man, if it belongs to you, I've got no complaint." I was looking back at the entrance design. "Is it about securing the border, or ambushing people?"

"That's the beauty of it. If people who aren't citizens respect our wishes, they turn around. No harm, no foul. But if they claim to be citizens, they proceed under the bridge. We get a good view of them from both sides and above. If we know them, the trucks at the end pull apart like a gate. If we don't, they have one last chance to leave or…"

"They'll be sitting ducks."

"Fish in a barrel," Conor said with a smile.

"Don't you think we need to be careful about using that kind of force? I mean, if a mistake is made, there's no coming back from it."

"Yeah. I heard about Liam. He complained to Dad about you, but then Dad interrogated him until he admitted what almost happened. But let's be honest, that guy doesn't really belong here anyway, right?"

"The other thing we have to consider," I ignored the question, "is that at some point in the future, the lights will come back on. When that day comes, everyone will have to answer for their actions. If we do anything more than absolutely necessary to ensure our survival, there'll be a reckoning."

"Yeah. Maybe. But the reservoir can't sustain too many

people. And your little stream is great, when it's running. Septic tanks will fill. Food will run low."

"I know all this." A hint of irritation in my voice.

"Here's the thing, bro. I get that we might be held accountable sometime in the future, but we need to make sure we live that long. That has to be priority number one."

"Conor! Get over here!" his dad hollered.

"What now?" I asked.

"Digging concealment positions. Gotta go." He turned and started to jog back toward his father.

I walked toward them. "Mr. Sinnot!"

"Pretty busy over here, son!" He was watching another volunteer digging the hard ground with a shovel. "Got those walkie-talkies Sebastian mentioned?"

"Simple single channel walkies, but they should do the job. One for each post, one for you, and one for Sebastian. Already gave Sophie hers." Conor glanced over as I continued. "Told her and Mr. Forrester to turn them on at the beginning of the next shift."

"Great." Mr. Sinnot grabbed them and tossed one to his oldest. "Thanks, Lukas."

"Thank my mom."

"I will if I ever see her," he said, pushing his glasses back up his nose.

"She's busy checking weapons before donating them to the community armory."

"I'm sure that's all she's doing." He looked at me knowingly before glancing at his mechanical watch. You've got about twenty minutes before you take over at the old road."

"Heading there now."

"Alright. You'll be relieved at twenty-two hundred."

"Ten. Got it."

"You've got food?"

"I do, sir."

"Okay. And I know this is asking a lot, but as you've probably noticed, several folks are allowing us to use their cars to block the roads. Sophie is moving our old truck to cover one of the lanes to the south. Could you block the other side with your mom's Bronco?"

"I think you'll need to make that request in person."

"Needs to be the Bronco. Your Toyota would lose a battle with a motorcycle."

"Remember," Conor interrupted, holding up his walkie. "If you need backup, don't be too proud to use it."

"I hope we make it through the night without that being necessary," I responded before climbing the incline up to the tracks and heading off to my post.

18.

THE TRACKS RAN NORTH TO SOUTH through Mariposa County, but took an eastern detour crossing the highway on the elevated berm just north of Skull Valley, gradually curving 180 degrees east of town, before heading back to the west, though the heart of town. After crossing the highway a second time, the tracks continued back to the west past the school and my family's property. The northern post had been established where the tracks crossed the highway. The eastern post, near where they crossed the old road.

I was walking the northern edge of the tracks from the northern post to the old road when I figured it was best to announce my presence from a distance. If William thought Liam was ready to stand guard, God only knew who was holding a loaded weapon up ahead.

"Lukas Taylor here! I'm here to relieve you!"

"Couldn't find someone more qualified?!" shot back a recognizable voice.

"Addison?" I looked for her. Then a tan tarp flipped back. Tossing some dirt and sticks that had been hastily thrown atop it.

She stood and wiped at the dust on her shoulders, left bare by her tank top and canvas pants, creating a sheen of mud with her sweat. "Jeez, it was hot under there!" She was gripping a .22 rifle. And she was right, she looked incredibly hot.

"This wasn't your shift."

"The meeting was boring. I went to the northern post. Was turned away. Came here to offer my services and found a taker."

It had been obvious her father's power grab had upset her, but if she wanted to talk about it, I'd let her be the one to bring it up.

"Well, your mom was looking for you."

"This isn't that big of a place. Could've found me if she was willing to walk ten blocks."

"True enough." I looked down at the tarp. "Ya think that's really necessary?"

"Well," she got back down and sat on her feet, "it's a pretty sweet vantage point. Tucked on a little rise next to the road. You can see anyone coming for a quarter mile. Give it a look." She patted the ground next to her.

"I'm sure it's great."

"Come *on*." She patted it again.

I rolled my eyes, pretending like this wasn't more nerve-racking for me than trying to keep Liam from shooting Trey.

"Now lay down and take a look."

I shot her a look that said, 'Are you serious?'

She returned it with a look that said, 'Just do it.'

The influence a high school upper-classman has over a middle school student—the influence I had used to disarm Liam—was only bested by the influence of a cute high school girl over any breathing high school boy—at least in my eyes.

I got down on my stomach and looked at her.

"Well?" She quickly tilted her head down the road. "Look!"

So I did. It *was* a good spot. My head was barely peering over the tiny ridge. Approaching people would never see me before I saw them. But William was right. For it to be an effective choke point, there would be some serious work to do. If improvements weren't made until tomorrow, tonight would be the most dangerous night the old road would ever see.

Addison laid down on her stomach next to me and looked up the road. Our shoulders touched.

I changed my mind about minding my own business. "Addison?"

"Lukas." She didn't look over. Let my name linger.

"You seemed pretty upset when you left." Her lips parted to say something, but I went on. "And I'm not asking you to say anything you don't want to. I just wanna know one thing."

She looked over at me, mere inches from my face, but somehow maintaining complete innocence, "And what's that?" I could feel her breath on my cheek. Or was that my imagination?

I couldn't return her look. I was afraid I'd be pulled toward her eyes, her lips. And I'd make a fool of myself. I kept looking up the road and asked my question. "Is there anything I can do to help?"

Out of the corner of my eye, I could see her continue to look at me for a long moment before looking to wherever I was pretending to look. "Lukas."

"Addison." I returned her name in the same quiet way she had returned my own.

"It isn't that I don't want to tell you. It's that I can't."

This time I looked at her. "Are you in danger or something?"

"No." She paused, "Well, no more than any of us."

"Then what is it?"

A third voice joined the conversation. "I find it's best that a lookout keeps focused."

I rolled quickly and looked back. Mom was standing there. "Hey, Mom."

She was a straight-up middle-age ninja.

Addison rolled the other direction. "Hi, Mrs. Taylor."

"Hi, Addison. It's nothing personal, but you are a very pretty girl and Lukas needs to stay focused."

"Mom." Irritated. "I'm focused."

Addison rose to stand.

"I'm sure you are." Mom took an AR from her shoulder and handed it to me. "Thought this might do you more good at long range than the CZ."

"Thanks," still embarrassed.

"Addison? It's always good to see you. And, Mr. Focus? Please turn on the walkie." She turned and began silently walking back toward the center of town.

Addison stood there, a bit awkwardly. "I better go."

"Addison." I quickly scrambled to my feet.

"I'm sorry I got you in trouble." She picked up her .22 and slung it over her shoulder.

"You didn't. Addison…"

"I need to get back home and make sure Trey and Emily actually get dinner." She flashed a quick grin and traipsed off.

"Bye," I said it more to myself than her.

I clicked on the walkie. "Old road checking in."

A click. "About time. North road here." Conor didn't use his name, enjoying this a bit too much. "Where the hell have you been?"

"Decided to go see a movie and grab some dinner in Prescott," I responded sarcastically.

Click. "This isn't a joke, Lukas."

Another click. "South road here." It was Sophie. "And he's being serious. Thanks for taking me, Lukas, but you really should've asked my dad first."

The girl was determined to get me killed.

Click. "If someone could here this channel, they'd be convinced our community is being guarded by a bunch of teenagers." It was William Sinnot.

"Uhh, Dad?" It was Sophie again. "That might be because it is."

"Conor and Lukas are more than capable."

William's sharp omission made the walkie-talkie go silent.

Conor finally came to her defense. "So are you, Sophie."

More silence.

"Hey, everyone." It was the fifth walkie. Sebastian Forrester. "Gotta quick question here. Then, we should probably conserve the batteries by staying off the air unless there is an emergency."

"Go ahead," William responded.

"Anyone see Addison? I'm sure she's fine, but I thought I should check."

"She's headed home." I answered before thinking.

Silence.

Crap.

I set down the walkie, checked the ammo in the AR and the CZ, and laid on top of the tarp as protection against crawling bugs. Loved the outdoors, but hated bugs.

It was time to settle in for a solitary six hours.

If we were lucky.

19.

THE SUN HUNG A HAIR ABOVE the peak to the west of town. I was looking east, down the old road, watching the shadows begin to stretch. The first full day of this brave new world would go dark within the next hours and I would stagger home and pass out as soon as my replacement arrived.

The radio clicked. Nothing.

It clicked again. Nothing.

A third click. "Am I about to be abducted by aliens or..." It was Sophie. "Or is someone too shy to say what is on their mind?"

I waited.

"Sorry. Needed to make sure before I freaked everybody out." Conor's voice sounded uneasy. "Dad? You need to get to the north road. Now." Urgency replaced unease. "Bring backup."

"On my way, son." William's response was instant. "Sebastian? If you are around anyone who can help, send them. Conor? Tell me what you see."

"Several vehicles lined up on cemetery ridge."

"What are they doing?"

"They appeared up on the ridge one at a time and stopped."

"Dad? Should I head that way, too?" Sophie's concern came through the radio.

"Conor." William ignored her. "If they come down the hill quickly, let them drive under the bridge and into the barricade. I'll be there by then and we'll be able to decide if they are friend or foe. If they approach slowly and you think they'll hear you, address them before they pass below you. Got it?"

"Got it."

"Conor, Sebastian here. Emily is headed your way and I'm heading toward the Taylors to get them."

I grabbed my radio. "I'm at the old road, but I can run the tracks and be there in a few minutes."

"Stay there just in case. I'm getting your mom." There was a quick break. "Never mind. I see her. We'll be there soon."

"Dad?" Conor's voice was anxious. "They're moving."

"Almost there, son." William's voice was breathless.

"Driving down the hill in twos. Side by side. There's six of them. No. Eight."

"That's a lot of people," Sebastian stated the obvious.

This was ridiculous. I was sitting here looking at a dusty road while a caravan was driving right toward our front door. I scrambled to my feet, tossed the walkie-talkie in the pack and threw it over my shoulder, gripped the CZ in my right hand, and began to sprint down the tracks as quickly as my adrenaline would allow while holding the heavy AR in my left.

As the tracks slowly rose on elevated earth like a levee, I glanced to my left, across a field, and saw who I thought was Sophie keeping pace with me, sprinting the highway in the same direction. After a few minutes more at full sprint, I got my first glance of the eight vehicles ominously crawling closer to Conor's post. I stopped, crouched, set my weapons down, and pulled out my walkie—which had either gone quiet or I couldn't hear over my running.

"Conor? This is Lukas. I'm to your east."

"I see you."

And I spotted him, laying prone across the tracks, facing our unknown visitors.

"Lukas! Who is watching your post?" William sounded furious.

He was right, of course. It was a calculated risk, and probably an unnecessary one, so I didn't answer. Even if it was a slight possibility, I didn't want to broadcast the fact that ninety percent of our perimeter was now unprotected. That's when I realized why the walkie had gone so quiet. All there would be to talk about at this point would be defense positions and strategy.

I stayed low and made my way to the south side of the elevated tracks. The first thing I noticed was our Bronco. Mom must've driven Sebastian to save a few minutes. I couldn't locate her, but Sebastian was standing with his back to her truck and looked to be holding the gun Mom had given him. My eyes found William crouched low next to one of the trucks creating the penned-in section. I couldn't be sure, but I thought Emily's head bobbed up for a brief moment through a truck window on the far side. There was no sign of Sophie, either.

I glanced back down the track. Conor was like stone. Unflinching. I slowly approached the north side to reestablish a clear view of the visitors. I aimed the AR and flipped off the safety. They were getting close now. Thirty some odd yards from Conor.

20.

ONE OF THE FRONT TWO VEHICLES, a familiar old rusted out F-150 in the right lane, slowed to a stop, as did the six assorted older vehicles behind it. Only the classic Mustang on the right kept rolling. It was the only attractive car of the lot. And one of the few I didn't recognize. As soon as it was a car length in front of the F-150, it too stopped in the road.

The driver side door creaked open.

Trevor Beck, the only celebrity Skull Valley ever produced, the man who rated having his name on the city limits sign—as in "birthplace of"—slowly emerged from the car.

After serving in the Army, he eventually moved to California and hit it big. A celebrity survivalist whose shows rivaled those of Les Stroud, Matt Graham, and even Bear Grylls. His fit frame, sparkling smile, and scruffy blonde hair gave him the appearance of a man still in his prime and made network executives swoon.

He had been in Prescott the night before, filming his homecoming special. By all accounts, most of Skull Valley and a huge segment of Prescott had filled the high school football stadium for the occasion. That was when the power went out.

And now he was standing on the edge of town with several guns aimed at his head.

21.

"**I** REALLY PICTURED THIS MOMENT DIFFERENTLY." He scanned the entire scene, hands held high. Then, he nodded toward the birthplace sign on the side of the road. "I'm that guy."

I flipped on the safety and lowered my weapon. I looked to my left and saw the barrel of Conor's rifle lower as well.

William fumbled over the hood of a truck and stood in the middle of the pen. "Trevor! My name is William Sinnot! Moved here a few years ago, but it's home now. You've got quite a crowd with you! Who are they?"

While keeping his hands elevated, Trevor gave a slight wave with his right hand. "Nice to meet you, William." He surveyed the scene before him. He seemed to spot me, along with everyone else. "May I lower my hands?"

"Oh! Yeah! Sure!" William seemed to consider something. "But we still need to know who you have with you."

"Only Skull Valley residents who attended my event last night and a few of my crew who don't have anywhere to go."

"Fair enough." Another moment of consideration. "Here's what we are gonna do. Everyone gets out of their vehicles. Leave the weapons behind. Line up right about where you are now. Left to right across the road."

"Alright, William. Here's the thing. I don't know you. Can I go back and ask a resident if you are trustworthy before we impersonate a firing line?"

"Works for me."

Trevor turned around and walked back to the second truck. With the adrenaline receding, I realized it looked like Jimmy Espinoza's. The door opened and there appeared to be a very brief exchange before Trevor walked back to his mark.

He looked at his name on the birthplace sign. "Good news, William! Jimmy is vouching for you. Says you're a good dude. Salt of the earth." He turned around and cupped his hands to his mouth. "Everybody out and get up here! And leave the weapons!"

Slowly, every door began to open. People came out and made their way up to Trevor. My eyes darted from face to face. Some people I knew by name. Other faces were vaguely familiar. One I didn't. Probably just a crew member. *Wait. No…* A man wearing an Arizona Cardinals baseball cap looked familiar, but he wasn't a resident.

He was the guy I'd left tied up at Wilson's.

"Everyone stop!" I shouted loudly as I raised the AK, disengaging the safety.

The small herd all looked in my direction. When the guy saw me, he quickly stepped behind Jimmy's wife, Rosario and put a knife to her throat. Someone else grabbed the back of a skinny guy's shirt and stuck a gun to the back of his head. It was the big guy who escaped, Kyle. *Kyle and Stevie.*

"We don't want to hurt anyone!" Big Kyle yelled. "Don't make us!"

"What the hell, Trevor?" William yelled. "Who are they?!" I couldn't see my mom, Sophie, Sebastian, Emily, William, Trevor, or if anyone else had arrived on the south side of the tracks.

"Said they were residents!" Trevor's voice responded.

"Told me they were part of your crew!" Jimmy added. His eyes were locked on his wife.

"Hey!" Kyle reclaimed the conversation. "We will be taking the Mustang. No one needs to get hurt. Everyone lower your weapons." He easily backed up the guy he had his gun against. Stevie did the same with Rosario, but she wasn't cooperating with the much smaller man.

"Stop it, lady!" Stevie grunted.

Rosario slammed a fist into his groin. His knife moved a few inches off her throat.

A loud shot echoed.

A portion of Stevie's head disappeared and he collapsed like his bones vaporized.

A second shot exploded.

I looked around and saw the second hostage on the road in a pool of blood as the Mustang's door slammed shut and revved to life. Several more shots rang out, including my own. The car was peppered as it peeled out into the dirt to the left of the road, cutting off the line of sight for everyone on the other side of the tracks. It took off across the field before me and I fired off several more shots. They weren't true. My hands were suddenly shaking at the realization I was the only one with a chance to stop him.

I was certain Kyle had been hit, but the car kept going and, in the distance, circled back toward the highway. In a cloud of dust, it headed back up the ridge past the cemetery.

22.

A S I WALKED THE TRACKS TOWARD CONOR, I saw William run to the bloody man on the pavement. He didn't need to check for a pulse. The resident I only knew as "Tim" was gone.

Jimmy ran to Rosario who was now shaking and looking down at what used to be Stevie.

"What in the hell happened?!" William yelled at Trevor.

That's when my mother walked out of the brush on the far side of the road beside the city limits sign. She had a Winchester rifle and hadn't put it away quite yet. "Jimmy. Take care of Rosario. Trevor, who are your crew?"

I made my way the rest of the way to Conor's spot on the tracks, directly over the road, and sat next to him. From the perch above the road, we listened to the scene playing out below.

Trevor looked back up the road where the Mustang had fled. Two men stood next to him. "Put your damn gun away, Jennifer." He said it with a familiarity that made me uncomfortable.

"Not until we know everyone is a resident or one of yours."

"Fine." He nodded to a hulking man with glistening umber skin and a clean-shaven head who must've been about six foot, but whose wide, muscled frame reminded me of a professional wrestler. "This is my bodyguard, George." Then, he motioned to a lean, younger man with sunken eyes and sharp cheekbones. "This is Andrew, my sound tech. Nobody else from the team decided to come."

"Where did they go?"

"No idea, but I wished them well. Told them Skull Valley was our best chance, but they wouldn't listen."

Andrew hadn't stopped staring at Stevie, or what was left of him.

George hadn't stopped scanning the group. The bodyguard was still on the clock.

"Everybody else! Line up!" William hollered.

They all seemed to be in shock as they rambled into place.

"Alright. Emily! Lukas! I need you down here," William yelled anxiously.

I made my way around and down the berm. Emily emerged from under the tracks.

"I need the two of you to clear every vehicle. I'll lead everyone who isn't a driver through the barricade. When you're sure there aren't any more stowaways, we'll get the caravan through. Conor is your lookout from above. Lukas? The second everyone is through the barricade and it's secure, find me. I need a few answers."

"Where's Mr. Forrester?" I asked.

"He's been hiding behind one of the barricade vehicles," remarked Emily with a disgusted shake of her head.

"And Sophie?"

"I sent her back to the southern post," William said. "Liam has the old road until you get back. If you are up for it, I'm extending your shift until midnight because Emily here is scheduled to relieve you and I'd like her to get a bit more rest."

"I'll be fine," Emily interjected.

"Maybe, but I'd like you fully rested for the wee hours all the same. Now, let's get moving."

23.

WILLIAM WENT ABOUT SEPARATING THE DRIVERS from the passengers. Trevor was whispering back and forth with his two men.

Sebastian had finally emerged and was talking with Jimmy and Rosario.

"Follow my lead. I've got a little experience with this," Emily said quietly. "And safety the AR. Shoulder it. That CZ you've got in your waistband will be more than effective."

As we moved through the vehicles, her confidence with her movements, her silent, but clear directions that put me in perfect position to cover her, and the way she checked every conceivable place someone could be hiding, made it clear she was experienced.

After we cleared the final truck, I stopped her before she gave the all clear for drivers to return to their vehicles. "You sure seemed to know what you were doin'."

"Most of the people here might know you, but they don't know me. And in a situation like this, having a few cards up your sleeve can come in handy." She studied my face for a second before asking, "Are we good?"

"If you're good with me."

"Listen, dude. Trey told me what you did for him."

I shook my head. "Like I told him, I only wanted Liam's ammo."

"I'm sure." She smiled. "And what you saw? He's not a coward. He's the bravest man I know. But that? That's up to him to share. If you need to know about me, I'll fill you in."

"I won't ask."

She turned and yelled the all clear.

Within ten minutes, everyone was inside the perimeter.

Jimmy didn't want 'everyone' to include Stevie's body. In his temporary thirst for vengeance, he wanted us to leave it for a coyote, mountain lion, bobcat, or black bear. Whichever local predator found it first.

Although there were plenty of people who agreed with Jimmy, Sebastian wisely slowed our inevitable moral descent by asking volunteers to wrap the body and bring it into our city limits until we figured out what to do with it.

I hoped it wouldn't be an issue we'd face with regularity.

24.

WALKED BACK DOWN THE TRACKS to the old road as darkness began to settle over the first full day of the new world. As soon as the road came into dim view, I called ahead. There was an armed middle school kid with an itchy trigger finger up there.

"Hey, Liam! It's Lukas! Don't you shoot me!"

No response.

I kept approaching.

"Liam?"

"I'm a stupid kid." The shaky voice came from behind some shrub brush.

I walked toward the voice. "I don't think you're a stupid kid."

"You do. But I didn't know who that guy was. And he

looked like trouble." He walked out from his hiding spot. "I'm sorry, but he did. Do you want me to assume everyone is friendly? Like all the threats my dad talks about—and your dad used to—aren't real? Because if they aren't, what the heck are we even doing, Lukas?"

Liam didn't give me time to respond.

"But we know that isn't true! There are threats! Dad filled me in on what happened. That's why I moved to a spot with better concealment. If that guy comes back, he could use this road. And he's a murderer. And that other guy? Your friend? I didn't know him. He could've been a murderer, too!"

"Liam," I said his name calmly.

"I'm not a stupid kid," he mumbled, almost to himself.

"You were in an incredibly tough spot. You and I both know there can be wolves among the sheep. You were just trying to figure out what Trey was."

He looked at me with pleading eyes, "How could I have known?"

"You couldn't. But you didn't shoot him. You did good."

We stood there in awkward silence for a moment before Liam turned and walked back to his position.

He called from behind his cover. "Your spot was good, but I thought a bit more cover might be cool until we can build out a barrier tomorrow." I stood there until he went on. "Let me show you."

I walked around the scrub brush and found Liam laying

prone. I got down next to him and saw a small tunnel he cleared through the bottom of the bush. You could watch down the road and even stick a rifle in the gap.

"Did you do this?" I looked over at him, adding a smile.

"Yeah. Like it?" he asked, probably hoping he was proving to be more than 'a stupid kid.'

"I don't just *like* it." I paused so the affirmation would grow in its impact. "It's freakin awesome. I'm stuck here alone until midnight and I'll feel a lot safer now. Thank you."

The smile bloomed across his face as we stood. "Welcome. I mean. You can use the other spot if you want." He motioned to the nearby crest and the tarp on its backside.

"Are you kidding? It's great for tonight." Liam almost seemed embarrassed, so I changed the subject. "When is your next shift?"

"Six in the morning." He shook his head and rolled his eyes. "Dad has me watching the south."

"Don't take it personally." I patted him on the shoulder. "Every day that passes, the southern border will become more dangerous. You think Yarnell will be able to hold off the masses from Phoenix forever? Heck no. Millions of people without clean water, sewage problems. A whole bunch of them will be smart enough to head where every house has a well. And you are on that line."

"I guess," he grumbled, looking off into the increasing darkness.

"If there wasn't a threat, your dad wouldn't have asked me to move one of our family vehicles there tomorrow."

"Which one?"

"I'll be having a conversation with Mom about that over breakfast."

"So it'll be your little truck." He smiled widely.

"Maybe not. I can handle my own with Mom."

"No one can handle their own with your mom," he said earnestly.

There was another moment of silence.

"If you've gotta be rested and on the line at six, you better get home and try to rest."

"Yeah. I guess." He shouldered his weapon and grabbed his supplies sack. "Be safe." He started into the night.

"Hey!" I called after him.

He turned.

"Thanks again for making tonight a bit safer for me."

"Welcome." He turned and trudged off.

I was alone, privileged to once again witness the gradual accumulation of the thousand stars above.

25.

ABOUT FORTY-FIVE MINUTES AFTER LIAM LEFT, my radio clicked to life with his older brother's voice. "Hey, Lukas, Sophie. I think it might be important to check in about once an hour to ensure all three positions remain awake. Lukas? You good?"

I picked up my walkie and squeezed the button on the left. "The old road is all clear and wide awake."

Click. "Good. Me too. Sophie?"

There was silence. I waited—afraid I'd block her response. Continued silence indicated Conor was doing the same. His patience wore out.

Click. "Sophie?"

More silence.

Finally, a click. "Oh, hey, big bro. I didn't hear you.

I was having the most spectacular dream about sitting in a hot tub, watching an Audrey Hepburn movie and eating a small mountain of rocky road."

"Not funny, sis!" Conor was equal parts amused and ticked.

"Kids," William broke in, "it wouldn't be a bad idea to check in, but I need you to be personally accountable and remain awake without check-ins because Mr. Forrester and I have walkie-talkies, as well. We need to get some sleep, but we need to leave ours on in case any of you have an emergency."

"Well said, William." It was Sebastian Forrester's voice. It was groggy.

Silence.

"Okay everyone," Conor said, his voice slightly deeper, "only use the radios if there is unexpected contact."

As the minutes turned into hours, I didn't look at my watch. I figured I'd know it was midnight when I was relieved. All I knew was boredom. I trimmed the sniper's hole in the bush a bit more. Taped a thin flashlight to the barrel of the AK. Tried to pace my water consumption, but had finished off my liter some time ago. The isolation was palpable in the silent night. There were no cars rolling through town. There were no planes in the canopy of stars. There was no buzz in the electrical lines. There were only small creatures foraging in the safety of night.

Then, a loud crack.

I was faced with a choice. Remain silent and concealed? Or speak up and establish the origin of the sound? I opted to begin with further silence.

Silence resumed.

Another sharp crack. Whatever it was, it wasn't small. At most, it was thirty yards away. At worst, fifteen. Deep darkness mixed with complete quiet made it nearly impossible to judge.

I slowly rotated my weapon a bit to the left. Still laying prone, it was virtually impossible to be silent in the effort, but I had made up my mind. I was going to say something. If it was a smaller creature than I expected, it would scamper off. If it was as big as I thought, it would hopefully do the same. If it was a community member, they would answer and I'd warn them to remain within the perimeter, particularly at night. If it was a threat, I'd…

My heart was in my throat.

As I clicked off the safety, I said the words quickly and firmly. "Who's there?!"

A loud rush of clumsy noise.

The adrenaline overwhelmed my plan and I clicked on the light. The light reflected in two big eyes for a flash before it turned, yellow-gold body, and only the sound of heavy pats on the ground rapidly putting distance between us betrayed the creature's direction.

A mountain lion had gotten less than twenty yards from me before making a sound. My heart pounded at the realization.

26.

ROUGHLY TEN PARANOID MINUTES LATER, I heard something quietly approaching from behind. My heart ramped back up to full throttle.

"Easy buddy. It's Emily. I'm relieving you." A bobbing flashlight flicked on.

"Over here," I said, trying to sound calm.

The light found me as she made her way behind the scrub. "Nice spot, Rambo."

I stood. "It's all yours." I looked at the Winchester rifle she was carrying. "Ever shoot an AK?"

"I have." She cocked her head, curious.

"I'm going to trade you for tonight. I scared off a mountain lion about ten, fifteen minutes ago."

"You sure that's what it was?"

"I caught a glimpse." I showed her the flashlight taped to the weapon.

"Might be overkill for a kitty, but if you're cool with it." She reached out.

"It was a big kitty." I gave her the AK and she handed over the Winchester.

"Anything else? Boar? Coyote? Alien aircraft?"

"Little stuff. Nothing worth mentioning."

"Okay." Emily smiled. "Get home. You need to get sleep when you can."

I started, then lingered awkwardly. "You okay out here…" I trailed off.

"My mom's a cop. Usually works undercover so I don't see her much, but she's taught me well. Raised me by herself and she's my damn hero. That's why I just graduated from the academy myself."

"Wait. So you're a cop?"

"Trey and I decided to take a road trip to celebrate. Now we're here. So yeah. I'll be good."

"Is Trey…"

"No. Trey does something else."

"Yeah. Alright. Well. Be safe." I turned to escape my awkwardness.

"I'd like it if that stayed between us, okay?"

"Got it."

I made my way back across Skull Valley in the darkness. Mom opened the front door for me—which was a surprise since I'd been silent, but I didn't say a word. I walked directly to my room and fell onto my bed. Fully clothed.

It was as if my body knew what tomorrow would bring.

DAY THREE

"ALLIANCES ARE IMPORTANT,
BUT THEY SHOULD ONLY BE CEMENTED
AFTER CAREFUL DISCERNMENT."

—
MARK TAYLOR

27.

WAKING UP WITH THE SUN ALREADY in the sky, I startled out of bed.

"Mom!" I stumbled down the stairs to the kitchen. "Mom!"

She came up from the basement. "What?"

"Why didn't you wake me up?" I questioned irritably.

She made her way over to her boil and brew camping french press and took a swig. "You need your rest."

"You burn wood to heat up that water?"

"I miss my coffee, okay?"

"Why didn't you wake me?"

"I told you. You need your sleep." She headed back to the door leading to the basement stairs.

She left me in the kitchen. I shook my head to no one in particular and followed her down.

Our basement was a musty, cobweb-infested bunker. There were a few flimsy walls. The entire cavern was split into only three rooms. Each of the walls were covered with shelves. Some attached to the walls. Some, unattached shelving units. Most were filled with cans or mason jars of varied foods. In the center of the main room, there were several folding tables set up. It was the organizational center. In one of the smaller rooms—the one behind the locked door—there was a small armory. There were several large safes, box upon box of ammunition, a reloading press, a reloading scale, a tumbler, a dial, a few cartridge gauges, and more. The third room contained huge boxes of dried goods and supplies filling the shelving units shoved against each wall and balanced tenuously in the center of the room, like an oversized Jenga tower.

Mom emerged from the storage room.

"I think I'm done." She smiled as she wiped her brow.

"Already?" My surprise obviously pleased her.

"What's your next commitment?" She kept sorting some clothing items on the table before her.

"Mom, I could've helped you."

She stopped and looked at me. "Not your job." She went back to her work. "What is your next commitment?"

"I need to find Mr. Sinnot and ask about my next shift."

"I think he's working on the old road barrier." She didn't even look up. "You better eat something. Then, wash up in the stream and go find him."

"Mom? One other thing."

"Use your truck for the southern border."

I tried not to plead, "He wanted something bigger."

"There might be a day we need the Jeep and the Bronco because they don't need roads." She kept sorting.

I looked at her a minute. My truck was tiny. It was rusted. Most of my former classmates thought it was ridiculous. But it was my truck.

She moved a box into the storage room. Emerging back into the main room, she sighed and asked, "When are you going to admit your father knew what he was talking about?"

My temples tensed. "Even if a man gets lucky and wins the lottery, it doesn't mean it was a wise financial plan."

"Seems like it was for the winner."

I turned on my heel and made my way upstairs in furious silence.

28.

I FELT GOOD TO TURN THE KEY and rev my little Toyota back to life. It looked small enough to fit in the bed of some of my classmates' monsters, but it was mine. It was reliable. It got the job done. Now? Well, now it was just a sacrificial offering to the outer keep.

I shoved her into gear and kicked up defiant dust as I turned her onto the short road. I passed the stone gate and continued past the elementary school. The tracks drew nearer to the right side of the road until I came to a stop at the two-lane highway. I looked across the intersection at the makeshift mobile home park that made up the most densely populated portion of the community. Most of the people were outside. Children learning what childhood was like before cell phones and video games, I imagined. Not that I ever knew a time like that, myself. Parents watching said children. Now they were all looking at me.

In less than two days, the sight of a running vehicle had turned into something akin to seeing a mountain lion walking through town in broad daylight. I turned right onto the two-lane highway and watched as the mobile homes gave way to small, but well-kept homes. Yards that proclaimed pride of ownership. Garden beds. Flower beds. Trimmed lawns that wouldn't stay trimmed for long. I turned left onto the old road and rounded a bend. The homes grew larger, as did the fenced-in property belonging to each. White picket fences declared the acres of the families who used to vie for the title of the wealthiest family in Skull Valley until the mysterious Forresters showed up and built their fortress on the opposite end of town.

As the fences came to an end, the land began to roll ever so slightly. I turned another bend and slowed to a stop. Directly before me was a small conversation that stopped abruptly at the sound of my truck. Mr. Forrester, Mr. Sinnot, Rosario and Jimmy, and Conor were all looking at me.

I shut down the truck, but I hadn't even shut the door before Mr. Sinnot was inches from my face.

"What is this?" he whispered harshly.

"My truck. I'm moving it to the southern position, but I wanted to find you first to ask about my next shift."

"I didn't want this little—"

"Lukas!" He was cut off by Mr. Forrester. "Has your

mother finished cleaning the donations for the community armory yet?"

William looked down and clenched his jaw.

"Quite soon, sir."

Sebastian put his hand on my shoulder, "I know we can count on your family."

"Speaking of your family…" I turned to see Trevor Beck walking toward me, flanked by his formidable body guard, George. "You're the Taylor kid, aren't you?"

"Yes, sir. Lukas Taylor."

"Pleasure to meet you." He extended a hand and I quickly shook it, embarrassed to realize I was a bit star-struck.

"Pleasure to meet you, too, sir." I shook his hand a few seconds too long.

"For God's sake. Don't call me 'sir.' Name is Trevor. And this?" He tilted his head to the man made of muscle beside him. "This is George."

"Hi." Nerves in my own voice as I extended my hand.

He only nodded.

"George? You afraid he'll hurt you? Stop pretending to be all tough, ya big teddy bear!" He shadow-punched George.

George made a pained face, reached out, and nearly cracked every bone in my hand.

"Jennifer's boy." Trevor shook his head as he conjured a memory. "Good to finally meet you. Your parents and I grew up together."

"Yeah. You did."

"Yeah. We did." He flashed a grin that added a comma to his paycheck, before it vanished. "Hey, man. I'm sorry about your dad. He was a good man."

"Thank you." It didn't feel entirely appropriate to share my recent opinion of the man.

He turned to George. "Besides myself, I bet there isn't a man in the county better prepared for the situation we find ourselves in than the young man standing before you." He looked back at me and the grin returned. "I had to specify gender because if I include women, your mom might kick both our asses."

William was pretending like he hadn't heard that by cleaning his glasses.

"Trevor here was helping advise us regarding the best course of action for the old road," Sebastian announced like a child who wanted to join in a conversation on the playground.

"He also said he was impressed by how quickly we had set up a perimeter," William added.

"I did." Trevor's eyebrows raised as he nodded slowly. "Most other towns are waiting around for the lights to come back on or someone else to tell them what to do. You've set up a perimeter. Vital to keeping out dangerous outsiders. But also vital to making sure the wells don't get over-taxed and run dry. Making sure the septics don't get over-taxed and... well... the opposite of that. And crucial to extending food supplies. You've also established capable leadership in electing Sebastian your leader." Sebastian openly beamed at the affirmation as Trevor continued. "William has taken on the head security role more than capably. And you've fended off your first threat."

"I'm sorry about your arrival," William's voice said solemnly.

"That's entirely my fault. I should've identified who was a crew member and who was a resident in front of everyone. That would've flushed those two out. And not doing that?" He paused. "That is a mistake I'll have to live with."

There was another pause as if everyone was waiting to hear what Trevor would say next.

Finally, Sebastian filled the silence. "Lukas? There is another meeting at noon. School cafeteria. I expect you and your mother to be in attendance."

Before I responded, Trevor jumped in. "I wouldn't. She's probably preparing her house for war."

Crap. He *did* know my parents.

"Pardon?" Sebastian looked at him inquisitively.

"That family knows what they are doing. They don't need town hall meetings to be prepared."

"While I'm sure they have done an admirable job, the fact is, every family, including yours, Lukas, is better off working with the community."

Trevor nodded at Sebastian while the hint of amusement showed on George's face. "You're right, Sebastian."

Trevor conceded. "Power in numbers. Although it might not be easy getting Jennifer on board."

"We'll fill everyone in on shifts at the meeting," William informed. "It's important she's there."

"Very important," Sebastian reinforced.

"Do you need my help here or…" I began to ask as Conor was digging a hole in the hard soil twenty feet away, near where I'd hid the night before. He was sweating bullets and kept glancing over.

"No," William answered. "Drop off the truck. Sideways. Southbound lane. Bumper to bumper with the truck that's already in the northbound lane. Then head home and get your mom to be there at noon. We'll see you there."

"Yessir."

"Hey." Trevor wanted my attention. "Good to meet you. Talk soon?"

"Uh. Sure." I sounded like an eight-year-old. I climbed back in my truck and pulled away.

29.

I DROVE MY LITTLE TRUCK UP THE LAST INCLINE, before the highway rolled downhill and out of town. The two lanes had been cut about fifteen feet deep into the small ridge. This was the perfect spot for a stand on the southern edge of our little town.

William's old Chevy truck that had seen better days was already blocking half the road. I looked above the road to both sides and saw a resident poking his head over the edge.

I cranked my window down and called to him. "Getting the truck in place!"

"That tiny thing?" The voice carried back.

"It'll be an effective speed bump in a worst-case scenario."

"Worst-case scenario. I'm pretty sure that's what you'd call this," the guy said before he pulled back out of sight, leaving me to get the Toyota in place.

I parked my tailgate against the front bumper of the bigger Chevy. And jumped out to see Addison standing under the Arizona sun in the road behind me. Her hands were on her hips and she looked to be evaluating my truck.

"Well, I guess that'll stop someone on a skateboard."

"Funny," I muttered.

She broke into an apologetic smirk. "Was only a joke."

"I know. It's… It's the only truck I've ever had."

She cocked her head. "But it's still your truck."

"No. The second I parked it there"—I motioned to it—"I gave it away."

She looked beyond me to my former truck, then back to me. "Where are you headed now?"

"I'm supposed to try and convince Mom to attend a meeting at noon."

Her face flinched. "Dad?"

"Yeah. Your father wants everyone there."

"I'm not going." Her voice, almost hostile.

"Where *are* you going, then?"

"Right now? I'm going with you." Her eyes seemed to spark again.

"Why?"

"If you'd rather go alone…"

"No. I mean… No. Let's go." I looked up and called to the man on watch, "Let them know the truck is in place."

I patted the side of my truck for the last time.

30.

WE WALKED RIGHT DOWN THE CENTER of the highway, as if all of Skull Valley was ours.

"Are you going to ask?" Addison's voice was quiet.

I shot a look at her, but she wasn't looking back. "About what?"

"What everyone has wanted to know since we arrived."

"Oh. That." I took ten more steps before continuing. "Now that you mention it, what is your dad's ATM pin number?"

She didn't laugh. She didn't smile. She didn't even look at me as we approached the spot where the tracks headed back to the west at ground level.

I broke the silence. "We should take the tracks. It's faster." We silently turned. "I'm sorry."

"For what?" she asked.

"Upsetting you."

"You didn't."

I didn't believe her.

"My dad worked for some very important people. It was his job to put the perfect words in their mouths."

I didn't dare look at her. I was afraid she'd stop if I dared.

"Officially? He was a speechwriter for some very powerful people. I think that's how it began. But he must've learned some things. Heard something. Because he started looking worried all the time. Looking older. We had more money overnight. More stuff. But we saw him less and less. And when a certain man retired, my dad suddenly announced he had been given a huge bonus and was able to retire. It all sounded great, but then we found out we had to move."

"So, Dad hit the jackpot, but there was a cost?"

"Seems that way." She finally met my eyes. "In all honesty? I don't know much more than that. I'm not even sure how much Mom knows."

"Have you asked?"

"Of course. She turned it around and told me Dad needed our support. But they've fought ever since." She looked down the tracks. "She hates it here more than you do."

"I don't hate everything about it."

The words lingering made me feel like an idiot, so I quickly moved the conversation along.

"I don't know how to ask this." I swallowed for courage. "So you don't know if your dad—"

"Hey, kids." Sophie walked out from behind that same bush beside the tracks.

"Seriously? Again?" I asked. "You might need to get that checked."

"You're probably right." She shrugged and regarded Addison. "Hey, hot stuff."

Addison laughed it off. "Hey, Sophie. Whatcha doin' out here?"

"You don't wanna know," I interjected.

"Probably right," Sophie, matter-of-factly. "Not very romantic. But I'm done here. I'll leave you two alone."

"We were headed to his house," Addison explained.

"Wow!" Sophie's eyes went wide. "Well!" She started off.

"No, Sophie…" Addison tried to clarify.

"Don't bother," I stopped her. "Not worth it."

Sophie went whistling in the other direction as we walked the rest of our journey in silence. Not sure what was on Addison's mind, but my brain switched back from the awkward exchange. I had begun wondering what kind of man was now the most powerful person in Skull Valley.

31.

A S MY HOME CAME INTO VIEW, Addison reached over to slow me down.

"Should we make some noise or something? Your mom doesn't strike me as someone who should be snuck up on."

I kept walking. "By now, she knows we're coming."

She shook her head. "Has she always been such a badass?"

That gave me a laugh as we ascended the front porch.

Before I opened the door, I fixed my eyes on Addison's. "Thank you for trusting me."

"Always have."

I wanted to respond, but I was afraid I'd screw it up. I opened the door. "Hey, Mom."

She came down from upstairs, holding a coffee cup.

"Well hello, Addison. Always a pleasure."

"Hello, Mrs. Taylor," with a sweet smile. "That's not…" Looking at the cup.

"It is. And before my beloved son says a word, I'll burn down the entire forest to heat coffee. Totally worth it." She punctuated her comment with a sip. "You two going to the meeting in a bit?"

"I am," I quickly responded.

Mom looked to Addison, a single eyebrow raised.

"I can't. I have to…" She strained for a plausible excuse.

"Don't bother." Mom waved her off. "I'd rather skip it, myself."

"Then why would you go?" Addison returned the eyebrow.

"If I don't show up eventually, people are going to begin thinking I've joined my husband."

"Mom."

"I'm only saying I need to eventually show up and make sure the community knows I am part of the team."

"If you're going, do I need to?" I fished.

"If you think that I'm leaving you here, unsupervised, with the most beautiful girl in the county," she smiled broadly, "you've lost your mind."

Why did she have to make things awkward by assuming stuff I was still figuring out, and more importantly, talking about it in front of someone who might not feel the same way?

"That's very kind." Addison graciously filled the silence.

"It's the truth." She looked at me and seemed to realize she'd overstepped. "Before we head off to the meeting, and you," she looked back to Addison, "go wherever you are going, let me make us some lunch. We've cleared the fridge and now we are working our way through the thawing freezer. I'll even make a bit more coffee. Just need you to refresh the fire."

32.

ADDISON JOINED ME AS I BUILT a small fire in our pit about twenty-five yards off the far side of the house. As I constructed a small log cabin-style fire, she noticed my silence.

"You alright?"

"Yeah." I looked up from my squatted position adjacent to the pit. "Competing memories."

"Like what?" She squatted down beside me.

"One of them is of us sitting across the campfire from each other only two nights ago." I left out the part about how amazing she had looked. "It feels like a year ago."

"Mm. It does." She was looking at the unlit fire and was smiling.

"There's another." I stared into the past for a moment.

"Me, Dad, Mom. Sitting around this pit. Laughing. Eating s'mores. Dad would pick at his guitar—"

"He played?"

"No." I grinned. "He only knew a few chords. He'd pick at it softly. It was beautiful in its own way."

She didn't respond immediately. She seemed to intuitively know I needed to remember.

I went on, lost, back in time. "It was either the guitar or the dad jokes."

"Dad jokes?" she prodded like a hypnotist working her magic.

"He was an expert in the field." I came back to the present. "What do you call it when an apple hits an orange?" I grinned as I waited for her guess.

"Not a clue."

"Fruit punch."

She groaned. Then laughed. "That is horrible." She looked back at the pit. "Tell me another."

"Okay." I tried to recall another groaner to drive my point home. "How did Canada get its name?"

"Do tell."

I broke into my most over-the-top Canadian parody, sharp Os and all. "Okay. Here we go. We gotta name our land, eh? Everybody ready? We are going to pick letters out of a hat, eh?" I mimicked picking something out of a hat. "C, eh?" I paused, "N, eh?" I didn't have to go on.

Addison laughed loudly, flashing her irresistible smile

again. "Okay. That one's a bit better." Her eyes moved back to the pit and the smile quickly faded. She almost looked forlorn.

"Hey. What's wrong?"

"Uh." Her eyes met mine. "My dad never—"

"Are you two going to light that fire so we can eat to-day?" Mom was standing behind us with a tray holding a tinfoil ball of something delicious.

33.

AS MY MOM AND I WALKED DOWN THE ROAD toward the elementary school for the town meeting, it struck me that we were taking a risk leaving our home unguarded. If someone knew where to look, they might find a surprise or two. Mom stalling until Addison headed back toward her home hadn't escaped me.

"She's quite a girl." Mom let the statement hang in the air as we walked.

"She's a friend, Mom." More footsteps.

"Surprised her dad isn't forcing her to show up. Even without cameras, a supportive family is a powerful visual."

"I don't think Addison Forrester does anyone's bidding. But she still loves her dad."

"Hmm." Mom seemed to consider this information. "You like her?"

"She's a good person." We approached the stone gate that led to her house. "Too good."

"What do you mean?"

"Does the phrase 'out of my league' ring a bell?"

Mom stopped in her tracks. "I never want to hear you say something like that again."

I hated the effort conversations like this took and had become pretty skilled at avoiding them. "Okay." Nice, short, and general usually did the trick.

"Lukas. I'm serious. She's a great girl, but she's no better than you. I've yet to meet anyone who is."

I didn't engage. She was letting motherhood cloud her judgement and if there was one thing I hated, it was people overestimating me. I didn't deserve it. And it wasn't fair to set the weight of lofty expectations on a young man incapable of bearing them.

I changed my mind. I needed her to understand.

"That's not true, Mom. There is no category of any significance where she isn't a better human being than me."

"She hasn't been through what you've been through."

"She's been through a lot more than you know."

Her eyes quickly narrowed. "Is it something I should know?"

"No, Mom. I'm just saying. Everyone goes through stuff and I'm sure she's got a story."

I may have lied.

She studied me. "Okay." Then, her face softened from suspicion to something resembling compassion. "Your father's death—"

"Mom," I tried to object.

"Your father's death was difficult for both of us. Incredibly difficult. And because it was just the three of us, you and I have suffered two waves of grief. We've had to deal with our own and the pain of the other."

"Can we please just go to the meeting?"

"Your feelings toward your dad have been incredibly hard for me to carry, but I understand them. At least on some level, I do. But my feelings for Mark Taylor have never wavered. He is the best man I've ever known."

My breathing went shallow. I didn't want to hurt her, but the words wouldn't stay down.

"He spent all our money. When other kids played ball with their dad, I was learning to skin big game. When other families went to Disneyland, we practiced bugging out. Mom, he turned us into *that* family at the end of the road. Then? He went and died of cancer. Cancer! How freaking unoriginal is that? How much preparation did he need for that? How did his supplies and training and drills and knowledge help us then?!"

Shallow breath turned to nausea.

I realized Mom was looking at the Forresters' arch. Then I realized she wasn't. It was just somewhere to look other than in my direction.

I felt sick.

Her watery eyes made their way back to me. "Are you done?" Her deliberate words trembled as she asked the question.

"I'm sorry."

She reached out and pulled me in for a hug. The side of her head against my own.

She whispered, "Your hurt doesn't have to make you a bad person, an unworthy person. But it will if you let it. Please don't let go of the Lukas I know."

"Is everything alright?" Sebastian Forrester was walking under the stone arch, with his wife, Corinne, at his side.

"We're good," Mom said with a curt nod.

"I have to say, I'm surprised you didn't see me coming. Word around town is that nothing gets by you."

Mom let me go and squared up to him. "You must be pretty stealthy, because if I saw you coming, I'd probably get real close to my son and start whispering so you couldn't hear me. But like you said, didn't see you coming."

They stood there a minute, before Sebastian smiled. "Got it."

"I understand you wanted me at today's meeting," Mom said almost casually, but not quite.

"Is that where you're headed?" he asked.

"It is, indeed. Isn't Addison coming?" Mom knew the answer, but was gathering information, as always. Even if that meant gauging a reaction.

"No." Corinne's response jumped in front of her husband's. "We briefed her, so she could keep watch on our home."

"Oh. Maybe you could brief Lukas so he could keep watch over our home?" She didn't show it, but I knew Mom savored the moment.

"Well," Sebastian's voice got serious. "The truth is that while Addison means the world to me, her attendance is not as crucial as either of yours. The reason will become clear soon enough." He signaled his wife. "Shall we head off? Will you join us?" He looked to Mom.

We fell in behind them.

"I love surprises." Mom gave me a look as she said it loud enough to be heard by all.

"No surprises. You are skilled individuals, crucial to the future of our little community," he said casually over his shoulder.

"Happy to help in any way we can." Mom's voice almost convinced me.

"As you've said all along." Sebastian stopped. Turned. "Jennifer? I don't mean this to be awkward. But it is less so here than in front of everyone at the meeting because it might appear like an ambush." He took a breath. "And that isn't what this is. I trust you. I just need a status update."

"The guns." It was all she said.

"Yes. The guns."

"Good news. They're ready. Lukas and I will bring them wherever you'd like as soon as the meeting is over."

"Along with the corresponding ammunition?"

"Along with the corresponding ammunition."

"That's great to hear." The warmth that won the election. And as much as I hated to admit it, I caught a glimpse of where Addison got her smile.

He turned and resumed his walk. And I could've sworn it suddenly had a bit more bounce.

34.

THE CAFETERIA WAS PACKED. The lunch tables had all been folded and moved into classrooms. The blinds had been pulled and every window was cranked as far open as possible. The natural light and slight breeze made the cramped room only slightly less miserable.

Mom and I managed to wriggle our way to a spot near the back corner next to a window. The spot was inconspicuous, the open window could be used as an emergency exit, and there was the slight breeze to consider.

A murmur passed through those assembled.

I looked toward the door, expecting to see Sebastian making his triumphant entrance. He'd taken up a spot at the front of the school, greeting people as they entered. Practically shaking hands and kissing babies. But the murmur had nothing to do with Sebastian. It was Trevor, flanked by George and Andrew.

Only moments passed before Sebastian entered. It was as if he realized he needed to reclaim the spotlight. But his entourage—his wife and William—was considerably less intimidating.

The three of them slowly navigated their way to the front of the room before Sebastian ascended a single chair. A smattering of applause spread throughout the large room. I looked back to Trevor, who had stationed himself near the door on the other side of the back of the room, and saw him clapping more vigorously than most. I realized he was probably the one who had initiated the support.

There was Trevor. He could've taken the room in much the same way Sebastian had taken the room from William, but he seemed to have no interest in a coup. I found the humility actually kind of impressive.

As I watched him, he spotted me and gave the slightest nod of recognition before looking back up to Sebastian.

"Thank you. Thank you." Sebastian was trying to hide his glow. "That is completely unnecessary. I want you to know I deeply appreciate your attendance. We all have much work to do and the sacrifice of your time is not lost on me. This will be quick."

The room was a complex mix of discomfort with the heat and congestion in the room, excitement with the presence of the celebrity come home, and the curiosity of why the meeting had even been called.

Sebastian got to it. "I would be remiss if I didn't begin by recognizing we have someone among us we all recognize. Mr. Trevor Beck!"

The room broke into an applause that far surpassed the mild ovation that Sebastian had received only moments earlier.

In the midst of it, Mom grumbled, "Beckel."

I turned. "What?"

"Beckel. That's his name."

I didn't know what the point of that was. I was pretty sure Bear Grylls changed his name, too.

Trevor waved quickly, then stopped and nodded back to Sebastian.

"The best part..." Sebastian had begun speaking before the clapping ceased. "The best part is that we have already spoken extensively and he has asked that we don't treat him any differently than anyone else. He would like only to join his considerable skills to those of our community, for the good of his hometown in these extraordinary circumstances."

Another outbreak of applause.

"And this brings up two important considerations. The first is the nature of our circumstances. The second is citizenship. After consultation with Mr. Beck—"

"Beckel," I whispered to Mom with a smirk.

"—our circumstances are precisely what I believed them to be. Our immediate area has suffered the effects of an electromagnetic pulse. We have no way of knowing how widespread these effects are. At a minimum, we have to believe it extends to the Phoenix metropolitan area. If it weren't impacted, it stands to reason we would've seen emergency services by now. Even if the effects don't extend to Las Vegas or southern California, this means the crisis is of historic proportions. There are almost five million people in the Phoenix metro area alone. While they may initially have more food stores than we do, they will rapidly run out of potable water and begin facing serious health concerns involving sanitation in the worst ways imaginable."

The assembled began to whisper among themselves.

"The news, on a macro level, is likely even worse. If large areas in California were left unaffected, we almost certainly would be hearing air traffic as aid of all sorts was delivered to Phoenix. Yet, our skies have remained eerily silent. This means we are left to assume the worst."

Reactions varied widely. One woman began sniffling back tears. Some heads nodded, inferring they already knew what was being said. Others couldn't hide the shock.

"After careful consideration, we are locking down our perimeter, with the exception of locals who find their way home. Exceptions will be made for those already within our boundaries. This must be done to maintain our food supply and the integrity of our working wells and streams."

"But what about those of us with family who live in other places who might be trying to get here?!" a lady pleaded.

"I understand this is hard. But here are some facts. Several of our wells are not working. Only the most basic, shallow wells are currently operational. We are looking at what we can do to get the deeper ones functional again. This will take time. And we have limited streams. Fewer still, that run this time of the year. But even if everything was working, there are over two hundred thousand people in the Prescott Valley alone. Some of them are prepared for something like this. Most are not. Due to their proximity, we have emphasized security to our north. The eventual threat of being overrun from the south is a much larger consideration. The Phoenix metro area has almost five million people."

A buzz went through the room as people realized the implications.

"We could be overrun within weeks if even a slight percentage head northwest and we are not prepared to make our home a very dangerous option." Sebastian paused for effect. "It is natural to want to help everyone. It is. But I'd like my wife, my daughter, and all of you to survive before all others." A second dramatic pause. "And this is how we will do it."

The room was silent.

"We have established a perimeter. There are checkpoints at the three paved entrances into town. They will continue to be built out. It goes without saying that people could enter on foot anywhere else. This is why we must all remain vigilant. If you see someone you do not recognize, ask for the security code. We have made it as simple as possible. SV86338. SV for Skull Valley, then the zip code. That's it. If someone is caught, they are to be escorted from our land. Over the next days and weeks, we will develop penalties for multiple offenders. Again, it has to be this way. Again. The security code is SV86338.

"I'd now ask our head of perimeter security, William Sinnot, to speak a bit more about those checkpoints."

Sebastian stepped down off the chair and William hoisted himself up. He was sweating and had to push his glasses back up his nose, only to see them immediately slide a third of the way back down.

"Thank you, Sebastian. We have done an initial assessment of those within the perimeter who own a firearm and are properly skilled. I hope you understand, we don't have many people to protect such a significant expanse of land. If you have the skill set, we need your help. I have consulted with Trevor, and Sebastian, of course.

"We know the late night and early morning shifts are difficult, but we decided against rotating them. All times will be permanent, every day, until further notice. We hope this helps people adjust their sleep schedules as needed. The shifts will be as simple as possible. Midnight to six in the morning. Six in the morning to noon. Noon to six in the evening. And six in the evening until midnight.

"There will be four people on duty each shift. One at each checkpoint and one floater. Utilize the extra person when you need a bathroom break. And although the times will not rotate, the positions will. Hopefully, this will combat boredom and will help every person be familiar with each station. Sebastian has graciously agreed that the floater should have his walkie. As head of the perimeter, I'll have the fifth walkie and will be able to find Sebastian if he is needed. The board will tell you where to go for your first shift. Each day, you will shift to the next position. North to old road. Old road to south. South to floater. Floater to north. Any questions?"

He wiped more sweat from his upper lip and pushed his glasses back up, before continuing.

"Eventually, we may extend the southern check point to the end of Iron Springs Road. This would add significant farmland and bring those farms under our protection. We may also extend the northern and old road checkpoints as the distance would provide security. We are weighing the resources needed against the resources and security gained." He pushed his glasses back up and stepped off the chair.

I noticed people were glancing back at Trevor to interpret his facial expressions, but the man was playing poker.

Sebastian stepped back onto the chair.

"Thank you, William! Excellent job!" He surveyed the room. "I want to let you know, I decided anyone who is responsible for guarding our perimeter, will have significantly reduced responsibilities for the remaining eighteen hours of the day. They need to be focused and rested to ensure we have no unfortunate incidents."

Sebastian's face grew solemn.

"Now, we don't want to think about it, but there may come a day where we are all called upon to defend our land. We have already taken steps to convert the basement of my home into an armory. We have received donations from the majority of you, with incredible generosity in particular from the Sinnot family and the Taylor family. If we are overrun, make your way to my home. I'm almost embarrassed to say this, but it is not only the largest home, but the most fortified."

Mom chuckled under her breath.

"We do not have a need to consolidate food as of yet. But I must warn you, that day may come. For now, I beg you, be responsible and ration what you have. Please continue to eat the food that will spoil first. In other words, save the Twinkies for last."

A slight laugh—which was not a small accomplishment.

"A few last words. I've been asked to announce, since it is Sunday, if you'd like to join her, Ms. Clarke will be leading a small prayer service in this room thirty minutes after this meeting's conclusion. All are welcome. And we could certainly use the prayers of our faithful at a time like this.

"Also, if you have a special talent for bringing food forth from the ground, be it farming or gardening, please come speak to me as soon as we conclude.

"Finally, we will meet again in four days. It will be here and it will be at noon. Thank you, everyone!"

Mom whispered, "See you back at the house."

I watched as she maneuvered her way through the crush of people toward the nearest door. Trevor intercepted her. They spoke for a few moments, before she ended the conversation by continuing on her way. Trevor was left surrounded by others who seemed to want to get his reaction. Instead he looked over and found me with his eyes. He smiled and made his way upstream through the remaining crowd.

35.

"**H**EY, LUKAS." **HIS EYES SHIFTED** for a second to the front of the room. "That was quite a meeting, huh?" George and Andrew caught up. He turned. "Hey, guys? Wait for me outside? I won't be long." They started off before he called after them. "And check the schedule. I think we'll all be on it." I thought I caught Andrew swallowing hard. George simply nodded.

"What did you think?" he continued.

"About what?"

"Any of it. All of it."

I fidgeted. "I honestly think your opinion matters more. You're the expert."

He blinked with kindness.

"Maybe people know my name, but I had to go off and

learn my skills from the U.S. government. And you know why I did that? Your dad." His eyebrows shot up as he nodded. "Your dad just knew stuff. Even as a kid. He could start a fire without matches. He could field dress any animal. He could shoot any weapon his dad would let him hold. In short? He was ridiculous. And pretty much the coolest friend a boy could have."

"I don't get it," I whispered as I looked out the window.

"You don't get what?"

"He was just a guy." I felt my face become hot. "A guy who lived in the middle of nowhere, spent all his money, and made life more difficult on his family."

I looked back to Trevor and saw disbelief.

He shook his head, eyes wide. "Wow." He looked somehow disappointed in me. "Okay."

Without another word, he turned and walked out the exit, while a few lingering people tried to get a piece of him.

Maybe someone else finally recognized I wasn't such a great guy.

Took long enough.

I made my way out of the cafeteria and down the short hall. A few folks were still gathered around the board. I looked it over and noticed Conor and I were the only two minors left on the perimeter duty schedule. Sophie and Liam had been bumped. I also noticed my shift started in about five hours. The other ones on my shift? Trevor, George, and Andrew.

There was a tap on my shoulder. It was William.

He leaned in close. "Trevor has been nothing but helpful since he arrived. And he's only had two requests since arriving. He wanted to work the same shift as his buddies, since they are outsiders, and he wanted you to be the fourth man on the team. Said 'if you were anything like your dad, they'd be learning from you.'"

We were interrupted as Sebastian walked over and asked William to come with him.

I couldn't help but think Trevor already regretted his request.

3 6.

WALKED OUT ONTO THE FRONT LAWN of the elementary school and sat down under a tree, exhausted and overwhelmed. I didn't care much for the world before this all happened. And I was starting to think I liked it less now.

"Do you think if I shot you in the leg, they'd put me back on the wall?"

I followed the voice to the base of an adjacent tree. It was Sophie. She was drinking a Mountain Dew.

"Excuse me?"

"Do you suppose I'm the first reserve? Because if I am, watch your back." She smiled sadly and took another swig.

"Real talk?" I asked.

"Do I strike you as someone who can't take it?" She held out the can of warm soda.

I stood and walked over and sat beside her. I took the can and savored a sip, before handing it back.

"We both know that your dad, while a very good man, would never put you ahead of Liam, because you're a girl."

She punched me in the shoulder with impressive force.

"Ouch." I spun to her. "What the hell?"

"It might be the truth, but you didn't have to say it." She looked around at the last of the people making their way out of the school. "Maybe I'll have to shoot Conor in the leg, too."

"Well, I might be wrong about your dad, so shoot Conor first."

She seemed to enjoy the thought. "Deal." Then, with a smirk, "But I'll load two bullets, just in case." She finished off her can of soda and stood. "Because I don't do well waiting in line."

A boy I recognized, but didn't know personally, smiled as he walked by. "Hey, Sophie."

She gave him a flight attendant smile before it melted into neutral. "He hasn't talked to me in five years. Suddenly no cell phone or video games and he remembers my name? I need that power to come back on."

"Sorry. Don't see it happening."

"Crap."

She walked off, leaving me under the tree.

37.

I WAS WALKING BACK UP THE ROAD toward home when I saw Trey's giant frame carrying an enormous green duffel bag up ahead, short of Forresters' gate.

I made my voice an octave lower. "Mister! I'll need your security code!"

He groaned as he turned. "SV8...uh..." Then seeing it was me, he broke into a grin. "You little jerk!"

I continued with the voice, "SV8 what? I require the rest of that code."

He set down the bag. Trey was a bull, and even he was straining with the bag. "SV8SHUTTHEHEL—"

"Nope. Not even close."

"SV8IMGOINGTOPUNCH—"

"Now you're not even trying."

The sound of approaching steps revealed Emily making her way down the long drive.

"Hey, Grandpa!" She called to Trey, "You okay?"

Trey turned. "Listen, Pumpkin. Not trying to make excuses, but your bag was about a quarter as heavy as mine. And this little punk is giving me a hard time."

"Hey, Emily. Do you know this guy?"

"Oh for God's sake," Trey mumbled.

"I've never seen him before, but he's kinda cute, in a brutish sort of way." She winked at him.

"You think so?" I prodded her.

"Oh yeah. He's with me. SV86338." She walked over to him and laid a big kiss on him.

"Good enough for me." I grinned. "What's your name, big boy?"

"Your daddy." He said, unable to suppress a hearty chuckle.

There's something that happens when you realize someone else said something unintentionally insensitive. You wait for them to realize it.

Emily made a silent, apologetic face.

Trey's face sunk. "Oh damn, buddy. I'm sorry."

"Hey, man." I gave him an obviously forced smile. "Not necessary. Didn't even get along with him at the end."

"Yeah. Okay."

I pressed on. "What are you carrying in the body bag?"

"The last guy who asked me for the town's security

code." He smirked. "Sebastian asked me to carry William's donated weapons to the armory."

Emily chimed in, "Would've been two trips, so I decided to help carry some of the load."

"If it's alright," I ventured. "Unzip that bag and let me carry some of the load the rest of the way."

"I carry all this ninety-five percent of the trip, only for you to step in and steal some of the glory at the last second? No chance." With a grunt, he jerked the bag back off the ground, causing his tatted, dirty skin to bulge with mounds of engaged muscle.

"I'm the only one who can talk sense to this stubborn mule," Emily smirked.

His eyes lit up as he nodded at her and began arduously hobbling under the arch and up toward the Forrester home.

"Then would you? If he hurts himself, I don't think we have medical equipment big enough."

"Naw. He's got this." She turned and amplified her voice. "Don't you, honey?!"

"Walk in the park," he grunted.

"But if he falls," she laughed, "he'll need someone to help him back up." She motioned me to follow him.

"I heard that!" he yelled over his shoulder.

We fell in behind him up the long drive.

Trey stopped in front of the front door, allowing Emily to walk past him and open the front door. Felt a bit strange that they didn't even knock.

Trey set the bag down in the entryway for a quick breather as I made my way down the short entry toward the large living room replete with giant windows opening to a view of Martin Mountain, I wondered who was keeping an eye on the new armory. Certainly, people couldn't saunter on in and head to the basement for their choice of weaponry without anyone standing guard.

I turned the corner into the oversized living room, complete with an oversized couch facing an oversized television. It was a shame, really. The couch was faced away from the thick windows and toward what my dad used to call the idiot box on the interior wall. The windows were less than perfectly clear. Addison said they were for extra insulation, but I knew safety glass when I saw it, and this was top-of-the-line.

"I could shoot you for trespassing, ya know."

I turned to see Addison standing there, holding a paperback in one hand and a plastic bowl of potato chips in the other.

"Pretty sure you don't have a free hand."

She walked by me as she said, "So, what do you need?" She set the chips on the end table, dropped onto the couch and lifted the novel to her face.

"Hello?" Trey's burly voice behind me.

"Ah." I moved to the side. "Sorry."

Trey and Emily walked by, opened a door leading to the basement stairs, and headed down.

Addison didn't look up from her book as she continued, "It's a strange feeling sitting on top of every gun in town."

"Not every gun." I patted the CZ holstered at my waist.

She shook her head as she continued to read. She seemed upset.

"I'm gonna…" She wasn't even listening. I turned and headed into the basement.

It was a low-ceilinged, expansive single room with the exception of a bathroom in the corner. A pool table had been pushed against the far wall. Trey unzipped the bag and headed to the bathroom.

Emily started pulling out various rifles and adding them to others on the table. "You might want to head back upstairs. He's been known to ruin a zip code."

"Why do the two of you always seem to think I can't hear you?!" His voice rumbled from the small bathroom.

I noticed there seemed to be a method to the madness—to where she was placing each weapon. And under the table, there were stacked boxes of ammunition. I walked closer and confirmed they matched the weapons directly above.

An ungodly expulsion of gas seemed to rattle the bathroom door.

"Warned ya." Emily noticed I was admiring her handiwork. "Rifles on the table. Corresponding ammo underneath. Handguns on the top shelves over there. Ammo on the next shelf down. Shotguns in the corner. Shells beside them."

"Well done." I turned to look at the stairs. "Only way in or out of the room?"

From behind the door, a toilet flushed, a sink turned on, then off, and was followed by the sound of something spraying.

"Yeah," she responded. "I don't give Sebastian credit for much, but this room can be made pretty secure. But with only one exit, it would be a deathtrap in a fire."

"I doubt the architect built the basement with the idea it would be the armory for a small militia."

"They are more prevalent than you'd think."

Trey burst out of the bathroom and slammed it quickly. "If you want to live, do *not* go in there." He looked around and began striding toward the steps.

"Not very gentlemanly," I half-joked. "Making your wife do all the work."

He paused, his giant hand on the bottom of the rail, and looked back.

"Trey isn't my husband quite yet. And he carried it." Emily came to her man's defense. "The least I can do is sort it."

"I don't touch 'em anymore." It was all he said.

The gravity of the statement didn't escape me. "Oh…"

He turned and took a single step toward me. "My family had a lot of…issues." He waited and steadied his nerve. "I was no saint, but my little brother made some real bad choices. I had him move in with me as soon as I graduated.

I guess I thought I could turn him around."

"Trey, you don't have to…" I wanted him to know it was alright if he wasn't ready to share, even if I was curious.

"One night, I was home, falling asleep on the couch with the TV on, when an argument broke out in the front yard." He looked to the pool table, but was seeing something else. "I went to the window to yell at whoever woke me up." He swallowed. "But it was my brother. He was arguing with someone. I couldn't see either of them in the dark, but my brother was as big as me. Had a voice like a bear. I left the window and headed for the front door to calm them down."

Emily made her way over and slipped her arm around the back of his enormous waist and kissed his shoulder.

He took a deep breath. "As I twisted the doorknob, I heard the shot. I swung the door open, but it was too late. My brother was dead on my front lawn. And the other guy was just a running shadow. I should've…" He shook his head. "But I just ran to my brother."

"God, Trey. I'm so sorry."

"A man is supposed to protect his little bro, you know? But I failed." Trey looked down to Emily, smiled at her, and seemed to draw strength from her supportive gaze. "Anyway, like I said, he wasn't a saint. He was holding a gun. I don't know who drew on who. I don't know what happened besides one thing: my little brother was shot dead on my front lawn. And I'll never touch a gun again."

I stood there. Stupid. Without a single adequate word.

Emily looked at him again, but spoke to me. "I was on a ride-along when an officer got shot. I finally realized the danger my mom faces every day. The danger of what I was about to sign up for. Someone overheard me talking and the department mandated I get counseling. As part of it, I attended a support group for a few months."

"And an officer who showed up at the scene that night..." Trey seemed to have his strength back. "He followed up with me. Saw how I was spiraling. Could tell I didn't even think breathing was worth the effort anymore. Drove me to a support group for weeks. Until I started driving myself."

"And that's where we met," they said.

38.

WALKED BACK UP INTO THE LIVING ROOM. Addison was still curled up on the couch, engrossed in her book.

"Upset with me?" I came right out with it.

She let out a sharp exhale, closed her book, and met my eyes. "When we moved here, I jumped right in and tried to make the best of it. I did it because I love my dad, I wanted to support him, and yeah, maybe I thought the move meant I'd be getting him back." She swallowed. "But now this?" She waved an arm around in the air. "This? My dad is now president. My mom is the first lady. My best friends have traded in their first-person shooter video games for the real thing. But me? I don't want to be here. So instead of being a drag on my family and friends"—she slapped her paperback—"I'm choosing to live in here."

"Addison. I'm not playing a video game." My voice rose defensively. "This isn't a video game. People have already died. There will be more. I don't want it to be you or my mom."

"I don't want anybody to die."

That wasn't likely, but she wouldn't want to hear it.

There was a hard knock on the door.

"Expecting someone?" I asked.

"No one who would knock." She jumped up and moved to the hall. I followed.

She opened the door to one Trevor Beck, and I could *not* understand how he still looked like the cameras were on. It was the first time I saw him alone.

"Hi," he said through his charming grin. "Addison, I presume?"

"And you are Mr. Trevor Beck." She reached out her hand. He took it.

"And Lukas." His eyebrows shot up. "Didn't expect to see you here."

"Hello, sir."

"Seriously? How old have I gotten?" He laughed. "You have got to call me Trevor. Both of you."

"Okay…Trevor." Addison clearly wasn't quite comfortable with calling a man more than twice her age by his first name.

"Was it really that painful?"

"Just taught to respect my elders." She smiled a bit demurely. "How can I help you?"

"Can't even pretend I don't qualify, but it still hurts. Your father sent me over to choose a weapon."

Behind us, some doors opened and closed.

"House party?" Trevor asked with that smile again.

"No. We have a couple who were stranded on the highway staying in our garage. Trey and Emily."

"Two people you just met? And now they have easy access to the armory?" He looked legitimately concerned.

"I trust them."

"With your life?"

He had a point. I'd just met them. And it wasn't like I'd ever seen Emily's badge.

"Let me show you to the armory." Addison welcomed him in.

"Thanks." Before he moved, he focused back on me. "Mind waiting a couple minutes? I'd like to chat real quick."

"Asking me to wait until you're armed before we talk? Am I in trouble?"

"Nope. Just fortuitous that you're here."

"How so?"

"You were my next stop." He patted me on the shoulder as he walked by.

I felt awkward standing in the front doorway, so I made my way outside for some fresh air.

Standing still as a statue, twenty feet away, was a young coyote. *Was nature already beginning to take our town back?* It just stared at me. Into me. I stared back for a moment before it turned and scampered off.

39.

THE FORRESTER HOME MUST'VE COST A SMALL FORTUNE. Whatever Sebastian Forrester knew, he was lucky that someone had chosen to pay this much for his silence rather than paying a fraction to a hitman. Maybe someone didn't believe in murder. Or maybe Sebastian Forrester had an insurance policy—the type of policy that became public upon his death.

I turned and looked down the sloping landscape further to the southwest and located my house. Beyond it were the railroad tracks approaching from further south. I followed them up and to the left until they entered the town proper.

It was quite a view.

The door behind me opened. Trey and Emily emerged.

"Going for a walk," Emily explained.

"Trey?" I slowed them.

"Yeah?"

"Thanks for trusting me."

"Thanks for trusting us." He said it with a wink.

He must've heard the exchange with Trevor.

"Don't wait up, Dad," Emily quipped as they walked off.

I watched them go, holding hands, talking, laughing as they went.

"Never thought I'd see a couple of wannabe motorcycle gang members and think they looked adorable," Trevor said from the doorway behind me.

"Oh. They are much more than that."

"Hmm." He stepped up beside me. "You extend them some serious grace and trust."

I considered pointing out that I knew them better than him as we watched Trey and Emily walk behind some trees toward the tracks in the distance.

Finally, he broke the silence. "Maybe I wasn't so wrong."

"About what?"

"You, my friend. You." He looked around for a moment. "We've got time before our shift. Let's go for a walk."

We made our way down the drive in silence. Once we got to the stone arch, he stopped to look at me.

"A bit ridiculous. Or is it me?"

Did he know about the buried gun just a few feet away?

He looked over at the arch. "Does Sebastian think this would impress people? Good Lord!"

I broke into a smile. "I have the right to remain silent."

"That's what I thought."

We resumed our walk into town. And as we walked, I noticed his pants were stretched ever so slightly over one of his ankles. I was curious what was in the ankle holster.

We eventually made our way to the intersection with the town trailer park directly across the road. Trevor glanced around, saw a downed log, and motioned to it. We sat.

"I need you to know I'm not Catholic." I said it quietly.

"Okay." He looked confused. "Neither am I."

"Well, this feels like confession."

He chuckled. "Hey, man. I'm not about to tell you all my sins, but if you want to tell me all your deep, dark, and dirties... by all means."

"If it's all the same to you, hard pass."

"Mr. Beck!" It was someone I didn't know, a weathered lady of about sixty.

There's a common phrase that pertains to Skull Valley: 'Everyone knows your business in a small town.' It's true. But just because you know their business, it doesn't mean you necessarily know *them*.

"Hi." He said the single word in a way that was familiar and kind. His whole demeanor betrayed his experience with celebrity status.

"This is embarrassing, but could I get your autograph? My home is right over there." She motioned to the collection of mobile homes. "I'll go grab a pen and a magazine I kept with you on the cover. It'll only take a minute." She began shuffling off.

"Miss!" She stopped cold at his voice. "What is your name?"

Her aged face stretched into joy. "Phyllis. My name is Phyllis."

"Phyllis. Please don't think me rude, but I have to say no."

Her face immediately showed the offense she was taking.

Trevor went on. "I am, in no way, more special than any other member of this community. So, I will not sign a magazine. But I'd love to get to know you sometime." As he continued, her face changed seasons again. "Like I'm getting to know Lukas right now. Would it be alright if we did that sometime? Get to know one another? Become friends?"

"I'd..." she began, before having to gather herself, "I'd love that!"

"Okay. It's settled. I look forward to it."

She scurried off, most certainly to tell her family about her new best friend, Trevor Beck.

"Does that get old?" I asked him, genuinely curious about the cost of celebrity.

"Folks like that have given me a wonderful life." He smirked before continuing. "But it did seem a little over-the-top considering the current state of affairs."

"Trevor. I want to apologize for earlier. I...I wrestle quite a bit with my feelings about my dad."

"Hey, listen. I'm the one who needs to apologize. I met you and the first thing I did was judge you based on bits of very old information. Decades ago, I lived right over there." He looked across the road to the trailer park. "Your dad lived in the same house you live in today. And it might not look like much now compared to some of the homes off the old road, and especially in the shadow of Sebastian's eyesore on the hill, but back in the day? It was the big house at the end of the road. It was the best house on the most land around these parts."

I tried to process this inverse reality where my address was the exclusive one, not the excluded one.

"Your dad was kind to me. And it wasn't like he had to be. I was the scrappy kid from the trailer park. I followed him around like a puppy and begged him to teach me stuff."

"Like what?" I seriously wondered what my dad could teach Trevor Beck.

"Hunting. Fishing. Survival. Creativity. Everything I know. Well…" He stopped himself.

"You aren't saying something," I prodded.

"That's why I need to apologize. I knew your father well. He was one of the kindest men I ever knew. He was also the most naturally-gifted outdoorsmen I've ever met. And I've met every outdoor specialist on the Discovery Channel, the History Channel, National Geographic, and the internet. But he's also the most stubborn man I've ever known."

"You *did* know him."

"And I tried. I tried so hard to help him. To repay him." He shook his head. "I reached out to see if he would be a consultant. The paychecks he would've cashed would've changed quite a bit for your family."

"He turned you down?"

"I can only assume. He never even took my call. Your mom passed along the message. And the thing is, if he would've just talked to me, I had a bigger plan. I thought once the network folks realized what they had in him, his knowledge, and he was almost as handsome as I am..." He waited for a laugh I wasn't feeling. "Sorry, kid. Just a joke. But he was a good-looking dude—in a rugged sort of way. That shouldn't matter, but it does. And I was going to put in a good word for him. Combine all that, and he would've had a pilot ordered within six months. From there? Those paychecks get exponentially bigger. Trust me. And then somebody, probably William, has to change those God-forsaken signs to include your dad's name."

"Shit." The word just came out.

"Aww, man. I didn't mean..." He shook his head. "My point was that I shouldn't judge you for struggling with your dad. Everyone around here says you're an amazing young man."

"They don't know what they're talking about."

"Nine times out of ten, I'm trusting you. But all things being equal, I think I'll trust everyone else on this one."

There was a long moment of silence as I weighed whether or not he would even want to hear what I had to say.

"He…"

Trevor waited me out, silently signaling his interest. Or at a minimum, willingness to listen.

"It's infuriating, you know? I loved him. Still do. But that doesn't mean I can't be mad at him."

"Hey. Of course."

"You say of course, but it's not like that. If I say a bad word, my mom gets upset. It's like Dad's a saint. But he shouldn't be. And now that all this has happened? It justifies everything he did in her mind."

"But you know why your mom doesn't want to hear anything negative about your dad, right?" I could feel him looking at me. "It isn't about you. It's about her. She can't handle one of her great loves criticizing the other." He tossed his arm over my shoulders. "But that doesn't mean you aren't justified in your feelings. It only means she might not be the one you should talk to about them."

"I don't have anyone else." I said it before realizing how pitiful it would sound.

The extended silence that followed only magnified my awkwardness.

"Last I checked, I'm not going anywhere. I knew your dad. We were close. But I've never put him on a pedestal. Would it be presumptuous of me to volunteer?"

"I wouldn't want to bother you with my drama."

"The only thing that'll bother me is if you place me on a pedestal."

"In my defense, I'm pretty sure I just saw someone ask you for an autograph and your name is still on the town sign."

"That's not me on that sign, kid. That guy is Trevor Beck, a guy you see on your television. Every fire he starts with his bare hands takes less than a minute. Every shelter is built between commercial breaks. My name is Louis Trevor Beckel." His eyebrows shot up for a brief second. "That doesn't roll off the tongue quite as well, does it?"

"When did you lose the 'Louis' and change the last name to Beck?"

"Network negotiations. And by negotiations, I mean, they said 'If you want a show, your name is now Trevor Beck' and I said, 'When do we start filming?'"

We both chuckled for a moment before settling back into silence.

"Thank you, Louis."

"Let's stick with Trevor. I think the network execs might've been right on that one."

"Okay." I grinned as I said, "Thank you, Trevor."

"Hey. No worries. I might bend your ear once in a while, too."

"Deal."

"Alright. I've gotta go get a few things done before tonight's shift." He stood. I stood. He shook my hand. "It's good to know you, Lukas."

40.

DECIDED TO TAKE THE TRACKS HOME in an effort to avoid people lingering near the elementary school-turned-government capital. I was three-fourths of the way when Sophie walked out from behind her favorite manzanita.

I shook my head. "This is becoming ridiculous."

"What? You stalking me every time I pee? Yeah. You've got some pretty serious issues." She started walking away. "I might need to report you to my brothers."

I decided this time I'd wait a minute.

As soon as Sophie walked off, I made my way around the scrub. I looked around. Thankfully, I didn't see moist dirt. Instead, tucked under the bush, a small crucifix held upright by a small pile of rocks.

41.

AS I APPROACHED MY HOUSE, I imagined it several decades ago. The elementary school hadn't been replaced with a bigger version yet. The Forrester family hadn't built their abomination yet. This beautiful farmhouse was at the end of a long, exclusive road. An amazing place to live.

It didn't feel anything like that anymore. It needed a coat of paint. It needed some wood replaced. And as I ascended to the front door, the squeaking stairs agreed.

I walked through the front door and Mom called up from the basement. "Lukas? That you?"

"A roaming marauder here for the last of your coffee!"

"Have to kill me first!" She emerged from the basement. "I love you, but you can be an idiot."

"Love you, too." I headed for the kitchen.

"I'm going to build a fire out back soon. Cook up some good stuff. And I'll bring dinner to your watch position."

"Sounds great." I looked at the table. It was where Mom placed what needed to be eaten first. There was some bread, butter, and bananas. Banana sandwich coming right up.

"Expected you quite a while ago." She was leaning against the door frame. Waiting for an explanation.

"I helped carry some of the Sinnot guns to Addison's. Chatted with her a bit. Ran into Trevor there."

"Trevor?"

"Yeah."

"What did he want?"

"He didn't *want* anything. We talked. That's it."

Her face betrayed displeasure. "What do you two have in common?"

"Well, he knew Dad. I knew Dad. He loves the outdoors—"

"What did he say about your father?" she interrupted.

"Nothing much."

"What did he say?" she demanded.

"He said Dad was the most talented outdoorsman he ever knew."

She studied my face. "What else?"

"Come on," I pleaded.

"Lukas."

"Fine. He said Dad was the most stubborn man he'd ever met."

"He needs to keep my husband's name out of his mouth." She was suddenly venomous, but this time I wasn't having it.

"Is it true Trevor tried to get Dad a consulting job?"

She looked stunned.

"Is it true Dad wouldn't even talk to him?"

Silence.

"Did you know Trevor was using that to get Dad in front of the network executives because he believed Dad had what it took to have a show of his own?"

"Bull."

"Mom. He explained the entire plan. But Dad, the guy you don't think was the most stubborn man in the world, wouldn't even take his call."

"That's not fair, Lukas," her voice quiet. "You're trusting a guy you just met."

I matched her quieter tone. "He didn't put Dad down. Trevor admired him. What isn't fair is Dad passing on what would have been life-changing money!"

"Some things are more important than money."

"Oh, sure. Like preparing us for earthquakes, civil wars, population migrations, super volcanoes, foreign invasions, self-aware robot takeovers and monkey uprisings."

"And electromagnetic pulses," she said without missing a beat.

"He doesn't get credit for that! If a meteorologist predicts snow seventeen days in a row, and it finally snows, it wasn't much of a forecast."

"Like I said, I love you, but you can be an idiot." She turned and stomped out the front door.

"I love you, too." I replied to the empty kitchen.

42.

I LEFT THE HOUSE EARLIER THAN I'D planned because there was no use sitting around with no television or internet, knowing my mother was outside, chopping firewood with a little something extra.

Instead of heading directly to my post, I stopped off at the Sinnot residence first. It was on the highway about five-hundred yards short of the southern post. Set in the rolling land that eventually formed the natural southern border, it was a newer home with a modest amount of land. The narrow driveway opened to a large gravel parking area. To the right was the home. Single story and expansive. Directly ahead, several locked storage units. Beyond them, a small seasonal stream bed. To the right, a rise in the land with a concrete frame encasing a secure metal door. The natural bulge of earth contained William's pride and joy: his bunker. No one had ever been allowed inside except for his children. Until the EMP.

Since Skull Valley had become its own independent nation, no secret stores were allowed. It didn't matter how hard a family had worked, or how much they sacrificed for a moment such as this. It didn't matter if other families spent their money on new cars or kitchen remodels. It was seen as somehow "unfair" if families like ours didn't share with those in need. The door to William's bunker had been swung wide and what it revealed increased the entire community's chances of survival by the slightest fraction.

There had been additional guns of every size, one thousand rounds for each, food in jars, food in boxes, packaged MREs, a stack of chemical toilets, Faraday cages containing spare parts for the water well, several hand-held solar chargers, batteries, lights, and a crank radio, water purification tablets, matches, lighters, hand tools, fifty gallons of gas he had been rotating, fifty gallons of water and more. It was remarkable to almost everyone in the town. Almost everyone.

As I looked at the door from the outside, I knew the guns were gone. The ammo was gone. And some of the other supplies had begun to be claimed "for the good of the community." Poor William. He had prepared exceptionally well from a logistical standpoint. But he failed to prepare for the social game. Everything he did was out in the open.

"Get off my land, a-hole!" a voice shouted from behind.

I spun to see Conor standing in his doorway. He was laughing because I jumped about a foot.

"Aren't you supposed to be sleeping?" I walked over to him and shook his hand. Only teenagers, I realized we were falling into the roles of soldiers rather comfortably.

"Aren't you supposed to be at your post?" he shot back.

"Not for another thirty minutes. What's your excuse?"

"I relieve you. Midnight till six. Sleep seven in the morning until about two in the afternoon. More than enough." He looked me over. "Sticking with the AK, Mr. Overkill?"

"Saw a mountain lion last night. Got too close for comfort."

"Well, that should work." He laughed before eying my small backpack. "Whatcha got in there?"

"A spade, toilet paper, some bread, bananas."

"Eating up the stuff before it goes bad. Us too." He straightened. "So, what brings you by?"

"Is your dad home?"

"At the school. Liam too. But Sophie's in her room."

"Can you shut the door for a sec?"

Conor looked a bit confused, but complied. "What's up?"

"I'm worried about your sister."

He raised his face and folded his arms. "Why?" He looked down at me in a sudden transition to big brother mode.

"She..." I searched for the words. "She has a hidden spot off the railroad tracks."

"I don't understand."

"I usually walk the tracks into town from my house. I caught her coming out from behind a bush on a few occasions. She said she was peeing." He was tensing and I knew I needed to get to the point. "But I knew that wasn't it, so one day, when she wasn't there, I looked. There's a small crucifix held up by a pile of rocks. Conor? It looks like a small grave. Did she lose a pet?"

His neck and shoulders relaxed, "No. She lost our mom." Now I was the one who didn't understand. "Nothing's buried there, man."

"Then why there? Privacy?"

"Listen, dude. Sophie pretends to be tough, and don't get me wrong, she is as strong as they come, but she's also incredibly sensitive. When Mom died, it changed her. It changed us all, but Dad and Sophie most of all."

"So she needs a hidden spot to cry?"

"You said it's off the tracks?"

"Yeah."

"Mom used to jog next to the tracks back home. Every morning. One morning, she didn't come home. We found her lying there, but she was already gone. We were told she died of sudden cardiac arrest. She was in great shape. Not like Dad. And she was the one whose heart switched off."

"Family history of heart trouble?"

"No idea. She was adopted. No contact with birth parents."

"God. I knew she died, but didn't know the rest. Conor. I'm sorry."

"I wish Sophie would talk to me."

"And your dad moved you here? Less than a half mile from tracks?"

"His way of holding on to her without realizing it? I don't know." He inhaled and I noticed it shook. "When Mom died, he never saw it coming. So, I think he decided he'd never be caught off-guard again. Moved us here. Made our property something special. Tried to make our community something special, too. And made sure we'd be ready for anything."

Behind Conor, the door opened and Sophie poked her head out. "Come by to finally ask me on a date?"

"Sophie." Conor glared at her.

"Well, my answer is no. Not until you show up with flowers."

"Sophie!" His voice rose.

"Well, I'd normally demand flowers and chocolates, but considering the state of the world, I didn't want to be unreasonable." She turned to me. "Flowers." And she shut the door.

Conor stood there. Glaring at me. Any brotherhood I'd been feeling evaporated.

"Well, I should head that way." I excused myself from the standoff.

"Yeah. I need to go for a jog. Thanks for stopping by."

"See ya at midnight."

43.

'D BEEN WATCHING THE HIGHWAY STRETCHING south for hours. George had stopped by twice. The first time, he scared the crap out of me. Walked up, nodded without looking at me, and quietly vanished back into the dark. The second time, I heard him coming. Again, nothing more than a nod and he was gone.

Outside of the breeze and a few buzzing insects, the night was silent. And the thought got the Christmas song stuck in my head. I was humming when my walkie crackled.

"Guys?" I didn't immediately recognize the whisper.

"Talk to us, Andrew." This voice was Trevor's.

"I'm not alone. Don't respond." There was a pause. "Hang on."

The next seconds seemed to take hours.

Then, finally, another whisper, "Requesting backup."

"There in two minutes." George. Out of breath. "Along the tracks from the north."

He didn't want to accidentally get shot.

As soon as the thought crossed my mind, a rapid succession of loud reports echoed across the darkness. Then another.

"Andrew!" Trevor yelled. "Report!"

Nothing.

"George!" Trevor again. "Report!"

"Almost there," George responded between quick breaths.

"If you need me," Trevor again, "I'm closer than Lukas."

"But your post gets more action. Are you sure I shouldn't head over?" I asked, unsure if I should tie up the channel.

"No. You stay. If I head there, cover the north."

Made sense. Trevor could get to the emergency quickly, while I could make my way from the post with the least chance of action to the one where Kyle was last seen.

Silence returned to the channel as we waited to hear from Andrew or George.

Finally, Trevor's voice, "Guys? I need an update within fifteen seconds or I'm on my way."

I counted out loud.

One.

Two.

Three.

Four.

Five.

Six.

The channel crackled again.

"We're good, boss." It was George. "There's blood, but based on what I'm seeing, it ain't human."

"The hell *was* it?" Trevor, looking for details.

"Let me guess," I jumped in. "Mountain lion?"

"Tracks match up," George confirmed.

"Had the same visitor on the old road last night."

"Thanks for the warning!" I couldn't tell if Andrew was pissed or amused.

"Aww." Trevor obviously fell on the side of amused. "Sounds like Andrew has a pet kitty."

"I hope I killed the bitch." Andrew still sounded freaked out.

If there was only a little blood, he didn't.

"Okay." Trevor sounded like he was trying not to laugh as he reassured Andrew. "Sounds like we're all clear. Don't think your pet will be back tonight. Although don't be shocked if the blood doesn't attract other friends."

"Fantastic."

"George? You good to hang with him for a bit?"

"Can do. South post. You good solo for now?"

"With all these insects and tiny mammals?" I answered. "I think I'll make it."

Trevor chimed in. "I'm sure Andrew would be happy to lend you his kitty."

"I'll keep protecting us from the impending mass invasion from Yarnell," I quipped.

"Give it a month or two," Trevor responded. And this time, he wasn't laughing.

44.

"WITH A MOUNTAIN LION ON THE LOOSE..." A voice whispered from directly behind me. I spun to see my mom standing in the moonlight, "you should be focusing a bit more on your surroundings and less on banter."

"Mom. You should've warned me you were coming."

"And exactly how would I do that?"

I gave her a look in the dark.

"I thought you could use some warm food." She held out a sealed bowl and a spoon.

I opened it to the smell of warm vegetable stew. "Thanks."

She sat. "Hey. I know Dad is a source of tension for us, but I will love and protect you until my dying day. You know that, right?"

"Yeah." I was downing the soup in gulps. "Of course."

"But can I ask you for one thing?" She was looking at me intently. "One thing before I walk back home?"

I set down the bowl, sensing something big was about to be asked of me. I waited.

"Can you admit that we are much better prepared for this current situation because of what your father did while he was alive?"

The night became silent again as she waited longer than she should've had to.

I knew what I should say, but there was a big part of me that didn't want to give any ground. Admitting this seemed akin to helping Mom put Dad right back on his pedestal. A pedestal he didn't deserve.

"Okay." She got up. "It's fine." She quickly headed back into the darkness.

I went back to the soup. I took several more spoonfuls before a sudden change of heart gripped me.

"Mom?"

It was too late.

45.

'D BEGUN TO FALL ASLEEP WHEN a boot tapped my leg. I startled and looked up. George was silently standing above me.

"You fall asleep?" he asked as he scanned the darkness to the south.

"Waiting on Conor to relieve me. Should be soon, no?"

"Yeah. Less than fifteen minutes. Don't shoot him."

"Didn't shoot you, did I?" I responded.

"No." He shook his head. "It's hard to shoot someone when you're asleep."

"Wasn't sleeping."

"Sure, kid. See you tomorrow." He left me in the darkness.

Determined that a third person wouldn't sneak up on me, I waited and watched until I heard only the quietest of footfalls.

"Conor? You finally decide to show up?"

"Yeah. Heard the shots about ninety minutes ago. Heard that Andrew guy might've nicked a mountain lion."

"You heard as much as I did."

"That kitty comes my way and the town will be eating a high-protein breakfast." He peered down at the two-truck barrier blocking the road that had been cut into the hill. "No activity, then?"

"Nothing. I was more afraid of falling asleep than anything else."

"No doubt." He sat in the grass next to me. "Well, bro. Get home and fall into a coma."

"Sounds great." I thought for a moment before deciding to embrace my inner death wish. "Conor? I'm sorry about earlier."

"What? My sister?"

"I swear I've never…" I didn't know what exactly to claim innocence for. When it came to Sophie, I hadn't done a thing.

"Hey, man. No worries. Must be nice to know a girl likes you. Just wish it wasn't my sister."

"I get it." I didn't want to say another word and screw it up.

I liked Addison. I liked her a lot. But I was starting to realize I cared about Sophie. No one noticed her. No one gave her any credit. Except Conor.

No wonder he was so defensive of her.

"Anyway." Conor put an end to another awkward encounter. "I've got this. Go get your rest. Tomorrow night might not be this quiet."

DAY FOUR

"IN A SHTF SCENARIO, PEOPLE WILL DIE.
MOST OF THEM WILL BE GOOD PEOPLE."

—

MARK TAYLOR

46.

MOM WAS IN THE KITCHEN, opening two jars of simple overnight oats. She handed me one without a smile.

Certain almond milks didn't require refrigeration and we kept a small stock we could rotate, always using the half gallon closest to expiration. And almond milk, with a touch of honey or remaining fruit, would soak oatmeal overnight and create a delicious treat that required no firewood, matches, or any of the precious propane we still possessed. The bananas that had gone completely mushy made this morning's batch a particularly delicious treat.

"Listen. Mom…"

"I'm going to need you to collect firewood for a few hours this morning. We're getting low. Take the wheelbarrow and head up the ridge a bit. If you hear the bell, leave it and head back."

I didn't know if it was a punishment, but it certainly felt like one. "Fine."

"And take a .45 with you in case you come across that kitty."

47.

BEYOND OUR HOME WAS A FORESTED RIDGE. The plan was to fill the wheelbarrow, build some additional piles that could be gathered as needed, and even pick up something extra.

I loaded down the wheelbarrow in a flash and found myself enjoying the rare solitude. I decided to continue with my firewood pile idea.

As I stacked the piles, I thought about Mom. She deserved to hear me say something—anything—nice about Dad. And so I would. But I couldn't help but see all the differences between him and Trevor.

I assumed Trevor would have a big ego. And he was the most humble guy I'd ever met. He was even *embarrassed* by the sign with his name on it. My dad? Everyone thought he

was humble, but he was too proud to take a call from someone who only wanted to help.

As soon as he could get here, Trevor arrived and couldn't
wait to pitch in and be another member of the community.
Dad trained Mom and me to distrust every other citizen of
Skull Valley. Now? I found myself feeling increasingly guilty
about the few secrets we still held.

Despite all this, I decided I'd find something kind to
say about Dad. Mom's heart needed it. And that was what
mattered.

It was then, I stumbled on the prints. Tracks—too many
of them—about two inches wide and a bit longer than
that. Oval-shaped with four toes, each with its own claw. It
looked like I'd wandered onto a coyote super highway. I'd
never seen this many tracks this close to the house.

Why were they here? I cleared my mind.

Smells drifting from Skull Valley had probably multi-
plied without garbage pick-ups combined with the first
food spoilage. Yet, sunrise had been hours ago and my odds
of seeing them were fairly low. If I did, I wouldn't run. I'd
make as much noise as possible. I'd try to save every bullet
possible.

I scanned every direction slowly until I noticed something else entirely. To the distant west, as far as the eye could
see, dissipating dark smoke. Some land was on fire. I was
probably the first person to see it because no one had ventured this far west of town since before the power had been

lost and the wind was carrying the smoke northeast. There wasn't a population center of any size until Williams, and the smoke wouldn't be visible traveling that distance. No one would even know.

I decided the distant fire didn't make my top ten list of concerns. The coyotes, on the other hand… It was time to get the full wheelbarrow home and grab a bite to eat before my shift.

48.

MOST PEOPLE HATED THE NEW WORLD because of a lack of air conditioning, food options, or entertainment. I'd always enjoyed camping and reading a good paperback, so these supposed hardships didn't bug me in the least. But, as someone who found most conversation exhausting, I was starting to realize I missed other people's cell phones. It kept them glued to their screens and out of my business.

Suddenly, people were making eye contact and relying on one another for entertainment. When they asked someone how they were doing, they actually wanted to know. Video games were out. Board games were in. It was an introvert's nightmare. So I took the tracks again, making a quick stop at Sophie's cross, and avoiding the group that had congregated in front of the elementary school when they weren't working on projects or cooking.

It only put off the inevitable.

"Young man!" A voice called out from a gathering at the edge of the trailer park. Several tables had been placed end-to-end with assorted residents seated shoulder-to-shoulder. Two other tables were off to the side and held several camp stoves, heating various pots and pans. "You one of the people guarding our perimeter?" It was an older gentleman, tall and thin, with a face full of history, shuttling back and forth from the stoves with hot food.

"Yes sir," I responded with my best Boy Scout impersonation.

"Well," he smiled warmly. "It ain't six o'clock yet. Get over here and grab something warm."

"Oh, no thank you. I ate a few minutes ago, and given the current state of things, I think it would be wrong to eat on a full stomach."

He nodded thoughtfully. "Can't argue with that." He slid what appeared to be some ground beef onto the plate of the woman who had asked for Trevor's autograph. "Grateful for what you are doing."

"Some are," muttered another woman with a gray-streaked feathered hair, also serving food and close in age to the man.

"Rose." He said her name like an admonition.

"Waaaalt." She answered with the same tone, not a woman under any man's thumb, especially one I suspected she was married to.

He changed his approach with a simple plea. "Please."

I realized this wasn't going to be pleasant, but I couldn't move. I hated offending my elders. If this lady had something to say, I was going to be here for it.

"It's…" The lady searched for the right words. "What if a family who desperately needs food and water walks up to your post? What do you do?"

"Rose." Walt jumped back in. "You are the smartest woman I know. You have got to understand, we might not have enough food or water for the people who are already here. If we let more people in, we all die sooner."

"And you are the most compassionate man I know. And I know you would rather die having lived rightly, than live a life of selfishness."

Walt turned to his wife. "I will never believe loving you above all others to be selfish."

Rose turned back to me. "Listen, son. I'm sure you're a good kid. But please put some thought into what kind of community you'd like Skull Valley to become."

"I'm sure he has," Walt defended.

"Promise me." Rose didn't look away.

"I promise." *I mean, what else was I going to say?*

Walt exhaled in exasperation. "Sure you don't want something for your shift?"

"Food goes to the hungry, sir."

"Like I said. A good kid," Rose commented. "You'll figure it out."

With that gentle dismissal, I left for the northern post to pick up my radio.

49.

TREVOR WAS HUDDLED WITH ANDREW AND George in the middle of the highway behind the automotive barrier. He glanced my way and finished his thought before greeting me.

"Lukas! Ready to walk a few miles tonight?" George and Andrew turned. George looked somewhere beyond me while Andrew bit his lip.

"I am."

"Good." Trevor smiled while looking at his crew again. "Don't mind Andrew. He's afraid he might get attacked by a bunny tonight."

"A mountain lion is a bit different than a freakin' rabbit," he snapped.

"Anyway. We were going over the strategy for tonight," Trevor explained. "If there is a call for backup, whoever is closest will be the first to respond. If you are the closest, everyone else maintains position unless additional backup is required. If you are on the opposite end of your rotation, I'll respond and you replace me. This ensures the fastest backup. Make sense?"

"So when the call goes out," Andrew interjected, "call out your position so we know if you or Trevor are closer."

"Got it," I confirmed.

"But hopefully," Trevor said what I assumed we were all thinking, "we have a quiet night and are asleep by twelve thirty."

"Sounds good," I agreed.

"Are we done?" George asked impatiently.

"Yeah, Mister Happy, we're done," Trevor said, shaking his head.

George turned and climbed the embankment to the tracks with astonishing agility for a man his size.

"Does he ever smile?" I asked, hoping I wasn't overstepping.

"Legend says he smiled as a young boy," Andrew offered, "but alas, we have no photo evidence."

"He's a good guy." Trevor jumped to his defense. "He doesn't believe in unnecessary words."

"Or emotions," Andrew chuckled, forgetting his worry for a moment.

"Alright. Andrew and I better get to our posts." He looked me up and down. "I don't see your radio, but if you've got it, walk with me."

"Still waiting on whoever has it this shift to show up," I answered. "If you want to wait a few minutes..."

"Nah. We'll catch up when you get to my post. Later, guys." With that, he turned and scrambled up the same route George had taken. He took the curve of the tracks from north to east. The reverse of the route I had run to assist Conor.

"Be careful tonight," Andrew whispered before he turned and headed the opposite direction down the highway.

"You too!" I called after him.

50.

AFTER I GOT THE WALKIE, I made my way up to the tracks. George was sitting in the middle of the bridge, atop one of the metal tracks, staring up the highway at cemetery ridge, a vein curling between his right eye and the temple behind it. My presence wasn't acknowledged, but I was certain it had been noted.

Given the choice of trying to force an awkward conversation with someone who had no interest in such trivialities, or turning the other way and heading for Trevor at the old road, I decided there was no time like the present to begin my rotation.

As I walked the tracks, I approached the spot where I had shot at, and apparently missed, Kyle as he made his escape two days before. Parallel bare markings could still be seen in the plain to my north where the spinning tires of the escaping vehicle had stripped grass from the land.

To my back, the sun was rapidly dropping toward the crest of the mountain which caused sunset earlier than would occur with a flat western horizon. I resumed my walk toward Trevor at the old road post. I walked at a faster pace than I would later in the night. Although I'd make many approaches throughout the next six hours, I found myself more afraid of getting shot by startling one of the posts than by an intruder, or being attacked by wildlife. Getting to Trevor before complete darkness would eliminate at least one of the dangerous encounters.

I began to make a bit more noise as I neared the old road. Heavy footfalls. A tossed rock. An unnecessary clearing of the throat. Little warnings I was planning to repeat upon every approach.

"Hey, brother. We need to talk." Trevor emerged from behind some brush. His tone was serious, urgent.

"Sure. What's going on?"

He put his hand on my shoulder. "Promise me you'll remain calm."

"Yeah. Sure. What is it?"

"You know how we were talking about George earlier? How he's a pretty quiet guy?"

"I'd go with 'muscle-bound monk.'"

He didn't so much as smile. "He is a listener. And a watcher. And while he was patrolling last night, he was walking past the trailers when he overheard a conversation.

Two men were talking about William and Sebastian."

"Okay…"

"It was about their working relationship." He waited. I had nothing to say. He went on, "Lukas. It isn't good."

"But they seem to be getting along pretty well."

"William wanted to run the show. Everyone knows that."

"Of course." I was studying his face. It was worried.

"Let me put it this way—given the dynamic, it would be natural for William to be resentful. And it would be natural for Sebastian to be threatened."

"But it seems like they're working it out." I thought for a moment. "What did George hear?"

"Only every few words. But they were whispering about who should really be in charge."

"If that was the conversation, I'd think your name would've come up." I meant it.

"I appreciate that, but my name isn't on the ballot. Only here to help. The thing is, if those two are going at it, our community's chances of thriving go way down. Then? Me and my boys will have to get outta Dodge. And you and your mom will have to retreat to the inner keep."

My face must've confessed something involuntarily.

"Relax," Trevor reassured. "I told you, I learned a lot from your dad."

"Mom doesn't want me to talk to anyone about…" I trailed off.

"It's cool. I don't want you to betray her trust." He

suddenly looked around, having heard something that I must've missed. "Did you notice? Neither of them came to help during Andrew's kitty incident last night?"

"Must trust you a lot."

"Maybe. Maybe not." He kept looking into the thickening darkness. "I saw something on cemetery ridge before Andrew's message. It looked like two silhouettes. As George responded, I kept watching. The silhouettes ran west."

"You think Sebastian and William snuck out to the cemetery, beyond our perimeter, to have it out?"

"Either that. Or it was one of them meeting with someone else." He finally gave the hint of a smile. "Or maybe it was a couple of circus coyotes standing on their hind legs. But there has to be a reason they didn't respond."

"I don't know…"

"Listen. I'm not accusing anyone of anything. It's best for all of us if Sebastian and William can coexist. I hope they can. I really do. I'm only asking you to keep your eyes and ears open."

"I can do that."

"Good. When you get to the southern post, we should be far enough into our shift for a radio check-in. Have Andrew start it."

I was still digesting everything.

"Lukas?"

"Okay."

"You good?"

"Hundred percent."

51.

WALKING PAST THE SINNOTS', I was startled by a quiet pop. I clicked on the flashlight and swung it toward the sound.

Sophie was sitting on a boulder, chewing a wad of gum. Then, I noticed she was holding the flowers I'd placed on her mother's cross.

"What are you doing out here?" I questioned. "It's not safe anymore."

"First. Don't be like everyone else. I'm not a helpless girl." With her free hand, she picked up a pistol and lightly tapped it against the rock below her. "Second. You obviously misunderstood me. I wanted you to bring flowers to *me*."

I stammered, "I...I don't know what you're talking about."

She lifted them as her eyebrows shot up.

"Pretty flowers." My face was granite.

Her face sank. "Lukas. I didn't assume you were going to propose to me. You did something nice. And I liked it."

"Then, why didn't you just say 'thank you?'"

"You pretend like you aren't as wonderful as everybody knows you are. I deflect with humor and my badass personality." She hinted at a smile. "I guess we both have our issues."

"Sounds like it."

She left the gun and the flowers on the boulder, stood on the hard rock surface, and hopped down, landing cooly on both feet. She walked up to me, closer than a friend.

She locked her hazel eyes on my own. "You were kind enough to give me something. I'd like to return the favor."

My ears felt hot. My face, flushed.

She grabbed my hand in her own. She reached into her jeans pocket with her other and pulled out a pack of peanut M&Ms and placed it in my hand.

"It's my last one. I must really like you." She let go of my hand, turned, and hopped back onto the boulder. She picked up her flowers and the pistol, before heading back toward her front door.

52.

EVER SINCE ADDISON MOVED TO SKULL VALLEY, I found her to be the kindest person I'd ever known. And she just happened to be exceptionally beautiful. A few days ago, I risked everything by stopping to pick her up before I left Prescott, so I knew she was special. She could say things to me, challenge me in ways no one else could without getting under my skin. And she cared about me. That was obvious. But she cared for everybody.

Then there was Sophie.

She'd begun flirting with me a few months before, and as far as I knew, she had never flirted with anyone else. I liked that. I hoped it didn't mean I was turning into a narcissist. Sure, she didn't look like she could walk into a pre-disaster modeling agency and get signed on the spot like Addison, but she had something—something undefinable that made me want to protect her, even if she was formidable in her own right. It wasn't about what she could or couldn't do. It was about how I felt about her. And that made her attractive from the inside out.

I realized the distance I'd covered and figured Andrew might be a bit jumpy after his incident with the big cat the night before, so I made even more noise than I had when I'd approached Trevor.

"Could you *be* any louder?" Andrew called out.

"Are you saying my ninja tryouts aren't going to go well?" I called back.

As he came into moonlit view, he asked, "The hell took you so long?"

"One of your friends had a lot to say."

He extended his hand and I shook it again. I grew to appreciate how Andrew treated me like a man, not some kid. It was different than Trevor, who seemed eager to mentor me.

"Guessing it wasn't George," he grinned.

"Know what he wanted to talk to me about?"

"Pretty sure I do."

"Thought you might."

Andrew looked back at the road a moment. "Did he tell you we'd start checking in when you got here?"

"He did."

"Better get to it." He pulled out his radio and took a deep breath. "Andrew at south station. Checking in. Lukas is here with me. Old road, you there?"

The radio crackled. "Trevor at the old road. Checking in. Northern post, you there?"

It crackled again. "George at the northern post. Checking in. Perimeter supervisor, you there?"

The radio came to life a third time. "William here. Sebastian is with me. I'm at the school. Be safe out there."

"William? You're still at the office?" It was Trevor. "Geez. How long are you planning on working tonight?"

"Don't worry about me. I'll be heading home in about thirty minutes, just like always."

"Good. You obviously need to get more beauty rest."

"Screw you, movie star."

"Television star, William." Trevor laughed. "Television star."

With that, the channel went silent.

I looked at Andrew. He looked back to the road.

"Well," I broke the silence, "I guess I should move along."

"Hang out a few minutes. Long shift and you know you won't be spending any time at the next station."

"Are you maintaining the position that George isn't a master conversationalist?" I sat on the dirt.

"You've lived here since you were born?" Andrew asked out of nowhere.

"Same house."

"Do you like it?"

"I was counting down the days until I left for college before this happened."

He nodded. "I think I kinda like it. But to your point, it is the middle of nowhere."

"The thing is, if I can't wait to escape it, why do I feel like I'd do anything to protect it?"

"Like family."

"Guess so."

The radio crackled to life once more. "Northern post. Saw a man. I shouted a request for the town security code. He ducked back into the brush on the west side of the road. Requesting back up."

"I'm on my way." It was Trevor's voice, calm as could be. "Lukas, get to my old road post. George. How far away was the man?"

I jumped up and began sprinting without saying a word to Andrew.

"About thirty to forty yards."

"Damn. That's close," Trevor replied. "William and Sebastian? If you've got a vehicle, mind joining us?"

There was a slight pause before, "Let's wait. Might be a frightened resident."

The unmistakable sound of three gunshots rang out across the night.

"Taking fire!" George yelled across the channel.

"On our way!" William, suddenly out of breath.

"There in a sec!" Trevor, not out of breath.

I ran back past the Sinnots' as Conor, Liam, and Sophie burst out the front door. To the northwest, the foreign sound of a truck revving to life.

Conor yelled, "Someone trying to kill more wildlife?!"

Another two shots, followed immediately by five deeper sounding reports.

"Doesn't sound like it! Sebastian and your dad are headed there!" I responded in a dead sprint.

"Where?!" Conor yelled.

"North!" Over my shoulder.

As I approached the spot where the old road met the highway, I slowed. If I turned right here, it would've led to the old road post. But if I continued straight ahead, it would eventually get me to the northern post. I raised my walkie. "Lukas here. Need more backup?"

Headlights flashed through the sky up ahead.

"Lukas! Get to north as soon as you can!" William, still out of breath.

"No! Head to the old road! Don't leave it vulnerable!" Trevor corrected.

"With all due respect, I'm head of perimeter," William again. "Lukas? Get here. Andrew get to the old road."

I ran up the road toward the mobile home park, and the northern post beyond.

"See your truck, William." Trevor across the channel. "Sebastian with you?"

"Yeah. Getting out of the truck now."

The channel went quiet—leaving only the sound of my shoes patting against the pavement. My progress through the heart of the community seemed to take forever. I had crossed the tracks on the southern side of the loop and was now approaching the mobile homes where several people had emerged into the night to investigate the gunfire. Walt held an old Winchester rifle.

"Need backup, son?"

Mingled shots rang out. At least three weapons. It was the freaking O.K. Corral up there.

"No sir," was all I could manage between breaths.

It wasn't far now, but it was still taking too long.

Several more shots pierced the air. Only a single weapon.

Now I could hear shouting. And something else.

I looked over my shoulder and saw Conor almost caught up to me.

"Watch where you're running!" he yelled. "We're too close for you to be looking back!"

He had a point.

Ahead there was no more gunfire. Only the sound of Trevor and George shouting.

I pulled up into a jog. Trevor and George were yelling at one another on the railroad bridge above.

I stopped and called up to them as Conor fell in beside me, "Is it all clear?"

The shadows spun and peered down. "Lukas? Who's that with you?!"

"Conor?"

"Conor!" Trevor shouted, "We need you up here right now!"

"Where's my dad?" he asked.

The silent response felt like an eternity and we both instinctively looked around. Conor saw him first.

"Dad!" His voice cracked, unnaturally high, and ran to his father. William sat on the dirt, back against the front bumper.

"Dad!" He knelt beside his father. "Dad!" Higher. Louder.

I jogged up, saw the horror, and turned to see George scrambling down from the tracks. I instinctively gripped my weapon.

Conor saw him too. Through his tears, he pulled a pistol from a side holster and aimed it up at George. Sniffling.

George stopped in his tracks and threw his hands in the air. "Put down the gun, boy. I didn't shoot your dad."

Still on the ground, cradling his father with his free hand, Conor sniffled again.

"Conor!" I yelled.

He looked at me, but I didn't see Conor. The shock had forcibly removed Conor from his own body. His trembling arm still extended the gun toward George.

"Conor Sinnot!" I tried again. "Put it down, man."

The gun slowly lowered to the dirt. As soon as his hand let go of the gun, his arm flew up to wrap his dad in a tearful, silent, shaking embrace.

George flew to the gun, clicked on the safety and stuck it in the back of his waist belt.

"What happened, George?" I quietly asked.

"Get up to Trevor. He'll fill you in."

I hesitated.

"Go! I got this." He stood above Conor, giving him the moment.

It was only when I climbed up the hill and looked over at Trevor that I remembered Sebastian. His body laid on the ground, about ten feet from where Trevor stood, looking at me with a shell-shocked expression, rifle slung over his shoulder.

"Trevor…" I embedded all my questions in his name.

He slowly lowered himself and sat on the tracks as I approached. "By the time I arrived, George had figured out it was that guy from the other night. What's his name?"

"Kyle."

"Yeah. Kyle. He must've circled his way back with a hell of a vendetta. Anyway. Shots were fired. George returned fire. Sebastian and William pulled up. I made my way down to them while George watched for the guy. William stayed at the truck, checking his weapon. Sebastian said he wanted to get up on the bridge with George. He said he'd been a coward last time, and a leader doesn't hide behind his people. I told him to be careful as I took up position behind the vehicle barrier. I told William to come up and take cover behind the barrier when a weapon went off. Immediately, another weapon fired and the bullet blew through him. I thought Kyle had gotten an accurate shot under the bridge somehow, and turned to make sure he hadn't somehow gotten a lot closer. Instead, I saw Sebastian on the bridge. Lukas? He aimed his gun at me. George shot him just in time."

"Wait a minute. Why would…?"

"Sebastian shot William. My best guess is that he thought George was too busy with Kyle, but then he saw me look at him and—"

Sebastian groaned.

"Damn!" Trevor yelled, grabbing his rifle and aiming it at Sebastian's body in a fluid motion.

I realized I'd pulled my gun and was pointing it at Sebastian too.

"Make a move asshole!" Trevor yelled at the body.

I didn't think there was the slightest chance of that happening.

We waited. Nothing more.

I knelt and placed my hand on Sebastian. He was breathing, but unevenly. The man wasn't doing well.

"He's alive," I looked up to Trevor, "but he isn't a threat."

He didn't lower his gun. Instead, he yelled, "George! Sebastian's alive!"

There was a sudden scramble below.

"Get back here!" George roared.

Conor crested and took aim at the man who just shot his dad. He held George's rifle.

I raised my gun at him and yelled, "Conor! Don't make me shoot you!"

Conor glared at me. "You are going to shoot me for avenging my dad?"

"Conor?!"

"You are going to shoot me for avenging my dad!" He screamed so fiercely, spittle flew from his mouth.

George crept above the edge behind Conor. He approached silently, but I dared not look away from Conor.

"Conor?" I hoped these words would work. "If you shoot him, we'll never know why he did it!"

"I don't care!" he spit with venom.

"We'll never know if someone else knew, if someone else was involved!"

"Plenty of time to—"

George forcefully disarmed Conor with a series of precise movements ending with a punch to the face, knocking him out cold.

I exhaled.

"Thanks." It was all I could say.

"Probably should've let him shoot the prick," Trevor added.

"No one takes my weapon," George responded under his breath.

We stood there on the bridge a moment. One man dead. Another about to die. One young man knocked unconscious. And three men trying to figure out what the hell had just happened.

53.

"**WHAT NOW?**" I ASKED.

Trevor let out a heavy exhale. "Alright. There are bound to be quite a few people heading this way. We have to hurry. You two get Sebastian to the truck. Keep him as stable as possible. Then, get him to his house."

"Should we really be moving him?" I asked skeptically.

"No, we shouldn't, but we've got no choice. If he's here when others arrive, and they judge he isn't worth saving, we won't be able to stop them. Moving him to the security of his home with George is his best chance. He knows basic field medicine."

George cleared his throat. "William is leaning against the truck."

"Lay him on his freakin' side." Trevor wasn't yelling, but

243

seemed out of patience. "I'll deal with Conor, his dad, and whoever shows up." He pulled out his radio. "Andy?"

It crackled. "Here."

"Get to the northern post now."

"Anything I need to know?"

"I'll fill you in when you get here."

"On my way."

54.

GEORGE LIFTED SEBASTIAN AND CARRIED HIM down the embankment with ease.

As we neared the truck, George instructed me to move William's body onto its side and off the truck. Then, I ran to the back and lowered the tailgate. George laid Sebastian down in the bed.

We realized neither of us knew where the keys were. George reached into Sebastian's pockets as I ran up and checked the ignition. Nothing.

"Any luck back there?" I called.

"Nope."

Crap. Was not looking forward to rummaging through a dead man's pockets.

I ran back over to William and checked his exposed

pocket. His radio, but no keys. Then, forced to gently roll him, I found them in his other pocket.

A girl's voice asked, "What the hell happened here?"

It was Emily, flanked by Trey's hulking—and panting—frame.

"Long story. Ain't got the time," George answered curtly. "Lukas! Let's go!"

"Is that Sebastian?" Trey asked, looking closer at the body in the bed of the truck.

"He shot William and was about to shoot Trevor. George had to stop him. But he's still alive so we're getting him back to his house before others arrive and we have a mob situation."

"Wait. What?" Emily blurted.

Sure enough, behind them, a large group of people were ambling their way toward the scene. I was pretty sure Sophie and Liam would be among them.

"Lukas! Start the damn truck!" George yelled.

Trey quickly strode up to me and grabbed the keys. "I know where everything is in the house. I'll be more help there. You know what's going on here. Stay and help sort through the aftermath." He crammed himself behind the wheel, revved the engine and backed out, before rambling the truck past the herd of the curious.

I was left there, standing next to Emily with the now-exposed body of William Sinnot. The others were only twenty feet away now.

She looked down at the body. "Who moved him?"

"Me. Had to. He was leaning against the truck's front bumper. And the keys were in his pocket."

"Where's Trevor? Andrew?"

Now the group was only fifteen feet away.

"Trevor is on the bridge with Conor and—"

"Conor?" She cut me off.

"He got here at the same time I did. Was going to shoot Sebastian. George knocked him out."

Ten feet.

"And Andrew?"

"On his way up the tracks from the old road."

Five feet.

"Disarm Liam and Sophie," she forcefully whispered, "now!"

55.

"**A**RE YOU ALRIGHT?" Sophie's face, concerned and locked on my own. Liam was steps behind her.

"Are you or Liam armed?"

Someone screamed.

Sophie leaned to look over my shoulder. I gently touched the side of her face to reestablish her attention. It worked.

"Are you or Liam armed?" I asked again.

There were gasps and shouting erupted behind me as the majority of the crowd had discovered William.

"No. Should we be? What's going on?" She still appeared to be primarily concerned with me.

"Sophie? I'm so sorry." I was suddenly shaking. "There's been an accident... "

"Lukas?" Her voice went stern. "Where is my big brother?"

Liam came up beside her. "Yeah. Where's Conor?"

"Conor's fine." I couldn't stop trembling.

Behind me, the commotion kept rising despite Emily's best efforts.

"So what's the problem?" Liam asked.

Sophie blinked through doe eyes. "No."

I stepped aside.

Her shoulders sagged as she looked over to Liam.

"Is that...Dad?" Liam's face melted into disbelief. He took an uneasy step forward before Sophie caught him. She hugged him tightly as he cried out, "Nooo! No! Someone resuscitate him! Has anyone even tried CPR? Chest compressions? Something?"

Sophie held onto her brother until the fight left him and lowered him to the ground. Sophie Sinnot *was* clearly the strongest member of her family.

An old voice behind me gently asked, "Are those his children?"

I turned and saw my new friend, Walt.

"Two of 'em. The oldest is up on the tracks with Trevor."

"Rose!"

She emerged from the crowd that had gathered around William's body and moved quickly to Walt. Years together had obviously helped her recognize his urgent voice.

"These are two of his children," he whispered.

"Oh God," her hand drew to her mouth. She looked down at the shaking boy being held tight by his big sister, breathed in, and said, "Okay." She approached gently and crouched beside them.

"We'll make sure they're okay, son," Walt said solemnly. "Tell the older boy. The trailer with the red horizontal stripe."

"Red horizontal stripe." I looked back at Sophie.

"I'm sure you've got responsibilities. We know how to help people grieve. Trust me."

"Thank you."

I turned and started for the incline to let Conor know about his siblings when Emily caught me.

"The scene has been compromised," she said with disgust. "The body was moved and now half the town has gathered around him."

"Why does that matter?" I asked irritably. "We know what happened."

"I believe in evidence more than witnesses."

"Don't start trouble. Tonight could destroy us."

"But we need to make sure —"

"You're not even *from* here!" I yelled before she could go on.

She pressed her lips together.

"Okay, but we need to figure out what to do with the body. And soon. But before he's buried, I'd like to take a look. I think it's—"

"I'm not telling his kids a woman they don't even know, who lives with the guy who shot their dad, wants to take a look at his body!"

"You know what? Never mind." She walked back toward the crowd.

That was when Walt and Rose slowly guided Sophie and Liam toward the body of their father. And to my right, Conor descended the hill. I moved to meet him.

As soon as he saw me, he stopped and waited for me.

"Listen, Conor—"

"I'll never forgive you," he somehow shouted through a whisper.

"I don't expect you—"

He cut me off a second time. "And if you don't stop making excuses and let me go see my father right now, I will not need a gun to murder you."

I wanted to explain. I wanted him to understand. But this wasn't the time. It might not be for quite a while. I walked by him and up the hill.

I needed to talk to Trevor.

56.

AFTER I ASCENDED TO THE RAILROAD bridge for the third time in a single night, I saw Andrew had arrived. He stood near Trevor, who sat on the tracks, head in his hands.

Andrew looked over. His face, ashen.

I walked over and sat next to Trevor.

Trevor dropped his hands to his sides. Tears welled up in his eyes.

He began slowly. "All because of me." Swallowing hard. "I knew. I knew they had problems."

"Wasn't your fault," I said.

"They were like two sticks of dynamite and I just sat back and watched while they jumped into a fire."

"Wasn't your fault."

His head lowered back into his hands.

From behind his hands, "I'm sorry. I know I just met William, but I saw Conor. And I could hear his little brother from up here. It's got me a bit… I'll be okay in a minute. It's just… I thought I'd come back and be able to help."

I looked over to Andrew. He looked up at the night sky, caught in a nightmare.

"Andrew?"

His mind was somewhere else. "This whole thing is a dumpster fire."

"Can you man this post the rest of the way if I take the old road?"

He stared at me blankly for a moment. "Uh. Yeah."

"Conor would've replaced me at midnight, so we will have to go without a roaming person until six in the morning."

"Yeah. Yeah. Sounds good," he responded. Still in a haze.

"I'll make sure we get the radio back."

"Huh?"

"From William's pocket," Trevor said from behind his hands.

"Oh. Yeah," Andrew realized.

"And I'll try to find someone in the crowd to watch the south until midnight," I added.

"Okay."

Trevor raised his head. "What about me?"

Trevor Beck was asking *me* what he should do. Everything about this was surreal.

"As soon as you're ready," I reminded him, "there are a bunch of people down there who need to hear from you."

Trevor let out a small, tragic laugh and shook his head. Andrew was shaking his head, too. Like they were regretting their decision to come to Skull Valley.

"Alright," Trevor finally said, "Tell them I'll be down in a minute."

57.

WALT AND ROSE HADN'T YET MOVED William's children from his body.

Conor looked from the side of his father. "The hell do you want?"

I hesitated and then spoke the truth. "I need the walkie-talkie. From his pocket."

He smiled the sort of disbelieving smile that reveals fangs.

Through tears, Sophie searched her father's pockets and removed the radio and tossed it to me.

"Thank—"

"Get the hell away from us!" Conor snapped.

I quickly looked to the onlookers. "Anyone able to watch the southern post until midnight?"

"I'll take it." The familiar voice came from someone behind them.

The crowd split down the middle to reveal my mother.

She stepped forward and looked to the Sinnot children. "I am so very sorry. If you need anything—*anything*—you let me know." Then she looked to me. "You okay?"

"I am."

"What's next for you?" she asked.

"Old road."

"And who'll be stationed here?"

"Andrew."

"Let's get to it then," she said before turning to walk off.

"Mom!"

She turned back.

"Your radio." I tossed it to her.

She caught it. "Oh yeah. Thanks." And she was gone.

I raised my voice to the crowd, "Trevor will be down to give you a first-hand account any minute."

As people whispered to one another, I headed off to my post. Hoping for quiet until midnight.

58.

"**J**UST HEAR ME OUT," EMILY'S VOICE WHISPERED shortly after coming to relieve me of my shift. "I listened to Trevor after you left and it doesn't add up."

The clouds had rolled in an hour earlier making the world invisible beyond our dim flashlights.

"Please." I needed sleep before facing what would inevitably be a horrible day tomorrow. "Not now."

She hesitated. "I'm not sure when we'll have another chance to talk." She paused again, probably listening for any hint of another human being. "Listen. I can tell you're a mature kid. But you are still a kid. And I'm sorry I'm laying this on you, but I don't trust anyone else in this town other than Trey. And he's an outsider, too."

Then there was a sound. And another. Something was approaching.

We both turned our lights in the direction of my mother, walking toward us in the blackness, but making no effort to obscure her sound. She winced as she threw up an arm to fend off the beams of light.

"I assume one of those blinding lights is my boy. Who's the other?" She kept approaching.

"Hey," Emily said as we both lowered our beams. "It's Emily. I'm here to relieve your son."

"Good. Because I'm here to retrieve him."

"Do you trust your mom?" Emily whispered, even more quietly.

"Of course." Now I was annoyed.

Emily waited until Mom was close. "Something about tonight doesn't add up."

"Okay." As Mom said it, she drew the word out until it meant, 'go on.'

"Well. The official story is that Kyle arrived. Poked his head out so George could see him. Why would he do that? Our perimeter is to stop vehicles and random groups of marauders. Not individuals on foot. That guy could just park over the ridge and take a four mile hike and walk right into our community and blow a few people away before we could even respond."

"Sure. But he might be an idiot."

"Not likely. According to your son, he knew to head

straight to a used camping supplies and firearms store with-in an hour of the outage. But that's the least troubling detail of the accepted narrative. George spotted him and asked for backup. Then, he began exchanging fire with the supposed moron. They asked William and Sebastian to join them. Trevor arrived on scene to assist. William and Sebastian drive there. Sebastian goes to the front line, even though he hid during the first encounter."

"He said he wanted to make up for it," I broke in. "He said he'd been a coward and he needed to be a leader."

"Were you there?" Mom asked.

"Well. Not yet. But Trevor told me."

"So he heads up to the tracks at the top of the ridge," Emily continued, "but William stays back, in front of his car, to check his weapon. William. The prepper. He didn't know if his weapon was ready for the situation. Meanwhile, Sebastian was ready to be Rambo."

"You are wading into some pretty deep water here Emily," Mom warned.

"I'm not making *any* accusations. I'm simply going through the official story."

"Alright. What did Trevor say happened next?"

"He started down from the bridge to warn William to take cover. More shots were fired. He saw William get shot. He spun to see Sebastian atop the bridge with his gun point-ed at William. When Sebastian realized Trevor was a witness, he turned his gun on Trevor, but George turned around

and, seeing what was about to happen, shot Sebastian first."
Emily turned to me, our flashlights still bouncing shadowy
light off the ground. "Sound right?"

"Yeah. Pretty much," I confirmed.

"So," Emily continued, "why would Sebastian shoot
William?"

"They were fighting for control from the start," I pointed out. "I mean. They were the only two candidates in the
election."

"They seemed to be getting along," Mom observed.

"They weren't," I stated flatly.

"But William won the election. He was the one already
in charge. So, then why shoot William like that?" Emily
questioned. "Did he honestly think he could fire a shot less
than twenty feet from George and get away with it? And
then, he was going to shoot Trevor?"

"He knew George was dealing with the intruder," I
countered.

"Kyle," Mom interjected.

"Yeah. Kyle. He was counting on George figuring he
was also firing at Kyle. If George's eyes had been trained on
Kyle, it would make sense that Sebastian would also start firing. Wouldn't it?"

"Possibly," Mom raised her eyebrows.

Emily sighed. "All I'm saying is, it seems strange."

"If we want to confirm Sebastian shot William, can't we
simply look at the blood?" Mom's training for disasters went

beyond having been married to Dad, she loved watching cop procedurals. "If the story is true, then William was shot from a downward angle and blood should've been in a spray pattern on the ground directly behind him. If he was shot from the same elevation, and he was standing in front of the truck, the blood would've blasted onto the front of the truck, no?"

"In a perfect world," Emily confirmed, "but William was leaned against the truck. Then, he was rolled onto the ground. Then, he was rolled over. Then, a mob of people showed up and kicked dirt all over the place. So that's lost. Hell. We can't even look for the bullet. So many were fired."

"What about the angle the bullet took through William's body?" I asked.

"Again. Wouldn't be conclusive. Was William standing upright? Was he leaning over to check his weapon? According to the story, only Sebastian and Trevor were looking. I already took the liberty of asking Trevor and he said he thought William had been bending over for only moments at a time as he looked back, which would make sense if he was checking his gun. So in the end, William's posture at the moment of impact isn't clear in Trevor's memory. And Sebastian isn't talking. Might never talk again."

"I don't understand the point of all of this," I interjected.

Mom stood there, thinking for a moment, before looking at me. "Well, I think we need to head home." She looked at Emily. "Do you go straight to bed after your shift?"

"Trey and I eat breakfast before we crash until about two in the afternoon."

"Come over. I'll have hot food waiting at quarter after six."

"You don't sleep much, do you?" Emily asked.

Mom smiled before looking back at me. "Let's go home."

DAY FIVE

"YOU'D LOSE EVERY HAND OF POKER IF THEY KNEW EVERY CARD YOU HELD."

—

MARK TAYLOR

59.

WOKE UP TO SILVERWARE CLANKING and the smell of bacon. More than enough to get me out of bed.

As I descended the stairs, I heard my mother's voice accompanied by those of Trey and Emily. They seemed to be having a normal conversation. And given the events of the night before, that was anything *but* normal.

"Good morning," I began. "What are you crazy kids talking about?"

"Let's see," Trey considered. "The cluster that was last night. Bits about our past. What we have in common. And what I have in common with pigs."

"And what is that?" I inquired, more than a little intrigued. "Wait. Let me guess. It's the weight."

"How dare you!" Trey made like he was angered and

fumbled to get at me while Emily laughed and pretended to hold him in his seat.

"Okay," I looked to the ceiling, as if thinking. "Your strong odor."

Trey shook his head slowly while Emily warned, "You keep this up and I won't hold him back."

"Then, I give. What do you have in common with pigs?"

"I make everything better," he said with glowing pride.

"Don't get it."

"Sandwich? Good. Sandwich with bacon? Better. Salad? Tolerable. Salad with bacon? Infinitely improved."

"Oh. Dude," I laughed. "You misunderstood. It's clear bacon makes everything better. I just didn't understand the part about *you* making everything better."

He jumped at me without the slightest interference from Emily. I spun and ran for the front door, the sound of Mom and Emily's laughter echoing from the kitchen. I burst out the door onto the porch and saw Trevor standing there at the bottom of the steps.

Trey rocketed through the door and exploded through me, sending us both flying over the steps and directly to the hard tack of the dust with a thud.

"God. You guys alright?" Trevor asked with concern as I laughed, pushing Trey off of me and trying to hide the effort I put into rediscovering my breath.

"Yeah." I hopped to my feet and thumbed to Trey, still on the ground. "And his nickname is now 'Bacon.'"

"Trey? You alright?" It was Emily, at the open door.

Trey let out a deep groan as he rolled over.

"That's not good," Trevor muttered and moved to Trey.

Emily and Mom descended the steps.

"Reaggravated my back."

60.

THE OTHER THREE TENDED TO TREY as I ran across the field toward
the Forrester home where George was still apparently
watching over Sebastian. The dry patches of grass crunched
and my breath heaved.

I slammed into the front door and swung it open without a knock.

"George!" I looked around as Addison descended curling steps from her top floor bedroom. "Where's George?"

He emerged from the master double doors at the end
of the hall.

"What?" His white eyes pierced me. Possibly for the first
time.

"Trevor told me to get you. Trey's on the ground. He
might've gotten the wind knocked out, or it might be worse."

His head moved toward the doors behind him a moment before looking back to me. "You stay here with Sebastian. If he wakes up, come and get me."

"Okay."

He bore into me. "Every second will count, Lukas."

"I said okay."

He glanced back again before jogging around the corner and out the front door.

Addison followed to the door and shut it behind him before walking back around the corner.

"Sit." She motioned to the couch in the living room.

"I'm supposed to be—"

"Mom's in there with him. It's fine." Her face looked like it was about to shatter. "Please sit."

I moved to the couch and sat. It was the first time I'd seen her since her dad shot William. I had no idea what to say. "How are you?"

She sat sideways on the other end of the couch, scrunched her feet under her thighs, leaned her elbow on the back of the couch and held her head up with the same hand. "What happened?"

"Trey and I were being idiots and—"

"I don't..." Addison stammered a moment. "I don't mean that."

"Oh." How do you tell a friend their Dad is a murderer? "That guy came back. Kyle. Near the railroad bridge. George was assigned to it. They were shooting back and forth. He called for backup. Trevor arrived on the scene. Then, your dad and Mr. Sinnot arrived. The shots continued and Mr. Sinnot got shot." I took a deep breath. "Addison? George and Trevor both saw your dad do it. Then, when he realized Trevor saw him, he turned his gun toward him. That's when George shot your dad."

"You didn't see it happen?" She asked, disturbingly calm.

"No. I did not."

She stared at me for a moment. Then, she abruptly got up and began walking toward her parents' room. She was more than halfway down the hall before she asked, "Are you coming or not?"

I rose to my feet and walked into the bedroom.

There, Sebastian was laid across the king bed. His slightly-bronzed face had been traded in for an older, ashen model. Each breath, labored and shallow.

To the left of the bed, Corrine Forrester sat in a chair. There was no makeup. No pretension. Her delicate hand extended, gently holding his right hand. No acknowledgement of my entrance. She was too focused for petty distractions.

"Mom?" Addison prompted, standing at the right side of the bed.

No response.

"Mom."

"What." It came out like a flat statement.

"Is Dad accurate with a gun?"

She shook her head. Less an answer than a dismissal of idiocy.

"Is he accurate with a gun?" Addison demanded.

Her mom looked up with contempt. "No. And you know it. He bought his guns and that worthless electronic safe when we moved. Made us all take a class and couldn't hit the broadside of a barn."

"In our family of three," Addison continued the interrogation for my benefit, "was he the least accurate?"

"It's why he hid during the first shootout. Then, when people whispered, he was determined. He told me, the next time, he was going to have to get into the action or people wouldn't follow him anymore." Her annoyance grew. "You know all this. Just leave us be." Her focus went back to her husband.

George walked in and surveyed the scene. I was shocked at how fast he'd returned.

"Hey. Trey's going to be alright, but he messed up his back. Trevor and your mom are moving him to your bed."

"Seems to me, you are the only one with the strength to do that."

"Had to hurry back in case Sebastian wakes up. Looks like you're getting moved to the couch."

"Fine with me." I wanted to hear more from Addison. "If you want a little break, I can keep an eye on Sebastian for a bit longer."

"No." Quick shake of the head. "I got him." Short.

Direct. No room for debate. "Oh. And Trevor is asking for a town hall on the front lawn of the school at noon."

"What about?" I asked.

"You'd have to ask him."

61.

MOM AND I LEFT FOR THE TOWN MEETING, leaving Emily to care for Trey. As we walked down the road, I considered sharing what Addison had told me, but thought better of it. Addison was hardly impartial. Instead of sharing hearsay, I decided to learn as much as I could.

"Mom? Can you tell me more about Trevor?" I asked without slowing our pace. "You know, from when you were younger?"

"Not much to tell. He was a year younger than me. Two younger than your dad." I waited for her to say more. After a few steps, she did. "Super shy. Your dad kind of felt for him. Showed him some pretty cool stuff."

"Like what?"

"Honestly? A lot of the stuff he taught you. Knots.

Traps. Basically? The stuff you learn in Boy Scouts turned up to eleven. But then…" She seemed to hesitate. "It got a little weird."

"What do you mean by 'weird?'"

She stopped and inhaled deeply. Slowly.

"In life, there are always people on the fringes. In school. At work. In communities. They act differently. Maybe they're shy. Maybe they have issues at home. Maybe they're on the spectrum. Whatever the reason, they're the ones who walk alone. And the rest of us are afraid to reach out. Not because we don't want to. We do. We want to be good people. We want to help. But we look at these people and realize they don't have anyone else. That means we can't be kind and move along. We'll be stuck with them. We will be their best friend. But we don't want a new best friend. We want to help change their lives, but not if it means a significant change to our own."

I looked around. Anywhere but my mother's eyes. Mustering the courage to say what my guts were feeling. "I don't want to live that way. I want to reach out, even when it comes with a cost."

"Like father, like son."

"Huh?"

"Your dad *did* reach out to Trevor. And Trevor became his pseudo apprentice. He even had a little notebook he'd write notes in when your dad taught him something. But then that scenario I mentioned? It happened. He wouldn't leave Dad alone. Ever."

"Maybe he was lonely."

"I'm sure he was," Mom responded. "But your dad had an introverted streak and needed to be alone sometimes. Plus, he was falling in love with a girl and was spending more time with her."

"And that girl was you."

"That girl was me." Her lips turned up the slightest touch.

"But Trevor didn't understand?"

"No. Quite the opposite. Trevor tried even harder to get your dad's attention. On dates, Trevor would *happen* to show up. One time, we were at a diner in Prescott and Trevor just appeared. He pulled up a chair, ordering before we could ask him for privacy. When he bought a movie ticket, found us in the theater, and sat on the other side of your dad, well, your dad finally lost it and told him to get lost. It was so uncomfortable. Your dad, who never yelled, went off on him."

"In the middle of the movie theater?"

"Yup."

"That had to crush him."

"It crushed your dad, too. He felt bad for weeks after that. Tried to reach out to him. So did I. But he wouldn't even look at us."

"Well. He sure recovered well."

"There's more to life than fortune and fame."

"I'm not even talking about that." I searched for the words. "He has only said kind things about Dad." I thought for a moment. "And he tried to get him that job."

"He did."

It was all she said.

62.

"**H**I, FRIENDS." THE SOLEMN, BUT REASSURING voice belonged to Trevor Beck, standing on a picnic table. The crowd surrounding him was much larger today than the day of the election earlier in the week. "I'm not going to revisit the events of last night. But please understand there were multiple witnesses to the unfortunate events. The guilty will be punished and safety will be restored."

As he paused, I realized George wasn't standing at his side. Must still be taking care of Sebastian.

"Last night, and again this morning, many of you have approached me regarding the future of Skull Valley." He surveyed the crowd before him. "Most are suggesting I take a leadership role. I thought I'd made it clear I only wanted to rejoin my childhood home. To rejoin my childhood home and help in whatever way I could. But now it seems this *is* the way you want my help." As he surveyed the crowd, he appeared exhausted. "I need to know something. Is this just a few of you? Or do the majority of you agree?"

The crowd murmured with assent. Trevor looked across the assembled, as if checking to see if he was going to be forced into this role he didn't want.

He was indeed.

His head sunk. "If I'm going to do this, I have some conditions. And they are non-negotiable because I'm not a politician and I don't know how to compromise. But I've got some ideas on how to get us through this." He waited for objection. None were forthcoming. "It will be temporary. Me. In charge. Once normalcy has been established, we will hold another election and I won't be on the ballot. Next? George will be taking over border security. I understand that the man isn't a local, but he's as loyal as anyone I've ever known and he will help reestablish the security of this community."

He paused a moment and took a drink from a water bottle.

"The facts are these. Men were killed the day I got here. I haven't grieved publicly, but I take responsibility for it. Then, George was almost killed. Within an hour of that, I had a gun pointed in my direction." He shook his head. "This has got to stop. We have people at every major entry point to the town. And that's great. More than most communities are probably doing. But anyone who has four wheel drive or can walk, can waltz into this place and open fire.

"Our greatest threat is that son of a bitch, Ken or Kyle or whatever the hell his name is. We killed his friend and he wants to make us pay. And even if we catch or kill him, there will be others. We have land and water. But I expect Prescott is in disarray by now. And anyone with an ounce of knowledge and a hard map in Phoenix has to know this is probably the closest fertile spot that isn't already filled with people. The clock is ticking. So the perimeter will be reinforced with more guards. In addition, every vehicle that has the ability, will be moved to flat ground along our northern, eastern, and southern borders. They will be fortified and supplemented with any junk we don't have use for. For now, we will have to settle for lookouts to the west.

"All firearms and ammunition will be collected and kept in the armory which is…" he swallowed, possibly realizing the irony in that moment, "the basement of the Forrester residence."

That *was* met with wide objection.

"Listen!" He reclaimed control. "I get it. I understand. It's the basement of the guy who murdered possibly the most-respected member of our community—"

"That's a lie!" Everyone spun to see Addison. Her face, less filled with anger than pleading. "It's a lie! He wouldn't! He couldn't!"

"Shut up, you bitch!" Conor's voice roared across the crowd, guttural and raging.

"No! Look!" Addison gulped down tears. "I'm sorry about your dad, but it wasn't—"

"I said shut up!" He shoved through the crowd toward her.

I darted between townsfolk, toward a point between the two of them.

"Listen," Addison pleaded, underestimating Conor's rage and moving toward him. "My dad—"

The crowd noise rose to the point where I couldn't hear them. Didn't matter. I reached Addison and moved her backward. I turned and saw Conor shove Sophie to the ground. She landed hard. Conor stood above her. Shoulders heaving up and down. Face contorted in conflicting emotions.

Sophie scrambled back to her feet and got in his face. "Really? Really?! That is who you are now?!"

"Conor!" Addison, still pleading.

"Not now," I whispered. "Not now."

"Damn it!" Conor erupted before turning and storming away.

Sophie shot a look toward me, then Addison.

"Thank you," Addison said.

"It wasn't about you," Sophie shot back.

She turned and strode after her brother.

"You better get her home." It was Mom. It didn't even realize she was right behind me. Then she whispered, "Then, run to the house. Everything of value gets locked up. Leave out anything people have already seen."

"You think that's necessary?"

"Go! Now!"

I looked around. The entire crowd watched us. Even Trevor, still standing on the picnic table seemed to be waiting.

"Come on." I prodded Addison toward the road.

"Yeah. Okay." She finally seemed to realize it was for the best.

As we cleared the crowd, Andrew stood alone under a tree. He mouthed the words, "Dumpster fire."

63.

I BURST THROUGH MY HOME'S FRONT DOOR and headed straight to the basement steps when I remembered Emily and Trey.

"Emily?" I called up.

"Lukas? That you?"

I moved to the stairwell leading upstairs and saw Emily at the top, leaning on the rail. "Hey. How's the big man?"

"He'll live. Meeting over already?"

"No. Mom forgot to take care of a few things."

She took a tentative step down. "Need my help?"

"No, no." I waved her off. "Keep an eye on your man. Need to make sure it doesn't get worse. I got it."

"Okay…" She moved back to the top of the flight. "Thanks for taking us in. I imagine things are about to get a bit weird at our last residence."

"You're probably right."

With Emily kept at bay, I collected every firearm hidden throughout the main floor. Only our personal weapons remained upstairs. I left a thousand rounds for each weapon we'd be turning over.

I flew down the steps to the basement, unlocked the door to the storage room, and closed the door behind me. I locked it and gave it a yank to make sure. I moved across the room to a large metal shelving unit against the far wall. I reached down and under its second shelf. I pulled out a magnetic key holder and removed the large key. Then, I pulled a thick rod from a hole to the left of the unit. Standing back up, I tried the shelving unit, and it slid easily about two feet to its left along the wall. An exposed rough hole in the concrete wall revealed a small but thick metal door. It looked like a large dial safe, complete with a three prong spindle safe handle and a keyhole. I turned the key and heard a bolt slide. Then, I dialed the correct combination—the day my parents met—before spinning the handle and heard a second, larger bolt slide. I gave the door a shove and the door gave. I crawled into the cramped underground shipping container that had been installed years earlier.

Dad had found a company through an online network of like-minded individuals who installed units such as this under the guise of large septic upgrades. It worked. No one wanted to drop by when septic work was being done.

Mom had done more than I realized. There was very

little that needed to be added. Much of the room was taken by food stores, water canisters marked with dates, the guns and accompanying ammunition, several chemical toilets, and clothes. I sincerely hoped we weren't going to be using this for anything more than super-secret storage, but even I had to admit, things were starting to get interesting.

I added the additional weapons, along with a bit more food. I wasn't sure what the current plan was, but Trey and Emily were now living under our roof. I placed a few more boxes of crackers on a shelf in the shelter. Trey was huge and had to eat a lot. God. I wasn't even sure Trey's shoulders could be pried through the door to this claustrophobic nightmare of last resort.

There was a violent knock on the other side of the storage room door.

64.

I **OPENED THE DOOR TO ANDREW.** "Hey." Couldn't say more because I was completely out of breath from getting back out of the shelter and closing the door and replacing the bolts and sliding the key into my pocket and sliding the shelving unit back and replacing the spike. All in twenty seconds while the knocking repeated every five.

"You alright?" His eyes weren't on me. They were darting around the cramped room.

"Yeah. Uh. Making sure we aren't missing any guns or ammunition before we lug it over to the Forresters'." I waited for him to meet my eyes. Eventually, he did. "No offense, but what are you doing in my house?"

"We've got a situation."

65.

IT FELT DOWNRIGHT GLORIOUS to be driving again.

We were rumbling down the road in Mom's Bronco, since it was going to be moved to somewhere along the perimeter anyway.

I asked Andrew for his walkie-talkie before clicking it on. "Who are they?"

"She won't say. As soon as we told them to stop, she began cursing at us and asking for you or Addison." Trevor's voice was impatient. It was obvious, even through the radio. "And I thought, given the circumstances, you were the better draft pick."

"Okay. Be there in two minutes."

As I handed the walkie-talkie back to Andrew, I couldn't help but realize the last time two people drove to the northern post, less than twenty four hours ago, one of them ended up shot and the other was dead.

"I knocked," Andrew said. "No one answered. I opened the door and yelled. Emily told me you were down there. Kinda surprised you didn't hear me."

I felt him asking the question. "Solid wood construction. Don't build homes like that anymore. At least, that's what Dad would've said."

"That's probably it." He looked at me as I drove. "Please turn in every gun and every round."

The abrupt change of topic seemed more than a bit odd.

"Yeah. I told you that's what I was doing."

"I know." He paused again, as we turned left onto the highway. There was a mass of citizens up ahead. Apparently, most of those at the meeting had walked down to see what was going on. We skidded to a stop behind the automotive barrier. Almost precisely where Sebastian and William parked the night before.

Trevor was at the top of the large berm. I climbed it for what felt like the thirtieth time this week.

"Hey there, Trevor. Never a dull moment since you arrived."

"Take a look." He stepped aside, giving me a clear view of the highway beyond the bridge, leading up the cemetery ridge above.

She stood in the middle of the road, about fifteen very exhausted middle school kids behind her. Only thirty yards from the barrier.

66.

"**JESSIE! WHAT'S GOING ON?!**"

"Hey, bud. Wanna fill me in on the password that'll open the front door?" she asked through a half-smile that looked like it was about to dissolve into tears.

I turned to Trevor. "Can I go down there?"

"Yeah. But those kids are going to see some guns. We aren't chancing an ambush."

"Trevor. I know her. She was a counselor at a camp with me and Addison. And those are camp kids. This is *not* an ambush."

"Where's the camp?"

"Just off Iron Springs Road just west of Prescott."

"So they had to walk here. Right past Kyle." Trevor waited.

288

"Yeah, so?"

"My point is, that they could've been compromised. They appear unarmed, so he could've easily intercepted them, threatened them, and is waiting for one of us to step a bit closer before he fires out of that brush to the left of the road."

"Point taken." I turned back to Jessie. "We need to make sure it's safe! One sec!"

"No worries. I'll make sure the preteens put away their bazookas."

Trevor had already spoken to George, who took off over the bridge and into the brush on the far side in an attempt to clear it. Then, he whispered something to Andrew, who unshouldered a rifle, got down with his chest on the tracks, and aimed his rifle well above Jessie and her charges.

"Not exactly a trick-or-treat-friendly neighborhood," Jessie remarked loudly.

"We've had a few incidents," I explained.

"Yeah. I can smell the PTSD in the air."

"Okay," Trevor whispered. "Let's go."

We made our way back down the inner side of the berm and hopped over the nearest pickup before walking back under the tracks. Trevor was to my right and a half-step behind me.

"Thanks guys." Jessie smiled. Relieved. "Could use some help here."

"Looks like it," I replied. "What's up?"

"Wait." She looked at Trevor closely. "You're…"

"Yeah. That's me." Trevor looked at the middle school youth. "How did you all end up on our front porch?"

"I stayed at the camp with the kids. Had nowhere to go anyway. Not like I'm making it back to New Mexico anytime soon. We did exactly what you said." She looked at me. "Started with whatever would go bad. Ate that first. Then, used as much as we could out of the refrigerators before it went sour. Finally, moved to the frozen food. We consolidated it so it would last longer."

"Sounds like you had it made," Trevor said. "I mean, compared to most."

"It wasn't bad," Jessie confirmed. "Kids were even getting picked up. Less than twenty four hours after lights out, the first family showed up. They looked like they were ready for World War Three. Picked up their two kids and were gone. Then, another family. Day after that, a caravan of four older cars and trucks showed up. A mom organized it. No idea how without telephones. Said the whole Phoenix area was getting sketchy quick. Police—who hadn't run off to protect their own—were doing their best, but it wasn't working out so well. The caravan was headed for a couple cabins further north."

"So Justin, Ben, you and the other staff were trying to hold it together until the last kid got picked up?" I asked.

"Not quite. Once a good number of the kids got picked up, Justin let the staff go. I think he was thinking there was a better chance the food would hold out with less mouths to feed. I stayed, cuz like I said, hell of a long commute. And Ben stayed, well, I think you could guess why."

"So, where are they? Justin and Ben?"

"They left me in charge of the rugrats yesterday morning. Said they were going to scout for more food. Never came back."

"They wouldn't ditch you." I wasn't positive, even as I said it.

"I'll probably never know for sure, but I don't think so because last night three people showed up on horseback. Two dudes and a woman. Kind of theatrical. Thought it was a joke. But they were well-armed. They had me show them where the food was. Where the pump was—"

"Water pump?" Trevor clarified.

"Old metal one. Worked great."

"Figures."

"Then they informed us it was time for us to move on. And it wasn't a suggestion." She looked back at the kids, now sitting in groups on the pavement, and whispered, "My best guess is that they did something to Justin and Ben. Anyway. That's when I remembered you. You seemed to think getting here was important. I figured if I got the kids here, it would be a friendly place."

"Did you come across anyone on your way?" Trevor asked.

"No. I guess most people up this way have already gotten to where they were going."

"Alright." Trevor cleared his throat. "Tell me if I've got this right. Phoenix is down and sliding toward chaos. Prescott is the same. You've got no food or water. I count seventeen of you. And some well-armed cowboys have taken over your camp."

"That just about sums it up." Jessie half-smiled. "Which is why we need your help."

"Absolutely," I said, nodding.

"Yeah," Trevor looked over to George, partially obscured in the high brush to the left, "That's gonna be a problem."

67.

"**H**OW EXACTLY IS THAT A PROBLEM?" I turned on him.

"Hate kids?" Jessie chimed in.

"Listen. I don't like this any more than either of you," Trevor sighed. "This town has appointed me to make the hard decisions, but I didn't think one like this would happen in the first few hours."

Jessie shook her head, eyes to the sky.

"I don't understand." It was all I could say. It was all I could think.

"No vacancy unless you know the secret handshake," Jessie said as she glanced back at her kids.

"Bottom line?" Trevor took the time to explain. "We've got a full community here and if additional actual residents arrive, we've got to take them. Lukas, have you seen the food supplies? We are going to run low very soon, unless you'd like to raid neighboring communities. And sure, I'll start teaching everybody alternative food options, but they aren't going to like them very much. And none of us really know how many people the water table can sustain. Your father would've made the same call."

"Dude." Jessie stopped him. "These are just kids. And you aren't even a resident."

"They've made me their leader. And leaders make tough decisions. But I'm not a monster. We can spare some supplies. Enough to get you back toward Prescott or uphill to find a water source. You'll want access before others. The point is, the choice is up to you."

"You have got to be kidding," Jessie was exasperated.

"What is going on out there?!" an older woman's voice yelled from the direction of the tracks. I turned to see Rose, her hands on her hips, in front of a crowd who had crept under the bridge. Walt tried to pull her back, but she was having none of it.

"Apparently we don't have the right passports!" Jessie shouted.

"Hey!" Trevor shouted. "Everyone get back behind the barricade! Now!"

"Wait. What?!" Rose was indignant. "You certainly aren't turning away a young woman and a bunch of kids!"

"Lady? I said get back!"

"Yeah. Mayor?" She said it sarcastically. "This isn't going

to work for me." Rose turned and left through the crowd, with Walt in pursuit.

George emerged onto the road and headed for the crowd. His muscular presence aided by a large rifle was more than enough incentive for the crowd to recede back behind the barricade. And something about it didn't sit right.

Trevor gripped my shoulder. "I'm trying to keep us all alive. It's not fun for me, but I'm sure leaving the camp full of kids wasn't fun for you, either."

"How did you…"

"Everybody knows. It's alright. You did what you had to for your community. I'm only doing the same."

"Like I asked," Jessie interrupted, "are you even a resident?"

Trevor pointed to the side of the road. "Name's on the sign, sweetie. Is that good enough for you?"

Jessie pursed her lips, as if to hold back a river of expletives. At least, until hope was lost.

"I'll be right back," Trevor said to me before heading back toward the crowd.

"So, the celebrity is in charge, huh?" Jessie more summarized than asked.

"We've had a rough few days and while I don't agree with this decision, he *is* the most qualified."

"I mean. I'll hit the road, ya know? I might have a chance. Just take the kids."

"I know." My head spun. "I know."

"It isn't like they're toddlers. They can work."

I made sure he wasn't headed back yet and did a double-take when I saw him arguing with my mother. Maybe Dad wouldn't have made the same decision. But there was no time to watch. I turned back to Jessie. "He's going to approve of giving you basic supplies. Some food. Some water."

"But that—"

"It sucks. It isn't fair." I cut her off. "But it is what it is. Take everything he gives you. Then, leave. Get over the ridge, a bit past the cemetery."

"But there's nothing there."

"And no fires tonight or tomorrow. A third night if you haven't heard from us."

"Lukas." She looked at me with concern. "What are you going to do?"

"I think I can talk to him."

"Here he comes," she whispered quickly.

I turned to his approach.

"What's the plan, boss?"

"Listen. Jessie? Right?"

"Yeah." She wasn't making any attempt to hide her scorn.

"Hate me all you want, but I'm going to help you as much as I can."

"I'm sure." It came out like poison.

He ignored it diplomatically. "We are bringing out a case of thirty-five water bottles. Roughly two each. It's enough if you make sure the kids don't toss the bottles. They'll be able to refill them in local streams. Only take from running water. We are also bringing out some matches, three tents, and a small meal for tonight. It's all we can spare."

"Could I get an autograph to go with that?"

"I gave you food, water, shelter, and fire." He seemed to really be trying. "You don't need my autograph."

An automotive horn began honking back behind the barrier.

"The hell is it now?" Trevor barked as he turned back.

"Stay here," I whispered to Jessie before intending to trail him.

"Hey, jerk," a young voice cracked.

I looked past Jessie and saw him sitting with a few others.

"Hey, Bobby." He looked scruffy and more than a bit shell-shocked. "You doing alright?"

"Am I allowed to complain now?" he asked with a hint of a smile.

"Hell, yes." I gave him the best grin I could muster.

"Still don't think you're supposed to swear in front of me." His face went serious. "Are you gonna help us?"

"As best I can. Promise." I took a quick look over my shoulder. "I really gotta go, but I'll see you soon."

Beyond the vehicles making up the end of the barricade, the crowd parted, revealing an old yellow VW bus. I'd seen it around town, but had never realized who owned it.

68.

R OSE ROLLED DOWN HER WINDOW AND YELLED, "Someone move those damn trucks!"

Trevor, not pleased with the newest development, "What the hell do you think you're doing?"

"Walt and I are going to help those poor kids." She wasn't asking permission. It was a statement of fact.

Walt, in the passenger seat, through his hands in the air as if to say, 'You stop her.'

"Here's the problem," Trevor proclaimed loud enough for all to hear. "You load out a bunch of your supplies. Your food. Use your fuel. You run out of all of it sooner. Now other members of this community have to help you."

"Come on, young man. Have you seen us?" Rose smiled. "We won't be around as long as most of you."

"So what's your plan?"

"I haven't the slightest!" Walt scoffed.

"We'll fill the van with as many of those tired kids as we can. Then, we'll drive next to the others until we find them a safe spot to settle."

"Then you think you'll come back? I'm sorry, ma'am. You leave, you won't be allowed to return until circumstances change."

"Are you making up rules as you go?" It was my mom again.

Trevor spun on her. "Listen. You know what?" He looked around to all the gathered. "I am being consistent. We are locked down. For both our immediate security and our long-term sustainability We need to ration our supplies, our food, and our water. More residents may still arrive. They must be our priority. And don't forget there is a nutcase with a gun out there determined to make us pay for killing his friend. So…" He took a deep breath and composed himself. "Let's vote right here, right now. You want me to keep doing my best to keep us safe today and sustainable beyond tomorrow, raise your hand right now. Right now!"

The group looked to one another. A low murmur. Then, slowly, about two of every three people raised their hands. Conspicuous abstainers included Rose, Walt, my mother, and I.

Trevor looked slowly at everyone, making a show of it to solidify his authority. And possibly—it struck me a bit too late—making a mental note of dissenters.

"Good. Then we're clear." He turned back to Rose. "You leave, you don't come back."

She extended an upturned fist out the VW's open window and slowly raised her middle finger. "Move the trucks, asshat."

69.

THE ADDITIONAL SUPPLIES WERE LOADED. There were a few tearful goodbyes and a few looks of resentment. Mostly, there was disbelief. How had the world changed so drastically in less than a week?

During the distraction, I made my way back out and updated Jessie. "The plan remains the same. Don't go far beyond the cemetery. No fires."

"Do you really think you can talk to him?" Jessie whispered.

"It'll be harder now that Rose forced him to take such a public stand, but I'll try to frame it as a good PR move."

Now atop the bridge with Andrew, George watched carefully as I walked back to the gathered.

The van slowly coasted through the barrier and under

the bridge. The trucks were moved back into place. The van stopped next to Jessie's group. Several of the kids who looked the most exhausted got in before it resumed a crawl up the ridge. Walt gave up his seat and walked with the few who hadn't been able to cram in.

Trevor walked over and silently stood next to me, watching the group until they slowly vanished over the cemetery ridge in the distance.

I spoke first. "Thank you for still giving them supplies."

"Lukas?" Hand on my shoulder again. "Everything I'm doing, I'm doing for this community."

"I know."

"Why'd you vote against me then?" He looked me square in the eyes.

"Trevor," I thought quickly, "it wasn't personal. Mom didn't raise her hand and she cooks for me." I tried to fake a smile yet again.

He returned the smile much more believably before he said, "Hey. I get it. I know you lost your dad and your mom is all you have left."

He walked off.

70.

THE CROWD STARTED TO BREAK UP and I realized Mom had disappeared again, as she was prone to do, so I decided to head back to the house to find her. We needed to talk. And soon.

I was going to take the road since it was a more direct route until I saw most of the crowd had moved back to the front lawn of the school. Because most of them had seen me acting as Trevor's right-hand man during the excommunication of Rose and Walt, every single one of them would have an opinion. And since one contingent would falsely think I wanted to refuse help to those in need and be upset I'd oust those who dare help them, and the other contingent would want to affirm a decision I didn't condone, I decided on the railroad tracks.

I was most of the way when I spotted Sophie sitting on the tracks ahead.

"I was hoping I'd find you here." Her voice seemed uncharacteristically void of emotion.

"Hey, Sophie." I walked up and went to sit beside her.

She rose to her feet. "Let's walk. I'm too agitated to keep sitting there."

"Alright. Where to?"

"How much time have you got?" She looked at me. Directly at me.

I wanted to say that I needed to get home. I had to talk to Mom. But Sophie was hurting and I wanted to be there for her. It was supposed to be me. And it had to be now. "Doesn't matter. Choose where we're going."

"I won't take advantage of your blank check this time," she began walking off the tracks, heading between the school and the Forresters', "but if you offer it again, I make no promises."

"Blank check? How old are you?"

"I'm an old soul, jackass." She stormed ahead. "In fact, I still haven't decided if you are old enough for me."

"Where are we going?" I asked.

"I'll tell you when we get there," was all she said.

I caught up to her and we walked in silence. We crossed the road with the school and the gathered crowd to our distant right, along with the Forresters' stone gate off to the left.

"Sophie?"

"Yeah?"

"Anything I'll say will sound stupid." I reconsidered my word choice. "Insufficient."

"Just say it."

"I can't imagine what you are going through." I swallowed hard. "How are you?"

"Sure you can." She looked up at the mountain we were approaching. "You lost your dad, didn't you?"

"But I've still got my mom. And you seemed to have a good relationship with both your parents."

She stopped and waited until I noticed and looked back.

"Lukas Taylor. You are usually so intuitive. But never when it comes to me."

"How do you mean?"

"In this particular moment? One of the many things we have in common is a complicated relationship with our deceased dads. Different complications, I'll grant you. I was his little princess. And he was amazing in almost every way, but he treated me differently. Which is fine. I guess. I am different. But not in the ways he thought."

"How do you see yourself as different from your brothers? They *are* who you are talking about, right?"

"I don't want to sound like I have some big ego."

"If it's the truth, own it," I prodded.

She paused. "Okay…Conor and—don't tell him I said this, but—even Liam can beat me at arm wrestling, but I'm stronger in other ways. More important ways. Conor is filled with rage. And bless Liam, but his heart is broken. I'm more resilient. I'm much more intelligent. It's not even close." She finally smiled. "And I'm pretty sure I'm a better shot."

I looked at her.

"What?" Her eyes flared apologetically. "See? I knew it wouldn't come out right."

"No, no, no. That wasn't it."

"Then what?"

"I think you are underestimating your arm wrestling ability."

I got a playful shove for that one.

"Lukas? What really happened to my dad?"

The question knocked the wind out of me for a moment before, "I wasn't there."

"I know." We took several more steps. We were further up the incline than the Forresters' now. Almost to where the tracks returned west before the mountain steepened and then back north. "What do you *think* happened?"

We reached the tracks and she stopped again.

"Apparently," I began tentatively, "Sebastian Forrester is profoundly inaccurate with a firearm. Which is why he hid when Trevor and his guys first arrived and shots were fired. It's why he ran up to the tracks the night your dad was killed. He knew he needed to be close in order to have any chance of hitting any…" I stumbled, recognizing my insensitivity a beat too late.

"Targets," Sophie whispered.

"Yeah." I took a breath. "Listen. Forrester is basically the president of Skull Valley. Your dad was basically the VP. Both were effectively removed from office. Now, I don't know if—"

"Hang on." She even raised her hand as she said it. "Who told you Mr. Forrester is a bad shot?"

"It doesn't matter."

"It was Addison," her voice, accusatory.

"Sophie."

"Oh God." She turned and began walking along the elevated tracks with the distant Forrester house to our backs.

"What?"

She whipped around on me. "Seriously? Could you have a bigger weakness? I mean, God knows she's hot, but come on!" She was walking away again.

I stumbled to catch up. "Sophie!"

Without turning around, "So, the only child of an accused murderer tells you her dad can't shoot straight, even though he owns several guns, and you take it as Gospel?"

"Addison is the most honest person I know!" The moment I said it, I regretted it. She stopped a third time. Except this time, she didn't turn back to me. "Sophie."

"No. It's cool." She stopped where one could see the mountain's base peel back to the left, exposing the backside of the thick brush and trees next to the northbound highway in the distance.

I made my way next to her. "That wasn't true."

"How do you mean?" She turned the words back at me as she studied my expression.

"Addison has never lied to me, as far as I know. And I do trust her. But I can't figure her out. Her thoughts, I mean." Sophie's eyes continued to search me, listening to every word. "But you. You say what you are thinking. You are honest on a whole different level. What I'm saying is, you are the most honest person I know."

"You're a dummy."

"See?"

Then something caught my eye. I stepped forward squinting to see what had distracted me. "Do you see what I see?"

"Where?"

I crouched down and motioned for her to do the same. "There." I drew near to her and pointed so her eyes could follow. "On the far left, behind that patch of overgrowth."

"The abandoned car?"

It was mostly obscured under branches that seemed to be tossed over the top of it, but I still recognized it. Parked where no one would see it from the highway. Where no one *would* see it unless they were standing precisely where we were standing.

"It's the Mustang Kyle used to escape." I remembered peppering it with bullets. "He's been hiding out less than five hundred yards outside our border this whole time."

"We've to get back and tell Trevor."

Then, from the distant trees next to the truck, Kyle emerged. And he was followed by George.

71.

W**E WERE PRONE ON THE TRACKS** as we watched George move along the tree line. Having left Kyle behind, he stopped every hundred feet, listening for even the faintest sound.

I'm not even sure we were breathing.

He crossed the tracks short of the bridge and disappeared down the berm, never even glimpsed by the man currently on watch.

We looked at each other and silently agreed. Jumping to our feet, we began running back past the Forresters' and on toward my house as fast as our feet could take us. Mom needed to know what we'd witnessed.

Emily was slowly walking Trey back toward our house. As Sophie and I approached, they turned and Trey managed to grunt, "What's the rush?"

Neither of us had the breath to answer and continued around the home and burst through the side door.

"Mom! Mom!" I searched every room on the ground floor, before realizing she wasn't there and took the stairs three at a time to the second floor bedrooms. "Mom!" Wasn't there either. I tapped down the steps to where Sophie waited. "Wait here." Took the stairs to the basement. "Mom!" The door to the storage room was open. I ran to it and froze.

Trevor sat on a folding chair without expression. He held the spike in one of his hands. Behind him, the shelving unit was shoved to the side, exposing the locked metal door.

And my mother was nowhere to be seen.

72.

"**W**HO'S UPSTAIRS?" He said it in a whisper.

"Sophie Sinnot. And Trey and Emily were practically to the driveway on their way back to the house."

"Do they know about this door and whatever is behind it?" Still quiet. And quick.

"I don't even know—"

"Don't. Just. Don't." He raised a hand holding a gun, but didn't point it at me. He was just letting me know he had it. "Do any of them know about the Taylor family inner keep?"

"No."

"Let's keep it that way for now."

"Lukas!" Sophie called down from above.

"Gimme a sec!" I yelled back before checking with Trevor.

"Tonight. During our shift, I'll come and get you. You'll let me in so I can see what you've been holding back from the community."

"I don't know how to get in."

"Either you do or you don't. You've got until tonight to figure it out. If you are telling the truth, you can visit your mom at the Sinnots'."

"What do you mean by 'visit?'"

"You don't get to ask questions from where I'm sitting." He stood. "Let's head upstairs. No mention of this. Got it?"

"Okay."

"Slide the shelf back." He tossed me the spike and headed for the stairs.

This wasn't good. Sophie knew about Kyle, about George, and, like me, had to realize Trevor was probably not who he had been pretending to be. And I had no way of warning her. But shooting him in the back wasn't the right play, either. I'd still have to contend with George, Andrew, and Kyle.

"Hey, Sophie," he said.

"Oh. Hi," her voice returned, sounding a bit thrown off. Or maybe I was reading into it.

I cleared the top step just in time to see him say, "I had a good conversation with Conor, but how are you and Liam doing?"

Sophie's eyes shot to me, probably a moment too long, then back to Trevor. "Losing both my parents halfway through high school? Dunno. Shock is probably a safe assumption."

"Understandable," Trevor looked so damn compassionate, and somehow, Sophie seemed calm as could be.

"The thing is? Right now?" She looked right at him as she went on. Unflinching. "The hardest part? Is coming to terms with who killed my dad. And resisting the urge to finish him off myself."

"Again. Completely understandable." He stepped forward and placed his hand on her shoulder. "But I appreciate your restraint. Let justice take its course."

"I feel confident it will."

"Sophie?" I jumped in, "Let me walk you home."

Trey and Emily walked through the front door.

"Oh. Hi," Emily chirped.

He gave her his best white-capped smile. "Hi, Emily. Trey."

"Hi, Trevor." Trey's normally relaxed face seemed to betray that Emily had shared her concerns. Big guy wasn't much of a poker player.

Trevor seemed to watch Trey for an extra beat before looking at each of us. "Well. I better head out. Expecting most of the firearms in town to be collected before my shift. See you then, Lukas."

73.

WENT TO THE WINDOW AND WATCHED as Trevor took a path across the field directly toward the Forresters'.

"Okay, fill me in," Sophie demanded.

"Wait." I kept watching. Once I was satisfied it was safe, I turned to my friends. "Trey. Stay on this floor. If anyone pays us a visit, stomp on the floor or drop something heavy. Something loud to warn us. Emily will have to fill you in later."

"I can do that."

"Ladies? Follow me."

The three of us made our way down to the basement, around the corner, and into the storage room. I walked over, pulled the spike and slid the shelving unit, exposing the metal door.

"What the—" Sophie began.

"I know, I know." I shook my head. "Mom made me keep it a secret. Dad taught her to trust no one."

"Well." Emily crossed her arms. "This oughta be good."

I brought Emily up to speed on what we saw with George, then I brought them both up to speed on the conversation between Trevor and I.

"What's your mom doing at my house?" Sophie asked.

"No idea and no time to find out, either. We need to clear as much out of here as we can."

"I'm guessing whatever's in there is bigger than a breadbox?" Emily asked.

"You'd be right."

"Well," Emily thought out loud. "Nowhere in the house, then. After finding whatever's behind door number one, they are bound to search every inch of the place."

"Twice," Sophie added.

"That leaves outside," I conceded. "We'll need to conceal it at least a hundred yards from the house, opposite direction from Forresters'."

"How will we get it out without being seen?" Sophie inquired.

"Leave that to me."

I turned, reached under the shelf and retrieved the key before entering the combination and opening the door. The girls moved forward and peered inside.

"Your dad did all this?" Emily asked.

"Contractors did, but to his specs."

"And people think my dad was prepared," Sophie mumbled.

"Hey." I turned to her. "As far as I can tell, your dad's only fault was underestimating you. And I'm starting to think the whole world is guilty of that."

She smiled through suddenly watery eyes before Emily jumped back in. "So, what's the plan to move the contraband, Romeo?"

I crawled into the room, moved to the far end, and grabbed a long metal pole with one hand before grabbing the latch on the far wall with my other. I pushed the latch down hard and pulled a second metal door, revealing a narrow vertical shaft with a metal ladder. It was designed with the bottom of the shaft about three feet lower than the entrance. The girls crawled into the main compartment behind me.

"Hang on a sec," I instructed before climbing the ladder to release a third hatch directly above me. As it swung down, a mix of dirt and dust fell over and into my face, but the majority of Arizona earth held firm as expected. I scaled down the ladder quickly and slid back into the main compartment, not wanting to test my luck. I reached in with the pole and began to jab at the underside of the hard crust. Little pieces began to fall, but it was harder to penetrate than I'd expected.

"You've got to be shitting me," Emily marveled.

"I'm not through yet," I grunted as I kept jabbing, barely making progress.

"You need some help there, cowboy?" Sophie taunted.

That was all I needed to hear. I jammed the spear with all the strength I had. It stuck into the earth above. I wiggled it hard and a dusty avalanche ensued, flying past my face and kicking up a nasty dust cloud as it filled the majority of the three foot drop. Light shone down from above.

"So we are going to have to replace all that dirt?" Emily asked.

"Yeah. Sorry. No avoiding it."

"Wish my man didn't have a bad back," she groaned.

"Us too," Sophie shot back.

"Okay. We've got to move. We need the weapons and the ammo. Then, we'll spread out the remaining items in here. Make the place look packed. And then we'll worry about the dirt."

"Okay," Emily said quickly, "you go topside and stash the stuff. Sophie? You and I will rotate between grabbing the stuff down here and running it up the ladder. Sound good?"

"I'll take the ladder first," Sophie agreed.

"Sounds great." I shouldered four rifles and carefully ascended the ladder, my shoulders barely supporting the heft of the metal. I reached up and grabbed at the dirt above and pulled myself out, not far from my father's homemade tombstone. I had a fleeting thought that I might owe him an apology.

Might.

The voice came from directly behind me. "At least now I know where you stand."

74.

TREVOR LEANED AGAINST THE BACK OF my house, a pistol resting in his right hand. "You might be able to drop back into that shaft before I get a shot off, but I doubt it. Besides, George has got a gun to your pal Trey's head back in the house. His back isn't doing him any favors. And if that isn't motivation enough for you to make this easier on all of us, your mom is currently locked in the Sinnots' shelter. So, get out of that hatch, close it gently, and stand on it."

As I did, Sophie lowered herself back down the ladder silently. Her face showed that she'd heard the exchange.

"For the life of me, kid, I don't understand why you're making this so difficult," Trevor squinted at the sky. "I don't want to shoot you and George doesn't want to kill Trey."

"What *do* you want?"

"At the moment?" He stood. "Take the rifles you are carrying and slowly set them at your feet. Please don't make me shoot you."

While I did as I was told, I asked, "Why is my mother locked up?"

"She thought she could take everything from me. She thought she could hide your inner keep. Like I'd forgotten what Mark had taught me." He took a few steps toward me. "All I've done since returning—everything—has been done to make my town the safest place possible." Another step. "I listened. I studied. I removed people who would've gotten every single one of us killed."

"By killing them?"

"Only one of them so far. But there might need to be more." More steps as he closed the distance between us. "I'm consolidating the weapons. Your actions, and those of your mother, will give me the authority to enable a curfew. The perimeter will be secure and, as a result, so will the lives of every individual who remains in my town."

"And why are you working with Kyle?" I asked the question without warning. An attempt to unbalance him.

"Did you really think they didn't see you up on the tracks with that Sinnot girl?" Another step. "Which, by the way, really makes me question your judgement. You could probably have the homecoming queen, but you are running around in the hills with Conor's little sister." He shook his head with a smirk. "And I had quite the talk with him.

He already wants to kill you for stopping him from offing Sebastian. Truth be told, I wish you hadn't stopped him. That would've tied everything up perfectly. But the real question isn't why am I working with Kyle, but why aren't you working with me? You could've been my heir apparent." He stepped forward again, to within feet of where I stood. "I could be the father your dad never was."

"Because you're a fake, narcissistic murderer who—"

The last thing I saw was his right hand swinging toward my chin, pistol in hand.

75.

THE SOUNDS AND SMELLS OF NATURE slowly crystallized as I blinked my eyes to help bring the world into focus. I found myself sitting on the ground with my back pressed into rough bark, arms uncomfortably pulled backward at the shoulders. With a tug, I realized my wrists were bound tightly in duct tape.

"Hey! That hurts!" Sophie yelped.

I looked over my shoulder. Then the other. My wrists had been duct taped to Sophie's who was in the same position on the opposite side of the tree. That's when I noticed my piles of firewood. We were a distance west of civilization.

"Not a good idea, brother," came Trey's deep voice. I looked back over my left shoulder, further off and saw that the same had been done to Trey and Emily around a separate tree. "They taped us up pretty good and it's killing my back."

"How long have we been here?" I asked, still trying to find my bearings.

"They left a couple minutes ago," Sophie replied.

"Trevor and George?"

"Yeah."

"Did they say anything?"

"Yeah. Trevor told us he'd be back after the town meeting."

"What the hell is he up to?"

76.

THE DAY WORE ON IN SILENCE. We couldn't strategize. There were too many places to hide. Trevor had already convinced us he'd left, just to circle back once before, and it wasn't a mistake I was willing to make a second time.

The sun shifted toward the west.

"Do you think he'll let us live?" Sophie whispered.

"Been thinking about that. He'll have to if he doesn't want a full-blown revolt. He can get away with imprisonment or banishment, but murder? No. The people aren't stupid and they loved your dad. If anything else happens, they'll all turn on him."

"But if he has all the guns, will it matter?"

"If he's smart, he'll prefer a town of sheep to a town of wolves."

"So imprisonment." Sophie seemed to consider it. "That's what he says he did with your mom."

"And I believe him. It gave him leverage. But four more of us? That's a lot of mouths to feed. I think we'll be banished."

"Screw him." Sophie's voice had a bite. "He thinks he can kill my dad, frame Mr. Forrester, lock your mom up, and kick us out of town? Not happening, compadre. Not happening."

There was the slightest rustle.

"Sophie?"

"What?"

"Stop talking."

"You stop talking, jackass."

Another sound. Faint, but real. Somewhere directly before me.

"Do you hear that?" I whispered.

"Okay, Trevor! George! Whoever! Ya got me! Congrats!" Sophie proclaimed. "You know I'm pissed at you! Shouldn't be a shocker!"

From over a slight ridge, a muscular mountain lion crept into view. And in the light of day, he was a big one.

"Sophie. It's a cat."

"A cat?"

"A big cat."

"Oh shit," she swore. "Hey, guys! We've got a big kitty over here."

Trey sighed loudly. "Worst. Day. Ever."

The lion turned to listen for something behind it. A long, red scar ran along its front shoulder.

"What's he doing?" Sophie asked, the slightest bit breathless.

"Distracted by something at the moment."

"What should we be doing?" Emily asked.

The cat's head snapped in the direction of Trey and Emily beyond us.

"Praying he ate a big meal ten minutes ago," Trey deadpanned.

"The good news is," Sophie began, "we aren't supposed to run."

"Think we've got that one covered," Trey, stating the obvious.

"The bad news is," I explained, "it is also recommended that we make ourselves as big as possible, wave our hands in the air, and if necessary, throw rocks at it."

"Let's get on our feet," Sophie suggested.

"What?"

"Come on. At the same time, let's drag our feet back and try to get on them. If we can squat, we can stand. At least we won't be chew toy level."

"I'm up for trying."

The lion was back to looking at me intently. No movement. My mind raced, imagining the predatory desires of the beast.

It wasn't easy, wrenching my knees and sliding the insides of each of my feet under, but I managed. The lion watching the entire ordeal, unflinching.

"Okay," I panted. "I'm ready. You?"

"Been waiting on you."

Without a sound, the cat began padding directly toward me.

"Wait, wait, wait," I whispered.

I was pretty sure I should yell, but there was the slightest chance it might provoke the cat. I waited and watched as it approached.

It slowed to a cautious crawl. And inched closer. Sniffed and drew up to my face as I involuntarily turned away from it. I was shocked by the sheer size of its skull.

It stayed there, head practically up against the side of my own. Hot breath, humid on my exposed neck in huffs.

"Hey!" Trey shouted. Again, the thick skull snapped in his direction, the huffs a fraction louder. With slow, intentional movements, it moved from my face and began creeping toward the other tree.

"No, no, no! Come back!" I shouted.

"Hey!" Trey yelled again.

It lept to the side, softer than a creature of its size should be able to, perhaps uncomfortable finding itself directly between the shouting voices.

It looked our way before resettling its focus on the tree anchoring Trey and Emily.

Then, a yip echoed from the forest beyond Trey and

Emily. A second yip.

"Worst! Day! Ever!" Trey roared moments before two coyotes trotted past them toward the much bigger cat.

They skidded short, front legs extended out before them, yipping and barking forward and up. With each subtle movement of the mountain lion, they scampered backward only to return a second later, doing their best to annoy the lion until it left their territory.

"Okay," I whispered, "Now we stand."

We pressed our backs into the rough, ragged bark, stretching our arms as far as they could go without dislocating our shoulders. In unison, we pushed and rose slowly, our backs and taped hands scraping on the way.

Then, about halfway up, my left hand caught on something. I looked back. There was a sharp knot sticking out about an inch.

"Sophie?"

"I see it."

We began to run the spot of tape between our wrists against it. Up and down, over and over. The pain was intense, but the tape began to fray.

The coyotes continued to provoke the cat only to retreat momentarily each time the cat flinched. One of the dogs wandered a bit close to Sophie and snipped at her. She kicked at it hard and missed, but its dodge sent it back dangerously close to the cat, who swiped and also barely missed.

The knot was starting to dull and despite fraying a bit

more, the tape still wouldn't tear.

"Hey!" I called.

"What?!" Sophie's voice, annoyed. "I'm trying to avoid becoming Puppy Chow over here!"

"Let me move your arm."

I moved the tape directly over the remaining nub.

"Okay. Now, I need you to pull as hard as you can," I instructed.

One of the coyotes ran from my left to my right not two feet in front of me. The big cat flew by right behind him before stopping on a dime just past me, turning back and catching the trailing coyote with a swinging paw that redirected the second dog violently toward my feet.

Sophie yanked my arm backward. Distracted, I had forgotten to brace.

"Ahh!" I wailed and pulled back into neutral.

"You told me to!" she replied.

The dog scrambled to its feet and snipped toward my ankle, but turned quickly, remembering the danger of the bigger cat, before scampering off. The other coyote had returned to yip a few more times. The cat was now back within a few feet, but turned the other way, facing the imminent threat of the persistent dog.

"Do it again!"

"Are you sure?"

"Do it again!" I steeled my arm.

A sudden pull and the fray gave way to a rip. We both

felt it and I resisted the urge to pull, instead holding my arm in place so as to not injure her shoulder or elbow. But she yanked with surprising strength and the rip went through.

The cat continued with another ferocious swipe at the dancing coyote.

We had to pull and twist as best we could because the tape stubbornly clung to our skin. Finally, Sophie's wrist broke free of the tape and she quickly swung around the tree to face the cat at my side, barely able to slow her momentum and maintain balance.

I reached over and ripped the tape from my other wrist. Taking her by the hand, I led her backward from the animals. Once clear of the spat, we backed much more quickly, but never turned and ran.

Once we reached the other tree, we both crouched, took an opposite side, and ripped off the tape.

In the distance, the remaining coyote finally turned and ran. The cat took off after it. Within a moment, they were gone over the ridge.

"I vote we don't wait for them to come back," Trey huffed, still looking around.

"Trevor's gang or the petting zoo?" Emily asked.

"Either," Sophie answered.

"Plus, I'm pretty sure I need to change my underwear," Trey smiled.

"Sorry pal," a shotgun was pumped behind us. "That'll have to wait."

77.

KYLE WALKED TOWARD US, GRINNING. "Was that not completely insane? I mean, I thought you were done for!"

"You were watching the whole time?" Emily asked.

"Well," he looked to each of us before continuing, "I missed the start of the show, but I walked up right as coyote number one ran off."

"And you just hid?" The look on Emily's face told me Kyle was lucky to be holding that shotgun.

"Well, yeah. Shotgun shells are a lot more difficult to replace these days." He held the shotgun with a single hand as he reached to the back of his waist and pulled out a pistol. "Along with these bullets."

"Freakin' coward!" Emily's voice crackled.

"Uh. Pumpkin?" Trey nudged.

"No. This guy isn't going to kill us. He was hoping the zoo would take care of us."

"Would've made things a bit easier. Not gonna lie," he said with a sneer. "Really looking forward to seeing this guy"—he looked directly at me and the smile vanished—"get it one way or another."

"I didn't kill your friend."

"You tried to kill me!" He yelled before composing himself. "Stevie was just a coworker."

"Sure he wasn't your cellmate?" Sophie quipped.

"Never been to prison, little girl." He smiled at her. "If you never get caught, you never do time."

"That your life motto?"

He looked at Sophie in a way I didn't like, before moving toward her. I instinctively stepped between them.

"Oh, my friend," the big man laughed. "Make a move."

"You wouldn't get a second shot off," growled Trey, deadly serious.

He took a step back and sized up Trey. "Well. Aren't you a ringing endorsement for steroid use."

"You said coworker?" He was sharing and I wanted as much information as he was willing to spill. "Where'd you work with him?"

He shook his head. "You seriously still don't get it."

"They worked with Trevor," Sophie realized.

"But… " I stammered.

"Put it together," he prodded. "I *believe* in you."

"You were at the stadium when the lights went out."

"When all hell broke loose and Trevor figured out what was going on, he remembered that old man's shop. He knew he wouldn't be able to slip away immediately, so he sent me along with his worthless cameraman to collect as much as we could."

"And that's where I ran into you."

"Once you left, I went back for Stevie and we raided that old man's place for everything we could find. Didn't leave us much."

"Why didn't you stay in Prescott?" I asked. "Trevor could've owned that town."

"Naw. Every politician was at that event. The sheriff, too. Anyway, Trevor told us if we made it here, we'd be running the show. So, we gathered up as many residents as we could find, let Trevor play hero, and headed here."

"But when I recognized you..."

"Everything went to hell and I had to improvise. Had to avoid getting shot and get to the vehicle that had most of the supplies."

I thought for a moment. "Trevor's the talent. George is the bodyguard. Andrew is the sound guy. Stevie. That was his name, right?"

"Stevie Drummond."

"He was the cameraman. And what did you do?"

"George and I were both hired by Trevor."

"A second guard."

"A bit of overkill, I'll grant you that, but Trevor liked the visual."

"Are there more? One camera doesn't seem like enough for a homecoming special."

"Ever see the show? Two cameras. One held by the star to make it appear more legit. Stevie got the establishing shots, the crowds, all the other stuff the viewer doesn't even realize are included."

"And how is it that every member of a small survival show crew can be downright psychotic?" Sophie asked.

"We're not psychotic." He leered at her again. "We just have the will to do what must be done to secure our spot. Our survival."

The shot rang out an imperceptible second before Kyle's chest blew out toward us in a deep red mist. The force jerked him forward, landing face-down on the ground.

78.

"**C**AUGHT HIM LOOKING AT MY DAUGHTER like that once." George said as he walked up. Rifle in hand. "All four of you. Take ten slow steps back and sit in the dirt."

We did as we were told. George hadn't once given us the impression he was anything less than serious.

Hunched over Kyle's body—including his shotgun and pistol, George pulled his radio. "George here. I fired the shot. Kyle captured the four and had them at gunpoint."

"Status?" The voice came back.

"Took him out."

"Well done." There was a pause. "I'm with a group of citizens at the Taylor house and they're grateful for your ability to keep us all safe." Another silence. "But we have an important decision to make. Give us a minute."

He pocketed the radio.

"He's putting on a performance," Emily whispered. "Letting the community think they are the ones making the call."

"What call?" Trey asked.

"Us," I answered. "What to do about us."

"But why kill Kyle?" Trey asked George, who was silently checking Kyle's weapons. "Don't you need everyone you can get?"

"As far as Trevor is concerned, loose ends," George muttered. "As far as I'm concerned, one less sicko in my little girl's world."

"Sheep and wolves," I said.

"Huh?" Trey was lost.

"He needs the town to be full of sheep. The second the town realized Kyle wasn't a good guy, his ticket was punched. They were using him as a common enemy."

Sophie nodded. "You can't control a town full of wolves with four men, but you can control a town of sheep with three."

I could've sworn I saw the slightest smile start across George's face when his radio crackled and he pulled it out.

"George? You there?"

"I am. Still with the four."

"It has been decided. Trey and Emily were guests. They would've been welcome to stay, like you and Andrew, but they had become close with the Taylor family and

337

certainly knew about the secret bunker and its provisions. As a result, they are immediately banished with no provisions. Unfortunately, due to his tremendous betrayal and possible collusion with Sebastian Forrester, Lukas Taylor is also immediately banished with no provisions."

"What the hell are they talking about?" Sophie asked.

I hushed her. I didn't want to miss a word.

"We believe Lukas doesn't know anything more. But his mom, Jennifer Taylor, will remain in our custody until we can be sure she isn't holding anything additional back. These are tough times and we need every resource within our boundaries."

"Trevor seems pretty scared of a middle-aged woman," I tried to provoke a response from George.

I didn't get one.

"As for Sophie Sinnot," there was a hesitation across the channel. "If she agrees to have a conversation with me and can assure me she was led into this…this insanity—I know she has been through a lot and is clearly not in her right mind—then we will welcome her back and she can resume her life with her brothers."

I looked to Sophie, her jaw trembling.

"But if not, she will also be subject to immediate banishment with no provisions. And banishment is permanent."

George looked up. "Well? What's it gonna be?"

We couldn't discuss anything openly with George right there.

"I think you should go back," Trey said. Defeated.

"Hell no. You'll never be safe there," disagreed Emily.

"He needs an answer," George warned.

She remained defiantly silent.

"It's up to you," I whispered.

She said the words slowly and clearly. "Tell him to go screw himself."

George lifted the radio. "She said no."

"I said go screw yourself!" she yelled.

George clicked it off a second too late.

"Disappointing." Trevor paused before continuing. "This could have gone very differently. Goodbye."

There was a click.

"I'm going to say this just once." George picked up every gun. "I'm about to kill all of you." Then, he shot just to the left of each of us. "Head west into the wilderness. Now. And if I see you again, you die."

"Why?" Sophie asked, taking a step forward before realizing it was a bad idea.

"Sophie…" I grabbed her arm.

"I didn't get into this to kill kids."

Sophie wouldn't let it drop. "Murder is murder."

"Sophie!" I snapped.

"And if karma is a thing, it might help my little girl." He looked over his shoulder for an instant, then back. "Don't make me kill you." He turned and headed back toward what used to be my home.

We stood in silence for a full minute before I put a voice to my thoughts. "Ready for a hike? We've got some ground to cover." I looked toward the brilliant sunset to the west. "And fast."

79.

WE TRAIPSED OFF THROUGH THE SLOWLY dissipating trees quietly. Cautiously. The sun had just set leaving the sky illuminated, but the land darkening by the minute. We were unarmed and wandering right through primetime for animal activity. In addition to the mountain lion and yipping coyotes, there were rattlesnakes and even the occasional bear.

It would've been safer to make as much noise as possible, but we kept falling into the instinctual silence. We wanted to hear a predator before it heard us. The fact that we knew it never worked that way didn't seem to matter.

We came upon a clearing where we found the railroad tracks as they curved north up a slight pass before continuing north. The plan was to take them to the far side of the mountain before veering right and hoping to find some friendly faces.

As we began the climb, it struck me that the last time I'd been here, was with my father. He had taken me out for a week. His idea of a vacation. We took no extra clothes. No food. Nothing but multitools. Mom went to visit a girl-friend in San Diego. We built a shelter and a fire. We ate disgusting plants that would fill a stomach until real food could be hunted. But tonight, the four of us didn't have time for that.

I found my breath suddenly shallow. My father had walked this spot with me. Mentoring me. Training me. Preparing me. For this.

"Whoa. Check it out," Trey whispered.

Off to our left, in the distance and exposed by our increased elevation, an orange glow was visible. And it wasn't the remnants of the sunset.

"I saw it a few days ago. Guessing a plane fell out of the sky a week ago and started a forest fire. Too far away to be any danger for us to worry about."

"Hadn't even thought about planes," Emily groaned.

Trey put things in perspective. "I guess I'd have more than a bad back if we'd booked a flight instead of taking the bikes."

"Well, I wanted a pony when I was a little girl," Emily laughed. "That would've been ideal."

I noticed Sophie's silence.

"Hey. You alright?" Again, it felt like the stupidest question imaginable.

"I'm going back. You know that, right? I'm going back and I'm going to save Liam and I'm going to convince Conor he's being lied to and I'm going to get your mom out of that freaking glorified cellar and I'm going to take down that smiling shark with alligator teeth." She took a deep breath before releasing it quickly. "You know that, right?"

"I do."

"So. Any ideas?"

"Working on it." That is what I said, but the truth was, I had no plan whatsoever.

80.

"**IDENTIFY YOURSELF!**" demanded the well-aged voice of Walt.

They were precisely where I told them to go. In a clearing over the ridge. No lights. Only hushed voices. The town cemetery along the ridge to the south and Skull Valley down the long sloping landscape beyond it.

"Four of us. Lukas, Sophie, Trey, Emily."

"You found us!" his voice, suddenly warm as he approached in the darkness. "We were hoping you would." He held an old rifle toward the ground now.

"How…" How could they even have known we were out here?

Rose walked up with an outstretched walkie-talkie. "Your mom slipped it to us before we left."

It was the extra radio she'd held back when she gave all

the others to Sebastian what seemed like a year ago. Having basically tapped the phones of those in charge, she'd been able to remain one step ahead until she saw the writing on the wall. Even in passing it along, she must've sensed where things were headed.

"Well," I smiled. "This changes things."

I made out the dark outline of the VW bus and the three tents they'd been given. The whispering voices of the young people were contained within them. It seemed Walt, Rose, and Jessie each planned on sleeping a couple feet outside the separate tent entrances.

"Pretty sure we heard you have nothing to contribute?" Rose lamented. "What was it? 'Banishment without supplies?'"

"Banishment without provisions," Sophie snorted.

"Oh, you," Rose hugged her before whispering, "'Go screw yourself?' If that wasn't just perfect!"

"Meant every word."

"Oh, that came through," with a weathered and beautiful smile. "Trust me."

"Got bad news." Walt pulled me away from the group. "They've got all the guns. Trevor used your betrayal, as he called it, to make sure the collection took place immediately."

"Forresters'?"

"Yup." He sighed deeply. "Sebastian isn't doing well. And his wife and daughter are refusing to leave his side."

"Anything else?"

"A curfew is being enforced. Sundown to sunrise. Trevor and Andrew are patrolling. No one else. Conor is guarding the armory."

"What about George? Think he's guarding Mom?"

"Didn't say. My guess is sleeping. Someone will need to be awake when the others are sleeping."

"Makes sense," I agreed. "Skeleton crew until they figure out who else to trust."

"Thoughts?" Walt asked, hopeful.

"That thing loaded?" I nodded to his rifle.

"Yeah." He cringed. "It has a bullet in it. Just one. Thought that'd be all I'd need for self-defense. Suboptimal vision forced me to give up hunting years ago."

"Less than ideal, but one bullet is a lot better than no bullets." I tried to project optimism, but the feeling didn't run deep. "Okay. We need to get some sleep. Tomorrow might be an interesting day."

"By all means. Pull up a patch of dirt."

DAY SIX

"PREPARATION IS THE MOST IMPORTANT PART OF A PLAN, BUT TIMING IS THE MOST UNDERESTIMATED."

—

MARK TAYLOR

81.

MY EYES FLUTTERED OPEN to the sound of a bear.

Well, not a bear, exactly. It was Trey snoring with the ferocity of one. Emily was curled up next to him, sleeping blissfully.

"Morning," Sophie's voice whispered from my other side. "I have a confession to make. I said a prayer that I'd wake up next to you one day. Only… I thought it wouldn't happen for about eight more years and this is definitely *not* how I pictured it." I looked over to see Sophie laying beside me, looking straight up into the hazy grey beginnings of dawn.

"How *did* you picture it?"

"I finally decided to marry you after years of begging." She didn't even smile. "And we both smelled a lot better."

"You've got it all figured out, don't you?"

"Make you a deal. You figure out how to take care of Trevor. I'll figure out the rest."

Rose quietly emerged from one of the tents. "Sophie? There's a girl who's pretty freaked out. Mind helping me with her?"

"Sure thing," Sophie whispered as she hopped to her feet. She looked down at me, "Honeymoon's over," and walked off.

I did my best to shake off the happy thought and take a mental inventory. Walt and Rose. A rifle with a single bullet. Jessie. About a dozen middle schoolers. A VW van. Some empty water bottles. Trey and Emily. Some matches. Three tents.

Trevor, a survivalist with military training, had two bunkers. An armory. Food. A badass bodyguard. Andrew. Conor. And the town.

The town.

Thirty minutes later, I was huddled with Walt, Rose, Trey, Emily, Jessie, and Sophie. There was no time to waste.

The same crew who I'd arrived with the night before, with the addition of Jessie, were about to set off on the same path, but this morning, we were headed back.

82.

WE HAD JUST GOTTEN BACK TO the tracks when Jessie whispered, "So you and Sophie have lived here your whole lives?"

"I have. Sophie moved here a few years ago."

"And you two…" The college girl's voice trailed off. I looked at her and she smiled.

"Nothing official."

"Huh." She appeared to be in thought. "A week ago, I would've sworn you had a thing for Addison."

"It's been a long week."

"So, things have changed?"

"Somebody get the hotdogs," Trey remarked. Off to our right, in the distance, smoke roiled up and drifted to the north.

"I don't think anyone will be putting that out anytime soon," I answered.

"You sure that isn't coming this way?" Trey asked.

"It would take quite a long time."

"Good."

We continued on.

83.

WE ARRIVED BACK AT THE WOODPILES with the sun beating down from directly overhead. It was warm. Almost uncomfortably so. Without a word of instruction, we huddled again.

"Remember," I began, "nothing happens until we see the signal. You've got what you need?"

"I do," Sophie nodded.

"And not until about three."

"I know."

I turned to Jessie. "You good?"

She adjusted Walt's rifle. "I know what the bullet is for."

"Alright, ladies." I sighed. "Promise me you'll be safe out there."

"Don't patronize the stronger gender," Jessie snapped. "You're better than that."

"I didn't mean—"

"Relax, cowboy. Kidding. But, don't even pretend like I'm the one you're concerned about." She smiled and tapped her fist against my chest before backing away.

Sophie stepped up and hugged me, hard.

"You be safe," she whispered.

"I know it would be faster to take a risk and sneak past the edge of town, but you have to resist the urge. You'll have no way of defending yourself until we hook up."

"Interesting choice of words," Emily observed with a trouble-making smirk.

"What?" I missed whatever it was.

Trey choked on something imaginary. Jessie shook her head. Sophie tried to suppress a grin.

"Seriously! What did I say?"

"You are such a boy scout," Emily laughed.

"See you in the morning." Sophie winked, before hugging Emily, then Trey.

"Let's go," Jessie insisted.

"Okay, Mom," Sophie cracked. "And one more thing, you three, look out for the cats and dogs."

84.

AS WE WAITED OUT THE DAY, we sat in silence. Listening. Not so much for the mountain lion or those coyotes—they weren't as much of a threat with there being three of us with our hands untied—but for a return of George, or even Trevor.

Any sound, any rustle, any little disturbance at all, and the three of us wouldn't breathe until the threat passed.

Trey and Emily took to whispering back and forth as the day seemed to stretch on forever.

Was my mother actually okay? I was led to believe she was being held in the Sinnots' shelter, but I didn't know with certainty. She might be anywhere in Skull Valley. And there was no guarantee that she was still even breathing. I tried to shrug off the thought, but it kept crawling back into my consciousness.

I found myself missing dad. Grieving, not as much for the loss of him, but having robbed myself of a warm farewell. Those years where I'd become angry and bitter. The years where I let our relationship suffer because my classmates played catch with their dads while my dad taught me to distinguish between edible and inedible plants. I was finally realizing he did what all parents do—he taught me what he knew.

I found myself hoping the world wouldn't lose the Addison I'd come to know and admire. That somehow she would be able to navigate her father being shot, possibly killed, and then framed for the murder of someone else.

I worried that I was about to get several amazing people killed. Jessie and those kids should've never been turned away. Walt and Rose should've been enjoying their golden years with some golf and early bird specials. This wasn't even Trey or Emily's fight. And then there was Sophie.

Sophie had lost her mom a few years ago. Now, her father had been murdered and she'd been lied to about the circumstances. She'd been cut off from her brothers. And now I was putting her life in danger.

With all this fighting for headspace as the day turned to night, I had begun to welcome every sound and rustle. Any disturbance to break up my steady stream of anxieties.

Deep darkness gradually set in and the plan had been to take shifts with the idea that two of us would sleep as the third remained awake until they realized they couldn't go any longer. Then, they would wake one of the others. The plan didn't work, because none of us trusted that we wouldn't all fall asleep. This was too important. So we sat in the darkness. Waiting for the sound of an explosion.

DAY SEVEN

"NEVER LOSE SIGHT OF YOUR MOST
IMPORTANT WEAPON."

—

MARK TAYLOR

85.

THE EXPLOSION NEVER CAME. But a single report from a rifle took its place. It echoed across the quiet night.

We didn't know if there was the proper percentage of gasoline in my beloved Toyota's tank to make it explode, so we had a Plan B. If the flaming rag stuck into the tank didn't elicit the perfect reaction, the girls were to load the back of the truck with dry brush, light it on fire, and use the bullet in the rifle to set everything in motion.

Using the single bullet meant they were unarmed, but there was no time to focus on that now. We had to get moving down the hill.

We descended single-file in the direction of my house when our radio crackled to life. "Was that one of you?

Report in." It was the tired sound of Trevor's voice. I turned
the volume down. I didn't want the radio to betray our loca-
tion if someone was guarding the house from the west.

"Conor here. Negative."

"Jimmy here. All clear."

A few seconds passed.

"Trev. It was a gunshot," Andrew sounded nervous.
"You want me to go alone?"

"Fine. On my way."

"No." Andrew hesitated. "No need."

"God, Andy." Trevor sounded disgusted. "Wait for me
in front of the Sinnot house if you want."

"No man. I told you. I'm fine."

The channel went quiet and my attention returned to
the dark path before me just in time to see it. Trey's considerable frame bumped into my back with enough force to
tip me forward. I spun and grabbed for Trey as I began to
fall backward. Trey stood upright, holding the weight of my
body as it leaned impossibly away from him, both my hands
clinging to his forearm.

"What the hell, man?" he demanded as Emily came up
to his side.

"Don't move," I instructed.

I pulled myself upright and swung to my giant friend's
side. I looked around and found a fallen branch and poked
at the uneven ground I'd barely seen in time. The light coat-
ing of dirt held up by thin, dry branches gave way to a ditch

dug about four feet deep-complete with several sharpened posts sticking up from the bottom.

"What the... " Emily muttered.

"A miniature deadfall," I explained. "Used to catch game or predators."

Trevor and his crew had been busy. And either he planned on more heroics by providing the faithful with some fresh protein, or he wasn't convinced George could be trusted with yesterday's task.

"That's messed up," Trey shook his head.

"Stay right behind me." I jammed the branch into the ground ahead of me as we made our way around the trap.

If all went according to plan, the next domino was about to fall.

"Hey, Trev?" the radio crackled quietly with Andrew's voice. "Something's on fire over here."

I stopped to listen.

"Come again?"

"Something. Is. On. Fire."

"I'm coming in the Jeep. Don't freaking shoot at me!"

A moment later, from the far side of the house, the Jeep roared to life and headlights made a grey outline of the old farmhouse visible. The Jeep tore through the night and down the road, leaving a dust cloud in its wake.

"Can't believe he's using Mom's Jeep," I whispered.

"Get over it," Emily whispered, "Let's keep moving."

I resumed the cautious advance around the pit, but as

soon as I turned the corner, the radio crackled to life again.

"Hey, guys? Jimmy here. What the hell?"

"Almost there, Andrew." It was Trevor. "What's going on, Jimmy?"

"There's a vehicle on the ridge. Headlights on." Walt was behind the wheel of the bus. I tried not to dwell on the danger my plan demanded of a senior citizen.

We were nearing the house now, but had no intention of stopping there.

"On the ridge?" Trevor confirmed.

"Yeah." Jimmy's voice was agitated.

"Let me know if it moves."

We were passing my house now and moving down the road toward town.

"Will do," Jimmy responded.

We still weren't sure where George or Conor were, so we remained on high alert as we approached the stone gate at the end of the Forrester driveway.

"It's moving!" Jimmy yelled over the channel. "I need backup! Now!"

"Relax, Jimmy," Trevor responded. "I'll be there in a minute. Nothing here but a bonfire in the back of a truck. Look alive, everybody. The retirees and their band of middle schoolers are probably pranking us."

We reached the arch and I got to my knees and started digging with my hands. Trey and Emily watched in every direction.

"Anything?" Trey checked.

"It's here."

"Loaded?"

I popped out the magazine. "Yup."

Trey took a deep breath and nodded.

"Trey? Emily?" I smiled in an attempt to reassure them, and myself. "Time to go knock on a window."

86.

"**IT'S HALFWAY DOWN FROM THE RIDGE!** Do I open fire?!" Jimmy yelled across the channel.

"No, Jimmy. Stay calm. Could be innocent people looking for a hand. We'll give them the opportunity to leave peacefully."

"Something feels wrong, man!"

"I don't care about your feelings! Just keep giving me facts."

Having turned our radio down to its minimum volume, we listened as we made our approach across the rolling front property to the west side of the Forrester home. Although we didn't expect any fortifications to the front of the home, we scanned the ground for more danger and the home for any lookouts. Anyone stationed here, be it George, Conor,

Liam, or another townsperson, would almost certainly be focused on the expanse behind the house up to the northern tracks and the mountain beyond them. They wouldn't expect threats coming from town.

I picked up a small piece of crusted dirt and tossed it at Addison's second story window. Nothing. I picked up a slightly larger piece and did it a second time. Still no response.

"Now what?" Emily whispered.

"I think I know. You two. Out of sight."

They crept up to the house and sat on the ground, backs to the wall. Trey held the walkie to his ear.

I walked up to another window and knocked gently, my pistol at the ready. I was virtually certain from my last time inside the house, this was the master bedroom. The curtain shifted and Addison's face appeared next to it. Rough and tired, but somehow still beautiful. Her face flashed with panic.

By way of hand motions, I asked if she could open the window. She vanished, replacing the curtain. And all I could do was wait.

"The van drifted off the road to the right and slowly tipped over." Jimmy reported over the channel. It was met with silence.

"Trevor? You there?"

He had to be putting it together.

"Yeah," Trevor responded. "Let me know if anyone

emerges from the van. I'm almost there. Conor? Plan B."

"Plan B. Doing it now."

I didn't like hearing they had a Plan B of their own.

The curtain shook again. Addison reappeared and flipped a series of several locks before sliding the window.

"Be quick," she whispered. "Conor is in the hall."

"You. Your mom. Your dad. Conor. Anyone else?"

"Don't think so. Haven't left this room except to get food from the kitchen."

"Okay. I'm not alone. Trey and Emily are with me."

"I'm not getting through that window," Trey whispered.

"I know. Turn off the radio." I looked back to Addison. "Trey's going to knock on the front door. It will draw Conor's attention. Emily and I will crawl through as soon as he knocks. I've got a gun."

"I don't want you to shoot him."

"We'll come up behind him. Make him drop whatever he's carrying."

"Lukas. I don't like this."

"Neither do we, but we need those guns, and until we have them, Trevor runs this town. And if Trevor is running this town, he can't afford for your dad to make a full recovery."

She looked over her shoulder. "This better work."

87.

N THE SOUPY DARK OF THE EARLY MORNING, it was easy to hear Trey slam on the door from around the corner of the house. Emily flung herself through the window. As I followed, I took stock of the room. Addison's dad was on his bed, wheezing with each breath. Her mom was passed out on a folding chair pulled up to the bed, bent forward, chest onto the bed, holding her husband's unresponsive hand. Addison stood before me with a look that seemed to be hoping I knew what I was doing.

There was another pound on the door.

We moved through the bedroom door and peeked down the hall. No hint of Conor. I slipped through the doorway and crept forward, approaching a door on each side. The one to the right led to the basement-turned-armory and the one on the left was a bathroom. Beyond, the hall opened to the large two-story living room and kitchen.

Slamming a third time.

Something was very wrong, but it was too late now.

I turned to Emily. "Stay here. I'll get to the door and let him in."

She nodded and crouched down.

I left her near the doors and moved to where the hall opened up, glanced up the stairs to the balcony that led to Addison's bedroom, circled the kitchen island, efficiently checked behind each part of the living room before turning the corner and unbolting the door. "It's me, Trey." I said it before opening the door.

As I swung it wide, Trey cracked, "Wanna buy some Thin Mints?"

"Get in."

There was the sound of a scuffle around the corner.

Without thinking, Trey yelled, "Emily!" as he lumbered past me, around the corner, and froze. He took a step back and raised his open hands.

I realized in my rush to let Trey in, I'd neglected to clear the hallway bathroom.

I stayed behind the corner. "Trey. What's going on?"

The sound of more scuffling.

"Just let her go, dude." Trey rumbled.

"I told you what would happen." It was George's voice. Calm. "Now, drop to your knees."

"No." The response from Trey came deep and hateful. "Not again."

"Last chance before I shoot her, then you."

A jolting metallic crash came from somewhere unseen. Trey broke toward George and Emily, out of view. Then, a gunshot.

I sprang forward to see what had happened and saw George and Trey locked in a struggle of titans. Behind them, Emily had picked up what I assumed was George's gun, but the two giants were flinging each other into the walls too ferociously for her to safely get a shot on George. Addison stood behind all of it with a dented folding chair.

I didn't raise my gun because even if the two behemoths slowed down long enough for me to aim, Emily and Addison were directly behind them.

"Put it down!" It was Andrew. He had nudged the front door open and had a pistol of his own aimed at my head.

George and Trey tumbled into the living room. Trey stood and blood had soaked his shirt at his chest. George charged him, head down, spearing Trey through an oversized chair.

"Put it down!" Andrew yelled. "Please, listen…"

Behind me, punches landed into what sounded like sides of beef.

I stood at the corner of the entrance and the hallway, the battle of the century rumbling behind me. I slowly crouched and set the gun down at my feet. Then, I stood back up slowly.

Something large crashed behind me.

"Here!" I said suddenly, before kicking the gun hard past Andrew's feet and out the doorway.

The second it slid, Andrew's eyes followed it and Emily tossed me George's gun. I aimed and fired. Andrew looked back just in time to comprehend his mistake and dive out the door.

Emily ran to my side and I handed her the gun back before I moved to the door, closed, and bolted it.

Behind me, in the living room, four shots rang out followed by about six clicks. I ran back to find Emily standing over George's bullet-ridden body. His eyes were open, but looking at nothing. Nothing in this world, anyway. Next to him on the floor, Trey's face was bruised and bloodied. The gentle behemoth gasped for air between coughs.

"Is...he...?" It was all he could get out, staring at the ceiling, unable to focus.

"Yeah. He's gone," I assured him.

The living room looked like a tornado had ripped through it.

"Pumpkin?" The crimson soaking his shirt continued to spread with shocking speed.

Emily snapped clear and crouched beside him. "Trey! I'm here." She sniffled. "I'm right here."

"I'm..." he coughed, his teeth red, "...sorry..."

"For what?" She gripped his huge chin and their eyes met. "You saved my life."

"I was going to ask…" Several more coughs.

Emily gasped back emotion before responding, "And I was going to say yes." Tears fell from her eyes to his cheeks.

"I wanted…" And the giant's face broke. His forehead wrinkled, eyes watered, and lips tremored as he must've realized what would never be. His head rolled slowly to the left. And he was gone.

Emily collapsed into the dead body of her man.

88.

'D ALMOST KILLED A MAN, LOST A FRIEND, and I needed to throw up, but there was no time for nausea. I steadied myself, and walked to the door leading to the basement. As I turned the knob and pulled, a shot rang out as the electricity of a fired bullet passed inches to the left of my ear.

I flung the door most of the way shut and dove into the hall. The grief and adrenaline had clouded my caution.

"Dammit, Conor! Is that you?"

"Lukas! There is only one way down here and I've got all the ammo I'll need! Trevor and the others are on their way!"

I dove back past the door, opened merely a crack, and yelled, "Addison! Shut your parents window and lock it up!"

A moment later, Addison appeared in the doorway at the end of the hall and nodded.

"Conor! You are helping the man who killed your father!"

"That's a load of crap and you know it!"

"He killed your dad. He framed Addison's dad. He locked my mom in your shelter. He took all the guns. He put a curfew in place. He banished your own—"

A shot blasted through the door.

"Enough!" Conor yelled. "You did all this! Forrester killed my dad! And if I would've killed him, it would've been over! But you just *had* to stop me! And the whole time, you and your mom were holding back! Lying! My dad? He helped the community. You and your mom are traitors. She *should* be locked up. So should you."

"Conor? Your sister and I saw George—"

Another shot blasted through the door.

"And then you dragged Sophie into this mess! She likes you and you know it! So you manipulated her! And where did it get her? Banished! You! You did all of this!"

There was an urgent knock on the front door.

89.

"OPEN THE DOOR!" SOPHIE SCREAMED.

I unbolted it and was knocked backwards.

Sophie and Jessie pushed in and slammed the door, Jessie replacing the bolt, before they both slid to the floor with exhaustion.

"Trevor." Sophie was out of breath. "He's driving your mom's Jeep." She took another breath. "He's pulling up."

"Either of you hurt?"

"Not a scratch," Jessie smirked.

"Oh God!" Sophie exclaimed when she saw Emily hovered over Trey's body. She scrambled back to her feet and ran to them. "Oh, Emily. Emily..." She knelt down and held her from behind.

"What happened?" Jessie asked.

"George pulled a gun on Emily. Trey saved her. And Emily killed George."

"Damn. Is that all?"

"No. I shot at Andrew. He's somewhere outside. Surprised you got by him. Conor's in the basement and he's not letting us down there. He doesn't know we're unarmed—"

"Unarmed?"

"Andrew's got two guns. Mine and his. George's gun is out of bullets. Emily used them all on him."

"Less than ideal."

"Pretty much." I thought for a moment. "Sophie? Get Trey's radio."

"What are you doing?" Jessie whispered.

Sophie reached for Trey.

Emily stopped her. "I'll do it."

She pulled out the radio and handed it over before Sophie handed it to me.

I lifted it to my mouth.

90.

"**J**IMMY, CONOR, AND ANYONE ELSE LISTENING, my mother and I have been guilty of holding back." I was careful not to release the talk button. This was about to be what my government teacher called a filibuster. "We held back because my dad taught us that you never know how people will react during a catastrophe. We decided it was best to wait awhile and see how things played out. We never intended to betray your trust.

"Mr. William Sinnot was one of the best men this town has ever known. I have come to believe he was shot by either Trevor Beck or his now-deceased bodyguard, George. They then framed Mr. Sebastian Forrester for the murder and intended on killing him, as well. My mother tried to warn me about Trevor's character. I did not listen. Addison tried to tell me her father wasn't capable of such an act. I did not take action. I am so sorry it took me so long to listen.

"Hear me clearly. Sophie and I saw George and Kyle beyond our town's borders. They were friends and coworkers. Kyle was with them from the start, until they killed him in front of Sophie, Emily, Trey, and myself.

"Now? William is dead. Trey is dead. Sebastian is clinging to life. And I need your help."

A loud report echoed from behind the house followed almost imperceptibly by an explosion and a white spider web crack in the middle of one of the two story vertical polycarbonate windows that made up the back wall of the living room. Someone had just tried to shoot me from up the slope directly behind the house and in my shock, I let go of the button. It was only for a moment, but it was long enough.

91.

"**C**ITIZENS OF SKULL VALLEY. EVERYTHING YOU just heard is a lie. You know this because Lukas and his mother have been lying to you for years. They had prepared for an eventuality like this for God knows how long, but hid it from you. Even when things went south, they hid it from you. Even when people died, they hid it from you. Even when children arrived, in need of help and supplies, they hid it from you. I was forced to make a decision without the full knowledge of what supplies we were in possession of. Frankly, I don't understand why this family hates me so much. All I can come up with is their jealousy. I took my skills and made good money helping others be better prepared for a time such as this. And they resent me for it. But I returned to help. Let me say that again. I returned to help. I wanted nothing more than to be a trench worker. I didn't ask to be in charge of anything. But you asked me to lead, to help you survive. But that wasn't what Lukas wanted. And after his mother's regrettable imprisonment due to her betrayal, Lukas went about recruiting others to their cause. He recruited two outsiders and young Sophie Sinnot. He almost got them killed when they were caught by that mad man, but George saved them. And how did they repay him? They apparently murdered him. Then, they shot at Andrew. And at present, they are holding Conor Sinnot hostage in an effort to steal our weapons. This is what we are up against, Skull Valley. I am the one in need of your help."

I waited for the walkie to click off so I could respond, but it never did.

Several more shots were fired in succession at the spider web halfway up the large window. As the web grew and cracked, the shots echoed over the open channel. Either Trevor must've used something to wrap the walkie-talkie, keeping the talk button pressed as he shot, or he was next to the shooter.

"The window won't hold much longer!" Jessie yelled over the blasts.

I grabbed the empty pistol off the ground. Trevor or Andrew or whoever shot out one of the windows didn't know it was empty. "Everyone! Get down the hall to the master!"

Jessie didn't have to be told twice. Emily didn't want to leave Trey, but Sophie kept persisting until she relented.

Sophie stopped at the entrance to the hall. She looked back and saw me walk up to a parallel window as ear-shattering shots kept assaulting the web. "What are you doing, Lukas?!"

"Just get in the master and shut the door behind you!" I shouted as the web gave and a hole the size of a basketball exploded from the window about twelve feet off the ground. The next bullets struck two feet lower. Whoever was shooting, was blasting an entrance. The echoes were still loud enough to cause distortion across the channel. The shooter had to be Trevor.

"What are you doing?!" She shouted right back.

Bang!

"Sophie! For God's sake! Get down the hall!"

Bang!

She vanished as a second web grew below the hole. I crouched low and found myself next to George's body.

We were running out of time.

92.

MOVED QUICKLY TO THE HALL AND YELLED, "Conor? Did you hear all that?"

"More lies!"

Another shot blasted through the door as the shots kept cracking the large window in the other room. I thanked God Conor wasn't using a shotgun.

I went back into the main room and searched the kitchen island until I found what I needed. Another shot blasted out the area below the first hole, doubling its total area. I walked to the unblemished window to the left of the one Trevor was working over, pulled out the white cloth napkin, and swung it back and forth above my head.

The shots kept coming. Now at a spot only six feet off the ground. Below the opening.

I kept swinging the white cloth over my head. Back and forth.

Bang!

I needed him to see me. Needed the shots to stop.

Bang!

Kept swinging. There was no other option.

Finally. Mercifully. Silence.

93.

"**W**HAT ARE YOU DOING, LUKAS?" The voice on the walkie was cool. The line was open, inviting a response.

"I'm giving up. I don't want anyone else to get hurt."

"Conor?"

"Here."

"Don't come up those stairs until I tell you to."

"Got it."

"Andrew?"

"Here with Jimmy."

"Head back to the front of the house. Just you."

"One sec." There was a momentary pause before he was back. "Here."

"Got eyes on the front door and garage?"

"Yeah."

"Jimmy?"

"Side of the house, eyes on the bedroom windows."

"Okay. No one leaves that damn house. I'm going to talk to Lukas now. No one else needs to get hurt."

As I looked out into the blackness behind the Forrester home, an approaching figure began to materialize.

Trevor strode down the long slope and toward the window. The arrogance, all over his face.

He stopped on the other side of the battered glass. We were less than five feet apart, separated by the thick polycarbonate. A spiderweb of cracks at eye-level with a gaping hole just above it. Trevor couldn't pull himself up and through without permission. There was a handgun at my feet, but he had no way of knowing the chamber was empty.

We studied one another for a moment. His head cocked. His AK shouldered. My hands casually in my pockets. I tried not to shake.

"So, what now?" he asked, grinning his million dollar grin.

"I thought we should have this conversation off the record."

"Oh, sure. But before we do that, I'm gonna need that radio."

My shoulders slumped and I pulled the walkie-talkie out of my right pocket before tossing it up and out of the hole blasted in the window.

He caught it with ease, gave it a glance and tossed it aside. "Okay, pal. What do you propose?"

"I'm guessing you can't let me live, right?"

"As long as I've got your mom as leverage, I think we could work something out."

Probably a lie.

"But I could never be your second in command anymore."

"No chance in hell after tonight. You burned that option to the freakin' ground, kid. Just be satisfied you'll be walking out of this with a pulse." He shook his head. "We could've run this place. But you were such a pain in the ass. George didn't listen and now I've got to improvise."

"And what about Kyle?"

"Once you outed Kyle, he could never have become part of the community."

"Makes sense." I waited a moment. "And Andrew?"

"Andy?" He laughed. "Spineless. He doesn't have the fortitude to do what must be done."

"So. Who will help you now?"

"Conor and Jimmy, I suppose. Not my first choices, mind you." He shrugged. "God. This community better pray I live a long time. But regarding the present, we need to decide a few things. You know Emily's got to die, right?"

"Because with Trey dead, she'll never play ball."

"And Sebastian, obviously. Which should be easy enough. He's nine tenths of the way there already."

But that's all, right? Not Sophie or Addison?"

He laughed. "Kid? You are gonna have to choose eventually." He shook his head before continuing. "They'll both be good. Addison still has her mom to consider and Liam seems like an accident-prone kid."

"So, I get to live. Sophie gets to live. Addison gets to live."

"And we can take care of Sebastian in the next twenty-four hours. His wife'll need to go to the bathroom sometime." He smiled his practiced smile. "It's that or everyone dies. Your choice. What's it gonna be?"

"Gosh, Trevor." I pulled George's radio out of my left pocket slowly. "I don't think it's up to me." I lifted it to my mouth while staring at Trevor. "Andrew? Are you too spineless to have an opinion? Conor? Cool with your little brother as bait? Jimmy? You still wanna follow this guy?"

Trevor's face contorted as I spoke.

He pulled his AK and began blasting at the glass between us.

I dove to the side as another hole shattered into the living room. I scrambled into the kitchen area as the bullets pursued me on the far side of the glass.

Conor bolted out of the hall with two pistols, tossing one behind the kitchen island and quickly ducking behind the overstuffed chair that had been flipped over in the earlier scuffle.

I slid behind the island, grabbed the gun, and clicked off the safety.

While Trevor replaced his clip, he bellowed, "This damn town belongs to me! My name is on the goddamn sign!" He resumed blasting between the upper and lower holes at close range. The bullet-resistant material didn't stand a chance at close range and came crumbling down.

As he stepped through the opening, I leapt up, and in my periphery, I saw Conor do the same. In Trevor's moment of indecision, we both opened fire.

Louis Trevor Beckel hit the ground without getting off another shot.

94.

THE COMMUNITY ACCUMULATED AROUND THE SCHOOL over the course of the morning, but I was behind my house, helping Emily dig. Earlier, when she finally looked at me and said she needed to bury Trey, I suggested out back near my father. After all, Trey had become family.

It was arduous work, trying to break deeper into the rough dirt, but it helped me burn through my emotions. I'd killed. It didn't matter the reason. I'd killed and I couldn't shake the sickness.

My mother came to get me in the afternoon. She told me the rumors were getting out of control and people needed to hear the truth of the past week.

Sitting on a picnic table, next to Sophie, we recounted everything as best we could. When I spoke of her father,

Sophie cried. When we talked about Trey's death, we both wept.

The strangest part of telling the story was how much it made me miss my father. I missed the man who taught us to be cautious. I missed the man who taught Mom to keep a radio in reserve. I missed the man who could discern the heart of another with such accuracy. I missed the man who loved me the best he could.

95.

WITHIN HOURS OF TELLING OUR STORY, now the definitive version of the past week, a few of the remaining town elders gathered, including Walt and Rose, and several important decisions were made.

The majority of the town had fallen under the spell of Trevor Beck. As a result, neither Conor nor Jimmy were punished for assisting him. Their guilt was punishment enough. Andrew, on the other hand, was another story altogether.

In the aftermath, he surrendered his weapon without incident and was questioned at gunpoint. He made it clear that he didn't approve of Trevor's actions. But he didn't make excuses and admitted he should've done something to stop him. Anything. But the most important factor turned out to be the mercy he'd shown me. He could've killed me without warning only hours earlier.

It was decided he would be given the choice of banishment or one year imprisonment with the chance at citizenship upon completion. To everyone's surprise, he chose imprisonment. I guess he welcomed the penance.

Weapons were to be given back to their owners, provided they had the means to keep them secured. Anyone who didn't have a functioning safe could keep their weapons and ammo in the Forresters' basement. The weapons could be accessed by the owner at any time.

The curfew was immediately rescinded. Furthermore, anyone was free to leave the community at any time provided they were able to maintain their responsibilities or find a substitute and provide an expected time of return.

A community bonfire was scheduled for that night. Although significant firewood needed to be collected before the temperatures began to drop in a few months, it was deemed an important step toward rebuilding the community. As one might expect, it was Rose's suggestion.

The sign on the north end of town was painted over before sundown. It no longer read 'Birthplace of Trevor Beck.' All agreed it should be replaced with 'Home of William Sinnot."

Finally, and most significantly, my mother was asked to assume a leadership role in coordination with the community's elders.

96.

ALMOST IMMEDIATELY, SEVERAL HOUSING decisions were made. The one that had the greatest personal impact was Mom asking Emily to move in. Like many of the homes in Skull Valley, we also took in one of the camp kids.

I requested Bobby.

I gave Emily my room, Bobby would take up residence in the basement, and I'd take the underground shelter. It was still connected to the house, but had its own exit, and I liked the freedom it would afford.

Addison suddenly found herself overwhelmed with responsibility. She would have to take care of her mother, an assigned camp girl, and her father in what appeared to be his last days. Jessie volunteered to move in and assist her.

And Sophie would move back in with her brothers. None of the three Sinnot children took their father's old room. They wouldn't even open the door.

97.

THE BONFIRE SLOWLY FADED to a remnant of its former glory
under the clear night sky. The orange glow flickering on
the faces of those who remained. Walt had left with their
new charge, leaving Rose to enjoy the socialization. She
whispered with Mom, their camp chairs scooted close to
one another. Jessie left to relieve Addison and, I imagine,
force her to leave the house. As soon as she arrived, Bobby
sat next to her on one of our remaining camp chairs and
tossed sticks into the fire. Liam stood on his other side, doing the same. Emily was passed out in my former bedroom.
Conor hadn't come, but Sophie was next to me on an old
log, although we sat largely in silence.

Earlier in the afternoon, Mom suggested we host the
bonfire. Walt tried to argue that it should be outside the
mobile home park, but Mom reminded him we already had
the large fire pit.

Bobby finally broke the silence. "When we go camping, my grandparents only burn pinion. It repels bugs and smells amazing. What is *this* stuff?"

"Oh, it's very special wood," I explained. "It's called flammable."

Addison shot me a look across the fire.

Bobby looked at Addison and said, "I get that the jerk probably saved the town, but how long do I have to be nice to him?" He looked pleased when his question drew chuckles all around.

"As long as you live in my house," I established.

"Well," Mom jumped in, "good thing you don't live in his house. You live in mine."

"Ohhhh." Sophie responded with a laugh.

"Hey," I looked at Sophie, pretending to be wounded. "Don't take my mom's side or I won't give you your gift."

"Wait. What? A gift?"

I looked back to the fire, stone-faced. "Nevermind. Too late."

Addison abruptly stood. "Hey, everybody. Thanks for the invite, but I'm pretty exhausted." She paused. "Lukas? Sophie? Thank you. Ya know... for everything." She put her head down and headed into the darkness.

"Addison?" My mother called after her. "You need anything—anything—you let us know."

"Thanks, Mrs. Taylor. I will."

Rose stood. "Bobby? Liam? Could you carry the four

chairs back into the house?" Then she turned to Mom. "Why don't we head inside? It's getting cold."

Mom looked over toward the log, a whiff of concern. "Alright. You two. Don't stay out much longer. You need your rest."

It was true. We'd both pulled an all-nighter and could barely keep our eyes open, but I'd been hoping we'd outlast everyone else.

I sensed I wasn't alone.

As Rose walked past us, she winked and I wanted to hug her.

98.

WE SAT THERE AS THE FIRE continued to die, each waiting for the other to say something.

"So. About that gift," she whispered.

"I thought you forgot."

She looked at me with animated shock. "You really don't know me at all."

"Well. I know what your favorite is."

"Pardon?"

I turned to her and leaned tantalizingly close. "I said...I know what your favorite is." As I said it, I pulled the small pack of peanut M&Ms out of my pocket and placed them back in her hand.

About two inches from my face, her eyes flashed at me, never breaking contact. "Oh my."

I didn't back off. "See? I *do* know you."

"But these were for you."

"I couldn't possibly enjoy them as much as you."

"How can I ever repay you?" Her eyes pulled at me.

I leaned a bit closer. My lips touched hers with soft, gentle electricity. I didn't want to, but I backed away.

She held her lean a moment. Eyes closed. Everything about her silently said, 'I wasn't done.'

But I had to be. And yet, I wanted her to know I enjoyed it as much as she had.

I whispered, "That. That is *my* favorite."

Her eyes slowly opened and lips curled into a wide smile. "Mine, too."

"Then can I have the M&Ms back?"

"Hell, no."

We both smiled for a ridiculously happy moment as the last flame flickered out and all that remained were glowing embers. We stared at it for almost a full minute.

"Just remember. I liked you before you became the hero of this town."

"What are you even talking about?" I brushed it off.

"You, me, and everyone in this town knows what you did."

"We did it together. Along with Emily and Trey and Walt and Rose and Jessie. Even Addison with the chair. And your brother at the end."

"Listen," her voice, serious. "I'm too tired to argue with

you, but we both know all those people followed your lead."

I looked at her face, dimly lit orange as she looked back at me.

"But I have to confess…I'm a tiny bit sad my secret is out," she continued.

"And what secret is that?"

"You."

THE END

If you enjoyed reading *SKULL VALLEY*,
leaving a review makes a big impact.
Thank you in advance!

Find entries from Mark Taylor's field journal at

DavidMartinLins.com

where you can also sign up to be the
first to know about upcoming projects,
find exclusive content, and get insider info.

Connect with the author at
facebook.com/davidmartinlinsauthor
instagram.com/davidmartinlins
twitter.com/davidmartinlins

ACKNOWLEDGEMENTS

MARYROSE. YEARS AGO, I SUMMONED THE requisite courage to tell you (yet again) that I needed to finish my novel. Instead of reminding me of previous failure, you encouraged me to get on with it. You supported all the early mornings, late nights, and mood swings brought on by the "there is so much to like...but" agent letters. That first, unpublished novel would've never been completed...and SKULL VALLEY would've never been published without your love and support. Thank you for walking through it all with me. I love you.

James Cook, I thank God I met you at that conference years ago. I have found your generous heart to only be surpassed by your love of puns. Thank you for all the little ways you continued to push me toward this day. Thank you for introducing me to the Round Table Company crew. Most of all, thank you for being my brother.

Lorin Petrazilka, I thank God I met you at that other conference years ago. You have patiently answered every question imaginable. You showed me that I didn't have to wait for someone else's permission to share my novel with the world (by releasing your own, VALE BORN). You created a freaking brilliant cover for SKULL VALLEY. Most of all, you have become my insanely talented literary sister.

Stephen Prat, I've known you for decades...and when I realized I had the need for a dear friend who could balance affirming strengths and magnifying weaknesses with brutal honesty...there could be no other. You are a Renaissance man if I ever knew one, but I beg you to continue to explore this gift.

To Mark Berent, J.D. Barker, and Barbara Hinske. I had lengthy conversations with each of you at perfect moments. To this day, I'm honored you took the time.

To my beta readers, your contributions have helped refine this work. It is truly a kindness to endure my writing in its most raw condition. I pray you saw the fruit of your collective effort in the final presentation.

To all my friends and (most of all) my family, who have been so supportive throughout the entire journey. And if my writing is found to be worthy and my readership grows, you will always be my "Inner Keep."

Mom? More than one beta reader commented on all the strong women that inhabit the world of SKULL VALLEY. I suspect it is because I've known one my entire life.

Finally, I need to thank God for allowing me to be a storyteller. It is a beautiful calling.

CPSIA information can be obtained
at www.ICGtesting.com
Printed in the USA
LVHW040823090621
689684LV00005B/145

Mom? More than one beta reader commented on all the strong women that inhabit the world of SKULL VALLEY. I suspect it is because I've known one my entire life.

Finally, I need to thank God for allowing me to be a storyteller. It is a beautiful calling.

CPSIA information can be obtained
at www.ICGtesting.com
Printed in the USA
LVHW040823090621
689684LV00005B/145